AF256920

BALD WENDY

by

Jane Palmer

DODO BOOKS

First published in Great Britain
by Dodo Books 2008

Copyright © Jane Palmer 2008

This is a work of fiction and
any resemblance to persons living or
dead is purely coincidental.

The author asserts the moral right to be
identified as the author of this work.

ISBN   978-1-906442-18-7

All right reserved. No part of this publication may be
reproduced, stored in a retrieval system, or
transmitted, in any form or by any means, electronic,
mechanical, photocopying, recording or otherwise,
without the prior permission of the publisher, nor be
otherwise circulated in any form of binding or cover
other than that in which it is published and without a
similar condition being imposed on the subsequent
purchaser.

Science fiction & Supernatural Fantasy
books by this author

**THE PLANET DWELLER
MOVING MOOSEVAN
BABEL'S BASEMENT
THE KYBION
THE ATON BIRD
HUNDER**

CHAPTER 1

Merryweather's exploded in a ball of fire. Tiles from its antique roof landed in Victoria Park's lake and the inside of the butcher's shop glowed like an Aga at Christmas, its enamelled tiles falling, one by one, into the inferno like swotted moths.

Those ducks that hadn't already been frightened off by the skirling sirens and clattering of hydrants took to the air before the smoke billowing across the lawns engulfed them. House martins performed an aerial ballet about the conflagration that was briefly punctuated by a blast of steam as the water in the loft tank vaporised.

Most of the houses in Victoria Street that faced the park were now derelict. The water pressure had been reduced long ago and the fire service control were unable to contact anyone in the water company capable of increasing it. For a short while the fire continued to roar like an angry monster, vaporising any water trained onto it. By the time the firefighters managed to run a relay of hoses from the High Street main so they could use jets, there was nothing left to save. The stench of burnt meat hung over the neighbourhood like Hell's barbecue. A couple of teenagers threw up.

The conflagration had been so sudden none of the customers could pinpoint the seat of the flames. All they remembered was a rush of hot, smokeless air, and Mr French, the butcher's assistant, ushering them out clutching their liver, chops, and joints as he locked the till and phoned the fire service.

An elderly woman holding a carton of chicken mince for her neurotic cat had refused to move since the fire started.

'But I'm sure Mr Merryweather was in there!' she wailed.

'It's all right Mrs Jenkins,' the community constable reassured her. 'The other customers say he was out the back at the time. They're checking the gardens and park. He's bound to be safe somewhere.'

The old lady kneaded the carton of mince in agitation. 'No! No! No! He was showing Mrs Niblock the locket Una wanted mending.'

A friend, eyes smarting from the smoke, tried to comfort her. 'Don't you upset yourself, Minnie. As soon as Mr French got us out he checked the parlour.'

'Then why haven't they been found?' insisted the old woman.

A fireman heard the outburst and caught the constable's glance with a nervous shrug.

For some while the clink of tiles dropping through the floors and the nauseous stench of burnt meat pervaded the area around Victoria Park.

The police found Una Merryweather between the aisles of pansies and petunias in the local garden centre. She was told, as gently as possible, that her home and the family business had burnt down. It took several cups of tea and five cigarettes before reality came back into focus, and she realised that she was sitting in the comfort lounge at the police station, talking to a plain-clothes officer with good looks that should have been illegal. He was investigating the possibility of arson but, as the middle-aged woman gradually became more fixated on him than the matter in hand, Una Merryweather was discreetly left with a bright-eyed young woman who had probably dealt with nothing more serious than lost poodles. She had certainly never had to break the news of a missing loved one.

'We can't find your husband, or Mrs Niblock. We've been told they went into the back parlour to look at a locket of yours, but Mr French says they weren't there when he checked.' She took a deep breath. This was quicksand without the stepping stones of a training manual. 'Is it possible they could have gone off somewhere together?'

The insinuation brought the butcher's wife crashing back to earth. 'Of course not! Deirdre and me are the best of friends. She's got a husband who dotes on her. And why would a vegetarian run off with a butcher?' Una took a sip of lukewarm tea. 'I never kept my locket in the parlour. Frank didn't pay any attention to things like that, but Deirdre knew it was in the bedroom, in the drawer with my stockings.'

The young PC's jaw dropped; if the couple had been upstairs, now she had two fatalities to deal with.

Una Merryweather had been a widow before. She pulled off her hat and thoughtfully parted the threads of its tassel. 'It's all right. I've lost most of my family at some time or other. The business used to be my father's. I inherited it when he died in a car crash ten years ago.'

The policewoman was nonplussed by her diffident manner. 'But, your husband - aren't you...?'

'Upset? Oh yes. But I've buried better men. You save your sympathy for Mr Niblock. He married Deirdre when they were teenagers, and they've not been apart for thirty-five years. Only albatrosses know devotion like that.'

***

Fire prevention continued to puzzle over the ferocity of the fire. Despite the shop being tiled, newly rewired, and Una Merryweather being careful not to use flammable fabrics, they were unable to work out the seat of the fire.

Then the fire service decided it was safe to lift the carbonised roof timbers. Under them they found the remains of two people.

***

A group of men stood at the end of Victoria Street and watched the ruins of the last independent butcher in the Moltonford Town centre smoulder. Like so many druids officiating at the wake of a newly extinct species, their presence lent the incident a sense of finality. Few of the men were local, but Moltonford had ceased to pay attention to the small gatherings of strangers examining street corners, Victoria Park and inoffensive dips in the lie of the town centre. As it sat in a valley, the borough engineer should have been more concerned about the one in five gradients either side of it. Many a resident had suffered a heart attack or broken hip negotiating the steep roads to buy the groceries or pay the council tax.

Only after the local onlookers had tired of the spectacle and filtered away, were two body bags carried from the debris of Merryweather's.

'Tragic,' one of the strangers muttered without much conviction.

A neat man in a grey trench coat was more businesslike. 'He was the last obstacle. Now the remaining residents in Victoria Street will be happy to sell up for fear of vandals wandering out of the park every night.'

A large man with the deadly smile of a hippo was examining some papers from his briefcase. 'Once we explain our redevelopment plans for the park and town centre, no one will object. Then we can condemn this street and Victoria Park as public safety hazards. After all, that bread left for the ducks only encourages vermin, the pavilion is full of down and outs, and the toilets - Do you know what goes on in the toilets?'

A tall, distinguished looking man standing a little way off from the gathering didn't share their enthusiasm. 'No. I wonder that you do, Mr Grablatt.'

'Councillor Makepeace, why must you be the only one unable to see the benefits of breathing new life into a derelict area that should have been razed years ago?'

'The only reason this area is derelict is because you persuaded the council not vote the funds to revitalise it as the local community requested.'

'Cutbacks. Did you want to see us rate capped like all the other councils who believe every deserving cause should be serenaded by a full orchestra when they really need to be drummed out of the back door?'

'And your little scheme is not going to cost us a penny, Mr Grablatt?'

The large mouth beamed wide enough to swallow an elephantburger. 'Gideon Enterprizes will supply the shopping centre. All we do is make a few concessions and provide the land.'

'Worth a rental value of millions per annum.'

'Enterprise, Councillor Makepeace. People want a shopping centre. Who else could we rent Victoria Park and a run down town centre to? The undead?'

Una Merryweather read the notes attached to the flowers placed before the remains of her family's business. At that moment she had nothing left in the world but a few credit cards, full board in a guesthouse for as long as she needed it, and a pot of bright yellow pansies.

The shock had long since worn off and with the insurance money she was almost indecently looking forward to a new life in the small fishing town where she and her husband had intended to retire. An overpowering man, Frank Merryweather had demanded that the world revolve round his mountainous frame. Now Una was able to stop running in circles, she could smell the moss roses left to run wild in Victoria Park and hear the squirrels squabbling in the branches of larch. Of course, she would have to keep up the act for some time yet and graciously accept condolences, secure in the knowledge that she wouldn't be around to be slowly marginalised as a widow. Having already been married to a grocer and butcher, what was wrong with trying out a redundant fisherman?

Una looked across the park. Through its damaged wooden walls, she could see something going on inside the derelict boathouse. A man wearing climbing tackle and a safety helmet was waiting while another with a silenced pneumatic drill tunnelled into its floor. She arched her neck to try and see more, and then felt that it was too early to show curiosity in such humdrum things as municipal maintenance. The workmen were probably only checking the sewers.

Una selected a long stemmed rose from the flowers, gathered up her carrier bag of toiletries and returned to the High Street to brave the sympathetic glances.

***

The Moltonford council chamber was surprisingly well attended, and the public gallery packed. Having failed to see modest redevelopment schemes approved, Neville Grablatt's proposal for a brand new shopping centre seemed an even better idea to the campaigning residents.

Of course, Councillor Makepeace radiated disapproval at the scheme, as he had done when speculators tried to muscle into Moltonford a decade before. Unfortunately he couldn't put into words what was so worrying about this new development, apart from it being proposed by Neville Grablatt.

There was an air of nobility in Conrad Makepeace's slightly stooped presence, like a self-effacing cricketer's about to be called to hit the winning six. His eyes were the same milky silver as his hair and it came as a surprise to hear that deep voice resonate from someone with such a narrow chest. Despite his crusading spirit, he possessed a calmness that persuaded people to trust him. Ex Inland Revenue, the councillor had a nose for projects that were not quite what they seemed.

It would have been pointless him getting up to confront Neville Grablatt, the champion of the huge shopping mall, to try and block his scheme. There were more grounds for complaint it being called Palace Parade, as not even the second cousin of a monarch had ever stopped in Moltonford to use one of their pink and cream urinals. Now the town could become the centre of the driving shoppers' universe. Gideon Enterprizes was American based; they liked the regal overtones and believed that no one could shop without a wheel at each corner. They had even designed, at great expensive, a rather vulgar crown that would no doubt appear over every entrance. Makepeace thought it should be called "Tacky Alley". As there was nothing he could do to outsmart the menacingly ebullient Grablatt, he closed his eyes and dozed. Perhaps something would crop up at the committee stage.

He woke as Grablatt was coming to the end of his triumphal speech.

'Oh, my God,' Makepeace groaned to himself. 'They've passed it. Where will the ducks and down and outs go now?'

The avuncular rumble of Neville Grablatt's voice was deceptively genial. 'And, bearing in mind government policy to discourage the building of out of town supermarkets, this development will house everything - and so much more - than other shopping complexes. There will no longer be any need to search for somewhere to park or struggle through the pouring rain and biting wind to buy life's essentials, or stand in endless queues at the post office when there'll be a counter in the same store where you purchase your loaf.'

Another scenario loomed before Conrad Makepeace. The man wasn't only going to plough up Victoria Park, he was going to back the closure of the local post offices as well.

Even the mousy mayor, vice chair, clerks, and chief officers had been spellbound by dreams of credit card heaven and Grablatt was too full of himself to be put off by one disapproving scowl. 'This is the future. The centre of our town will be protected from the elements, cushioned from the threat of street crime, and cater comfortably for everyone who needs to shop.'

There was enthusiastic applause from the public gallery and Conrad Makepeace half expected to hear the sound of pile drivers at any moment. From then on, it looked as though the champion of worthy causes would have to content himself with putting to rights the gripes he heard in his weekly surgery about the drains, traffic calming schemes, and barking dogs. Now the development had been approved, any debate about municipal incompetence would be edged out of council business by discussions on the colour of the paving bricks to pattern the forecourt of Palace Parade.

The meeting broke up and Conrad Makepeace's prostate insisted he pay a call before leaving the town hall. It was late and the bar had closed, so he wended his way past the enthusiastic groups of councillors and Palace Parade supporters and through the darkened lounge to the men's toilets. As he returned, he fumbled inside his wallet to find his member's card for the car park. Tugging it out, his family photos spilled across the bar counter and over the other side. Not knowing where the light switch was, Makepeace was obliged to get down on all fours and fumble for them.

Having retrieved the snapshots of his grandchildren, the councillor was about to pull himself up when he heard voices. One of them belonged to Neville Grablatt. The instincts of the tax inspector kicked in and he ducked back down out of sight.

Makepeace didn't recognise the businesslike voice of Grablatt's companion. 'I told you, Gideon is not going to commit without that surveyor's report.'

There was the familiar gurgle of perplexed amusement that resembled some huge carnivore digesting its prey. 'I keep telling you not to worry. He's in the bag. You heard the vote. No one can pull back now, not even if Makepeace besieged the town hall with tanks.'

'There's too much at stake here. Gideon isn't going to bring in plant before planning permission.'

'And you will have it.'

'And we don't want any trouble with the local builders.'

'There's only one firm of any size, and that's run by a woman. They never tackle anything more ambitious than the odd clinic.'

'I heard they built a multiplex in a neighbouring town?'

Grablatt grunted contemptuously. 'Oh that. Only some humdrum entertainment complex for a council estate.'

The councillor's business associate was obviously thinking something over. 'Has there ever been trouble between you and this woman?'

Grablatt sounded as though his estranged wife had accused him of going through her purse. 'Trouble? What possible trouble could there have been between me and a local builder?'

'Because if there has, she might feel inclined to start asking questions.'

'Suspicious or not, Mrs Zelinski can find out nothing. This is a tight operation. Do you think I wouldn't cover my tracks when dealing with a scam on this scale?'

The two men had reached the emergency exit and pushed its bar.

'By the way, you don't know who burnt out that butcher's, do you?'

Then, to Makepeace's frustration, the door slammed behind them.

CHAPTER 3

At approximately half past four the previous Tuesday, life had paused for Preston Niblock. Reality still seemed light years away, as though he had been nudged sideways into a different dimension where existence had a watery quality.

The jeweller watched the burly long distance lorry driver make token swishes at Deirdre's bric-a-brac with a duster as though he could waft away the ghosts clinging to her memory. The unlikely spectacle only heightened the unreality. Of well meaning souls, the husband of Preston's sister-in-law took full marks, but Ben hadn't been to that school which embroidered roses round the door of life and knew what to do when the stitches unravelled. If a jack, spanner, or new fan belt could fix it, Ben was your man. Unfortunately Preston's machinery needed the attention of a kindred spirit, not a lorry mechanic.

Barely five foot five, Preston Niblock had always been smart, though not dapper, and never wore his trilby at an angle. His cuff links could have been ruby and gold; instead he chose garnet. He preferred not to advertise his jeweller's skills with what he considered vulgar display. Finding that life wasn't so predictable after all had not persuaded him to review the way he saw the world; that would probably happen when the shock wore off.

Preston and Deirdre had seemed so compatible as they chugged along in life's two-stroke jalopy. Now, after ignoring them for over thirty-five years, Fate had lashed out with her hobnailed boot and left a cavernous dent in its bodywork.

To avoid confronting his grief, Preston tried to calculate how many hours on the road Ben was prepared to lose before being reassured that the jeweller wouldn't disappear through a rift in the floor to where purgatory was a solitary affair. Fran, Deirdre's sister, owned and ran the local garden centre, so she and Ben could afford to indulge themselves by doing the right thing. Preston wasn't sure whether he resented it or not. Though he didn't want company, he would have lost his sanity without it. Something kept insisting that if he went to sleep everything would slot back into place by the time he woke. After all, he was the one who should have collected Una Merryweather's locket. Deirdre knew nothing about jewellery. Given the crown jewels to look after, she would have polished the Kohinoor with Windolene. Loving the infuriating woman had never made any sense. It made even less sense now she was dead.

Ben looked at the alabaster carriage clock on the mantelpiece. It was a quarter to six. He boiled the kettle then filled a tray with sandwiches and chocolate biscuits in the hope Preston would eat at least one of them, even though the sight of food made the jeweller feel nauseous. It was just as well that the lorry driver hadn't attempted to cook one of the Greasy Spoon meals much beloved by his fraternity. Preston forced himself to sip some tea and Ben's large face lit up as though he had a winning scratch card.

Ben, whose presence could intimidate the most seasoned of picketing French farmers, tended to tower like a benign monolith and his chin always wore a five o'clock shadow regardless of how often he shaved. He had probably been a good-looking rogue when younger until Fran, and life in general, gave him a thorough going over. All that remained was a sly twinkle in the eye, the tattoo of a mermaid called Samantha, and the occasional stab of pain that made him clutch the small of his back where twenty five years on the roads of Europe had taken their toll.

By the time Fran arrived Ben had persuaded Preston to swallow some soup.

She took off her coat and waited while Ben washed up, secretly watching Preston's dark eyes, and tilted nose that gave him an incongruous air of defiance. There was no point in trying to say anything; the man was too intelligent to be soothed by platitudes.

'Do you remember that time the four of us went to Blackpool?' Fran eventually asked.

Reality still hadn't appeared on the horizon, so Preston didn't think the question odd. 'That was over twenty years ago?'

'Deirdre and me went to see this fortune teller while Ben tried to beat that Test Your Strength machine.'

'He did too.'

Fran hesitated. Preston wasn't helping her.

She took his hand. 'I never believed in all that mystic rubbish myself, but Deirdre was a sucker for it.' She swallowed hard before admitting, 'That fortune teller said she was going to die young.'

'She's fifty-two.'

'So Deirdre took out life insurance.'

'She never told me?'

'Did you tell her about yours?'

Preston shook his head. 'That's different.'

Fran took a letter from her shoulder bag. 'It's a lot of money, Preston.'

He pulled his hand free. 'I don't want it.'

'I know it doesn't matter to you now, but it's best you sign this all the same.'

'No.'

'It's what Deirdre wanted.' Fran put a Biro in his hand and guided it to the document. Shakily he signed his name. 'Good lad. Una Merryweather is moving to the coast on her insurance. Why don't you think about a holiday?'

'Without Deirdre?'

'We can come with you.'

'Ben has already lost a week's money running around after me and you can't leave the garden centre to run itself. I'll be all right.'

Fran sat back and looked at her brother-in-law. For a moment he sounded as though he meant it.

*****

Conrad Makepeace rapped the borough engineer's door. During weekdays its reception was usually open to field inquiries about leaky drainpipes on municipal buildings, blocked storm drains, and potholes in car parks. There was no reply, so he took out his glasses and read the tiny writing on the notice pinned to the door. 'Due to pressure of engagements, this office will be closed to the public until further notice. All enquiries can be made on the following phone and fax numbers.' Below was a list of answerphones that would take messages for everyone from the chief engineer to the office cat. The paranoia Makepeace was trying to fight back told him that they were probably plotting with the planning and architect's offices. Common sense insisted that they were bound to be busy after the announcement about the shopping mall, and nothing could happen until the borough surveyor had made his report. And if any of them were in the pocket of a corrupt councillor, he was no longer a tax inspector who could demand to see their books.

But what about the fire at Merryweather's? Two people had died and those instincts that had once led him to the dodgy receipt or embezzled millions were beginning to whisper "murder" into the councillor's reluctant ear. Despite being sure that the fire wasn't an accident, fire prevention were unable to say how it had started because the heat was so fierce it would have destroyed the traces of any propellants.

Then there was Preston Niblock. Conrad Makepeace had been acquainted with him for years. The jeweller had always engraved the names on his golf club's cups and mended many a family heirloom. How could he allow the man to believe that his wife had been murdered?

CHAPTER 4

A flock of pigeons pecking at a discarded beefburger took to the air and the occasional rabbit bounced from the overgrown hedges, wheeling this way and that in terror before disappearing into the neighbouring gardens. As the chain saws chewed through the trunks of their homes, squirrels angrily chucked at them. Larch cones cascaded down and, despite the risk to her perm, Linda Furnival darted in to collect the best branches for her flower arrangements. She secretly mourned the loss of her lovely, unkept park, yet for a shopping mall she would even forgive the council its road calming schemes.

Although planning permission had not yet been granted, there was nothing to stop the council felling trees or draining the lake. In the unlikely event of Gideon pulling out, Victoria Park could always be concreted over for skateboarders and car parking.

From a huddle of old raincoats and plastic bags in the derelict pavilion, three apprehensive faces watched. Their home may have been leakier than the squirrels', but it had kept them from the worst of the snow and wind. Now where would they go? Not into the town centre where the other down and outs were territorial and always drunk. As Merryweather's had burnt down, the rest of the houses in Victoria Street, derelict and occupied, would soon be demolished as well. Those residents who had held out could get compensation. Alice, Mabel, and Hector wouldn't get a sou. That's the way it always went.

Half a dozen duck catchers waded about the shallow lake trying to snare the birds whose protests could be heard in the High Street. A small band of onlookers gradually became a protest group, hurling imprecations at the abductors, even though they were trying to save the lives of the stupid creatures. Fortunately the lake hadn't been large enough to accommodate swans. For novices, ducks were difficult enough to handle.

The bird catcher's supervisor had been watching from the paddleboat jetty and came over to discretely ask the protesters whether they really wanted a shopping centre. His team was immediately left in peace to box the ducks and send them to a bird sanctuary where the geese would give them something to really quack about.

The Victorians had intended the shallow lake to be the focus of a pleasure garden in which children could safely sail boats and nannies wheel their charges. For many years it had been just that but now, many fancying a stroll past the philadelphus, weigela and moss roses, wanted somewhere to park. It was easier to drive the dog to the downs several miles away where their owners could sit in the car and watch their pooches defecate as they smoked and listened in comfort to the cricket.

Most children had deserted the playground for that all dancing, all singing, inter-active box in the corner that did their homework and provided monsters to zap. So only the vandals showed interest in the swings, seesaws, roundabout, and slide, leaving dangerous metal stumps that had to be removed. The gate carrying the notice about talking to strange men swung in the breeze, until an even stranger man knocked it off its hinges with a sledgehammer. The remains of the fence were quickly dismantled and rubberised surfaced ripped up.

Then the dredger arrived to remove the murky contents from the lake. A cover was taken off a nearby manhole and the water pumped into it until nothing of the lake remained but a deep layer of sediment, weed, and several items that had failed the audition for Cash Converters.

The pavilion was left until last.

Mabel, Alice, Hector, and Jenny had been comrades against the wide world in which they drifted; jetsam rejected by the virtuously employed and well off. Because they were inoffensive, in the main, and advanced in years they had been allowed to shelter in lock up garages and the occasional outhouse, though they had always returned to the derelict pavilion in the park. Because Moltonford Council had refused to approve the scheme that would have revitalised the area, it had stood mouldering away, giving shelter to the pigeons and doughty companions.

Now Jenny was gone. Alice assumed that the fairies had taken her, though Mabel refused to believe that she would have left for sweeter pastures without saying something. Hector had trouble remembering his own name, let alone anyone else's.

Jenny was a small, happy soul with no hang-ups or personal monsters. She had been born on the road and, when her family stopped travelling, had set out in her own camper until some council impounded it. The open air was her friend, and her only craving for material things was clothes. The last the others had seen of Jenny was when she had gone to collect a bag of cast-offs that would have helped them through another winter, and she wouldn't have run off lugging that with her. Hector might have done because of his tenuous grip on reality, and Alice was hardly any better because she thought she was a fairy and could fly, frequently ending up in the bushes when she tried. But Jenny - she was fitted with her own biological transponder that told her whereabouts in the world she was. The others were lost without her Traveller's instinct to find her way around, and daren't stray too far from the town centre and benefit office's counter.

Two social workers eventually turned up to offer Alice, Hector, and Mabel places in a hostel. Rounded up like sheep that had wintered on the moors, they gathered together their belongings and followed the social service shepherds.

Rotten to its foundations, the pavilion crumpled at the nudge of an excavator. The wood was burnt where it fell, casting another pall of smoke over the district and leaving nothing but the tiled floor donated by some Victorian benefactor. Moltonford's museum would have found storage space for it somewhere if someone had bothered to notify them what was happening.

Then metal jaws turned to the remains of Victoria Street. The coroner had given notice that the site of Merryweather's should not be disturbed until after the inquest. The police tape cordoning off the site had conveniently disappeared and, true to local authority communications, no one had told the demolition team. The address of the contractor's HQ was such a well kept secret that by the time the local police got wind of what was happening it was too late. If there had been a crime, all the evidence was now on its way to a landfill quarry. By the time the coroner heard about it, Victoria Street had disappeared - bar Henrietta Stevens who resolutely held out until forcibly removed. She had depended on the fair-mindedness of Moltonford's residents to object to an eighty-eight-year old being evicted from her lifelong home, without taking into account the overwhelming compulsion of apparently normal human beings to shop until their credit cards winced.

Given so many people had the craving to meander miles of supermarket shelving and see the ultimate in fitted kitchens, planning permission was promptly granted so the heart of Moltonford could beat in time to the footsteps of the consumer.

In Victoria Park, a scraper and three crawler dozers tore up the topsoil which was ferried away by a convoy of articulated loaders to cover the grounds of some executive director's barren estate. Then rippers and drills moved in to break up the pathways and boathouse's landing bay.

After the decades of sediment had been dredged from the shallow lake, its concrete bed was also broken up and carted away for use as hard-core. The park's trees had never been properly cared for and allowed to develop diseases and burr, so they were felled and burnt, watched from distant roofs by resentful starlings, and pigeons still trying to work out what was going on.

All the gardens backing onto the far side of Victoria Park were halved to accommodate an access road, and an old cinema and office block demolished. The landlords, who owned the jumble of offices, lock-up shops and restaurants in the centre of Moltonford, were paid generously to relocate, and their premises soon added to the brick dust billowing up and down the valley. When the demolition was complete, a swathe had been cut through the centre of the town as though some terrible juggernaut had ripped out its heart.

It was at this point that the owners of the shops in the adjoining streets started to wonder whether Palace Parade was going to be so good for their trade after all. They had assumed that the complex would bring more people into the town's centre. That was before seeing the final plans for the monster shopping mall. What they had been given to believe would be an open air shopping centre with a covered precinct, was now six storeys high with a glass roof to hermetically seal the customers from contamination by specialist outlets. It had just been a matter of moving a few key lines on a plan that was displayed for public perusal in the foyer of the council chamber, mostly inaccessible due to staffing cuts, so no one noticed until it was too late. Neville Grablatt's project was now a huge bubble to blissfully beckon people away from the real world.

CHAPTER 5

As she gossiped on the phone, Mary Bell gazed out at the tropical, turquoise ocean rippling like a sheet of thin silk. From the veranda of the mansion she could imagine turtles, manta rays, and the fish of the coral reef engaged in their life and death tango. Shoals of shimmering darts waltzed in the shallows like banners being continuously unfurled and sea birds hammered into the water, seizing lunch for their chicks. Catering to the strange whims of Julius Tucker the third was worth it just to bask in these exotic wonders. If paradise hadn't existed, he would have probably paid someone to invent it.

'You should be here Angie, it's beautiful. It's not like the house we had in the Barbados. This is right on the shore.'

'As long as he keeps sending the alimony, I'll be happy with Venice, Mary Bell. Now you remember what I said. Hang in there and you'll still be around when the old crook dies.'

Mary Bell resisted the urge to giggle. Though Julius Tucker didn't monitor her calls, she would have felt ungrateful. With the gifts he had lavished on the model, she could have bought her own island. 'Oh Angie, I wish we could meet once in a while, but I don't know what Juli would say? Would he be mad if he thought we got on?'

'Probably give us a medal each. He's a funny man. Blows hot and cold over stupid things. Someone with his money can afford to be eccentric, and then some.'

Mary Bell saw a launch drawing up to the jetty. 'My taxi's just arrived. I'm going shopping.'

'Have fun kid.'

Mary Bell always had fun shopping. She was genetically predisposed to pull out the plastic and purchase anything that glittered, jiggled suggestively, or fitted her.

She put on a flimsy, fluttery frock and huge sun hat. As she teetered down to the jetty in her sling back heels to the launch, even the gulls stopped fishing to watch, and the pilot had to keep reminding himself that he had seven children and very well paid job for a billionaire. Losing them for the sake of a quick grope would not have been a good move.

In a back room of the beach mansion, an architect paced round the scale model of his latest creation. He hated the thing, resenting the very balsa wood and styrene wasted to build it. He was an artist and should have been designing opera houses, libraries, art galleries - even the odd hospital. If the people who mattered realised that he had been responsible for this monstrosity he would never again be asked to create anything more adventurous than the kennels for a dog hotel. But this was a world where money was everything and professional integrity easily bought. He only hoped that anyone who went shopping in Palace Parade didn't share his ascetic sentiments.

Many aspiring architects might have been pleased with this creation of glass in which the escalators criss-crossing its interior resembled the teeth of gleaming rip-saws, and where cantilevered galleries were suspended like the running boards of some heavenly chariot crammed with cornucopian wonders. This architect had seen it all before. Enclosed shopping malls should have been consigned to the society's rubbish tip decades ago. Then, try telling that to someone whose only thrill in life was watching soaps and filling in lottery numbers.

Just before the sun went down, Mary Bell returned with a launch full of shopping. Lace edged pillow cases for their new love nest in London - Julius Tucker hated hotel linen - three gowns for a charity dance - she would decide which to wear on the night - and a box full of tourist mementoes to amuse herself wrapping as presents tomorrow.

Many might have said that Mary Bell's passion to purchase was due to some insecurity. Deep down, the model knew that she was really looking for that elegant Art Nouveau bracelet her mother always used to wear, and all these other things just seemed to get in the way. Five years ago that heirloom had been stolen from the family home and was never recovered. Now her mother had a terminal illness. Julius Tucker paid for an expensive nursing home and treatment that would give her several more years, and would have happily commissioned a copy of the jewellery, but Mary Bell was determined to replace the bracelet herself. It was the best way she could think of to show her love for a woman who had given up so much for her air-headed daughter.

CHAPTER 6

If there is any beauty in a cremation, it is in not having to cluster around a grave and give everything you had ever cared for to the muddy sod. Fire had killed Deirdre Niblock, so it was only fitting that it should consume what was left of her.

Preston Niblock felt as though he was going to float away on the perfume of the white and pink blooms that crowded the crematorium chapel. Fran was the local expert in arranging flowers for weddings, functions, and funerals. It was an ironical tribute to a woman who preferred the garden to be filled with forget-me-nots sooner than her sister's penstemons and petunias. Deirdre had been so different from Fran, Preston had often wondered about the wicked twinkle in their mother's eye. Now Deirdre had gone to join her, no one would ever know she did have that extramarital fling.

As he was well sedated, the congregation took the chief mourner's serene demeanour to be strength of character, not Prozac. Behind the impassive mask, Preston's thoughts were becoming more and more bizarre. Brandy and sedatives obviously did not mix. As long as he didn't fall flat on his face or let anyone smell his breath, no one could tell that visions of Old Testament magnitude were filling his mind. He was consumed by guilty memories of how he had treated Deirdre more like an inept child than an adult and never allowed her to follow through an irrational whim. Would it have hurt anyone if she had planted that hideous shrub with purple flowers in the front garden or built a hedgehog box in the rockery?

The jeweller sensed that the Universe was reading his thoughts. He had never felt so terrified of being found out. Even the flowers started to take on a life of their own, linking fronds to sway to the rhythm of the excavators only two streets away, and without so much as a stem of cannabis amongst them.

At the back of the chapel, Conrad Makepeace wondered what was going through Preston Niblock's mind. Would the jeweller have been so tranquil if he knew the truth about his wife's death? Well versed in the ways of such occasions, the councillor realised that the chief mourner was probably feeling very little at that moment. This service was for that monster, convention.

Una Merryweather was there, untranquillised and dabbing her eyes, more for her friend than husband. So were the Silvestri family who owned the health food store, Lucy Tribble the beadworker, Winston and Mercy Cuffe who owned Riotous Records, Monty Golden the bespoke tailor, Mr Singh the shoemaker with his wife, and many other shopkeepers from what was left of the town centre. At the very back of the chapel, trying not to look businesslike, were two plain clothes policewomen. Watching them from across the aisle, Councillor Neville Grablatt. Filled with an urge to reach for the man's thick throat, Makepeace closed his eyes and thought of cold marble.

The funeral breakfast was laid out in one of the conservatories at the garden centre.

Fran and Deirdre's father had been a grain merchant. Preferring flowers, Fran used her inheritance to set up a horticultural business years before buying plants became the Sunday substitute for Church and gardening programmes in colour had triggered ambitions in people once content to watch daisies invade the lawn. As soon as they had developed the compulsion to rake, feed and aerate their grass, then surround it with tubs of bamboo and datura, her turnover rapidly expanded. Now television had progressed and opened up luxuriant vistas to the window box minded. Fran had to anticipate the demand for trellises, artificial stone mix and F^1 hybrids like a supermarket stocking up with ingredients after a programme of Delia Smith recipes.

While the guests discreetly guzzled, munched, and made small talk, surrounded by Fran's tender stock of azaleas, gloxinias and calceolarias, Preston Niblock watched the sunlit scene and tried to find some niche amongst the bright colours in which to fit death. There wasn't even room for a graveyard spider, just sympathetic pats on the back, and careful grasps of the hand as though bereavement had transformed the chief mourner into fragile porcelain. Something told him that he couldn't float forever in this airy, expressionistic gathering and he would have to return to Earth at some time.

Ben noticed Preston's wan expression, sat him in a chair, and brought a cup of tea.

Eventually the limb of reality rose and dulled the colours. What was he doing here, wasting time?

'I have a brooch to set,' he announced to a neighbour who had been telling him about her Persian cat's new litter.

She hesitated before responding. 'Really? What stones are you using?'

'I promised Deirdre I would do it before her birthday. She wanted one for her navy jacket. Opal - the stones are fire opal surrounded by garnet baguettes - she wanted a dandelion. I didn't have the right colours, so I'm making her a dahlia.'

The woman knew she should let him ramble on, but felt impelled to sound interested. 'With rectangular petals?'

'I have some rock crystal beads.'

'Garnets sound nice.'

As he took a slice of cheesecake from the buffet table, Conrad Makepeace noticed Neville Grablatt zero in to offer his condolences. He left his plate to cut off the human bulldozer's approach.

'Councillor Grablatt, a word with you outside please.'

An annoyed flush filled Grablatt's huge collar. He daren't lose his temper here. Glancing around to find some way out, he instead saw Toni Zelinski, the local civil engineer, fixing him with a disconcerting gaze. He was unsettled enough to go outside into the avenues of compost to join Conrad Makepeace.

'This had better be good. This is a funeral y'know.'

'I'm well aware of that, and it's a pity we'll never know how the woman was killed now the crime scene has been levelled.'

Anyone else would have defensively pulled back. Like a true hypocrite, Grablatt quickly recovered. 'Crime scene? What are you talking about, crime scene?'

'The police told the coroner that the premises needed further investigation.'

'What rubbish, Makepeace. If fire prevention couldn't find anything, where was the point in waiting a couple more weeks?'

'A police forensic team were preparing to go over the debris. That's why they cordoned the area off. It was very convenient that their tape blew away before the contractors arrived.'

'These things happen.' Grablatt pulled himself up to his imposing height and dwarfed Makepeace, at least sideways. 'And why should all this concern me? Why bring it up here? Haven't you got any respect?'

'Just making sure you know that these matters do not go unnoticed.'

'Good grief, man! You're paranoid! Why would anyone want to kill Frank Merryweather?' Before Makepeace could assert that it was because he was in the way of Palace Parade, Grablatt snapped, 'I don't have time for this!' Then strode off.

'Yes, Mr Makepeace,' said a soft voice from behind a nearby trellis, 'why would anyone want to kill Frank Merryweather?'

He turned. 'Hello Miss Zelinski.'

Nobody really knew Toni Zelinski's age. Her husband was almost seventy, but she still ran up and down ladders, waded through muddy building sites, and glazed the odd window when she had no workmen on site unoccupied enough to order about. Not that anyone minded being ordered about by her. The civil engineer had an intangible charm that won over everyone from architect to apprentice brickie. It was odd to see her in a two piece suit instead of jeans and canvas jacket. Conventional clothes revealed how attractive she was in a mature dormouse sort of way.

Conrad Makepeace dutifully shook hands with the small, sturdy woman. 'I never saw you at the funeral?' he said.

'I only just arrived back from Scotland.'

'I'm sorry I couldn't do anything about the building contract. They wouldn't vote me onto the Palace Parade Committee.'

'That wasn't your fault. We all know that these things are fixed well beforehand - But murder?'

Makepeace gave an embarrassed smile. 'You never heard me say that. It was just to make Grablatt uneasy.'

'Really?'

'Every little helps.'

'No murder then?'

Makepeace examined the roses growing over the trellis. 'I think I'll take a couple of these for the porch. It might stop my wife painting it a different colour every year.'

Toni Zelinski smiled. In the business of building contracts, it paid to be able to read people, especially defensive members of local government.

***

That evening, while Ben snored in the spare room, Preston Niblock took the small family Bible from its box. He turned its gold edged pages as though expecting to find an explanation but the verses were for another time, another place, and more irrelevant than words in an avalanche. He had been without sensible thoughts for long enough and now wanted his mind back.

The jeweller watched the glowing embers of the fire Ben had lit more for comfort than warmth, and then tossed the Bible onto them.

CHAPTER 7

Hector tried to scratch his back. His rigorously manicured nails were useless and he let out a stream of monosyllabic profanity.

'That'll be enough of that!' snapped a voice from the high table.

'Bleeding Bible bashers!' cursed the old man, who rarely put more than two words together unless really roused.

'There are many who would welcome a place in this refuge.'

'Then why don't you bloody well go and fetch them?' Mabel declared in her plummy accent.

Alice tittered. She wasn't too sure what was going on but it sounded funny.

'All three of you have been nothing but trouble ever since you arrived.' Mrs Roy slammed shut the prayer book she had been vainly trying to interest her captive audience in, and stalked out.

'Bad move, bad move,' gabbled an inmate on the next table. 'Be bread and dripping for breakfast now, bread and dripping.'

'Don't need bleeding breakfast,' growled Hector.

When the social worker had promised the companions meals and beds they thought that she meant a hostel, not a reformatory where God's eagle eye gazed down from every tin lamp shade, and their small collection of worldly goods were fumigated before being impounded in a forbidding locker. They hadn't heard about Moltonford's brand new policy on vagrancy, which encouraged the immediate arrest of anything that looked as though it was about to settle on the pavement. It wouldn't have helped the companions to know that the feral pigeons had been poisoned and the dog pound was even fuller than Mrs Roy's emporium for waifs, strays, and the generally misguided.

Mabel straightened her hat as though about to attend a garden party. 'We had our own place, you know, in the middle of its own grounds.'

Alice tittered.

'Yeah,' said their neighbour. 'Well it ain't there no more. Big 'ole now.'

'Hole? What do you mean? Hole?'

***

A huge sheet of plastic flapped in the rising wind to reveal lights spangling the inky darkness below. From the depths rose the chugging of excavating machines.

'What's going on down there then?' a traffic warden asked his companion.

'Storage units. Be hundreds of them, each with their own lift.'

'Thought it was going to be car parking?'

'Nah. They're knocking down the bus garage for that.'

'Where they gonna park the buses then?'

'What buses?'

Having dug the hole of one section, the excavators started on the next, preparing the ground for raft foundations that would support the storage units, an access road, power cables, and water pipes.

From under the hood of her parka, Toni Zelinski furtively peered through a gap in the tarpaulin, down into a pool of light where East European tongues tried to make sense of the site engineer's instructions. Although she was an experienced civil engineer with similar ancestry, she couldn't understand what was going on either.

Eventually, Toni managed to calculate that a building half a kilometre long and several stories high, was going to rest on horizontal load bearing spans. The agitated discussion in broken English seemed to be about the proposed depth of the columns to support the centre of the structure. They were supposed to help spread the weight and balance the horizontal spans, but the engineer in charge wasn't allowing them to sink the columns any deeper than a metre.

Toni Zelinski replaced the tarpaulin, now thankful that she hadn't received the contract to build Palace Parade after all. It was also unlikely she would be shopping in the place.

***

Not one to get up early enough to read about the progress of Palace Parade in the papers, Emily shivered in the pounding rain as she waited for the last bus.

Without warning, a huge ball crashed through the wall of the bus garage opposite and added a hail of mortar to her woes. Not hanging around to find out what was going on, she pulled off her platform shoes and splashed over to the nearest phone to call a taxi. Where was a prossie going to take her clients after the shed at the back of the bus garage disappeared?

The following week, shafts were excavated in the bedrock to accommodate the outside columns that would support the whole shopping complex. To avoid time penalty charges, the builders continued to drill around the clock. Homeward bound revellers stopped to peer into the dimly lit holes and occasionally throw up.

Now the centre of Moltonford was empty of residents, it took on the eerie identity of some restless monster trying to flesh itself from the intestines outwards. On the balconies of council flats, people kept awake by cement mixers and pile drivers watched as, one by one, tall columns punctuated the night sky. Many were happy to substitute sleep with dreams of the shops that would nestle in their marble heart.

Preston Niblock looked down from his garret workroom, momentarily mesmerised by the frenetic pace of the building work in the valley below. Then he returned to the hinge of a locket. His hand was still unsteady. The shelf of half-finished settings and racks of pliers, needle files, triblets, and mallets surrounded him accusingly. 'Can't work? Won't work?' What use was a craftsman of fine jewellery when his hand shook? He needed a holiday.

Preston Niblock had bought his shop and home thirty years ago when the steep road down to the town centre had trees and grass verges until it was widened. The owners of the properties below him had sold their back gardens to a contractor who built a row of lock up garages. The jeweller kept his land. He resented being woken in the mornings by neighbours revving up their frozen engines.

Preston had never been sure whether Deirdre liked living next to the shop. It was a sizeable house and he had often sensed that she preferred to be in some unpretentious terrace with window boxes. As always, she never said anything, knowing he wouldn't want to give up the garret workroom that overlooked the centre of Moltonford.

The jeweller took a diamond catalogue from a shelf and tried to invite some sparkle into his life. It was no good. All he could see were the cat's eyes of a bland future stretching away into the night like an unlit road.

He went downstairs and made yet another mug of Ovaltine. Nothing worked. Sleep was another country. He examined his haggard reflection in the kitchen mirror. The hard fluorescent light ricocheted off a bald forehead too high for his slight frame. Preston was suddenly aware that the length of his remaining dark hair was annoying him. Used to Deirdre giving it a trim before it reached his collar, he picked up the kitchen scissors. Before he managed to cut a piece from his ear, he replaced them in the drawer and decided to leave it to the hairdresser.

CHAPTER 8

The chairman of the Palace Parade Development Committee, Neville Grablatt, brought the meeting to order with a bell borrowed from the council chamber. As he rose, his overpowering presence silenced the gathering of shopkeepers, and tenants of Moltonford's small industrial units.

From a distance, Neville Grablatt might have been mistaken for the sort of gentle giant who helped old ladies across the road and patted their overweight Labradors. As a councillor, that was how most saw him – fortunately from a safe distance. Those who knew better had sense enough to give the thug the wide berth his police record and size demanded. All except Conrad Makepeace, of course. During his life as an Inland Revenue inspector he had shrugged off worse threats than Neville Grablatt and was tall enough to look the man in the eye, not that he wanted to know what was going on behind those heavy lids. Grablatt had trained his expression to be bland, his tone conciliatory and garments to hang on his huge body without so much as a renegade crease. No one would have dared question how he could afford a wardrobe of hand-tailored clothes to cover his expanse, unlike many other councillors whose expenses only ran to the pick of the charity shops.

'Business people of Moltonford, let me welcome you to this meeting on behalf of the Palace Parade Development Committee. I am here to address any apprehensions you may have about the improvements to our town centre.'

Suddenly the air was filled with apprehensions. The bell once again tinkled.

'One at a time, please. Shall we allow Mr Becker to start?'

As he was one of the few to remain quiet, having been immersed in ideas for of the layout for his book on church furniture, this took the bookseller by surprise. 'Yes, er...' He suddenly remembered where he was. 'When will we know the cost of the units in the mall?'

Having thought his selection a clever one, Grablatt now regretted it. 'Ah, yes. That will not be known for some time yet. Rest assured that anyone unable to meet such costs will be compensated for any resulting loss of business.'

An ominous silence fell over the tradespeople.

Mr Becker promptly leapt from the cathedral of his preoccupations as he recalled Gideon Enterprizes testament to

Moltonford. 'Loss of business? I thought this shopping mall was supposed to enhance our businesses?'

'Indeed we hope so but, at this stage, nothing can be guaranteed.'

Winston Cuffe, who owned a record shop, was less diplomatic. 'All surveys carried out have found that small shops suffer when a large enclosed mall is introduced into a town centre. Our businesses will only remain viable in an open shopping precinct, as the residents had been demanding for over ten years, and were given to believe would be part of the development.'

'Now this is some-'

'Yes! Who decided to enclose everything in this massive aquarium?' blurted out Mercy, his sister.

More people leapt to their feet.

Chaos rained again until, taking the coward's way out, Neville Grablatt pointed to an accountant who was fortunate enough to have an office that would face the shopping centre. 'Miss Priddle, do you have any objections?'

The accountant polished her apricot nails on a matching satin collar. 'Yes, Mr Grablatt. I can't hear myself speak on the phone for those pile drivers, and all the pigeons not caught by pest control are roosting on my roof.'

The councillor was momentarily wrong-footed. Whatever powers he had in this little empire, pigeons were not subject to them. 'That wasn't what I meant.'

Miss Priddle leisurely scratched her head through her bouffant hairdo with a gold pen and looked the monster in the eye. 'Mr Grablatt, I have been asked to represent the Co-operative renting the industrial units in Archway Road. My clients are dependent on trade from the railway station traffic.'

There were murmurs of agreement in the background.

'Yes, yes. But this is a different matter-'

It was too late. The accountant's peach tones were pared aside to reveal the stone underneath. 'So why has the council abolished all parking in that area and doubled the rents of the units?'

Howls rose throughout the small hall.

'This is not relevant!' Grablatt bellowed above the din. 'Those units are unsafe! Structural repairs must be made! The new rents will only come into force when this has happened!'

Miss Priddle was finding the shouting competition tedious and would have rather been drinking wine with a vintage amour. The accountant rose like an equatorial sunrise and the audience fell silent. 'And, Mr Grablatt, while these repairs are taking place, does the council intend to allocate alternative premises to my clients? Or would it be more convenient for them to just go out of business?'

With a unified roar of rage, the metal craftsmen, a potter, shoe maker, baker, and electricians stood up, quickly followed by the rest of the audience. Even the thug in Neville Grablatt was unnerved, so he slipped through the platform curtains and out of the town hall to safety.

Without an Aunt Sally, the meeting was obliged to adjourn untidily to the nearest pub where the arrival of the angry crowd persuaded some students to vacate the benches in the garden.

'Is there anyone here who still doesn't believe something is going on?' Winston Cuffe aimed his question principally at the Cupit sisters who made children's clothes in one of the Archway Road units.

Vivian Cupit was highly strung and, once she believed her own conclusions, was prepared to attack anyone who disagreed with them. 'Why should this affect us? It will bring more people into Moltonford. I don't know why everyone's getting so emotional?'

'Sit down Vivian,' ordered Sonia Cupit. 'Mr Cuffe is right. There is something more than town centre redevelopment going on here. Look at the speed they're putting the place up. I doubt if the rats were able to get out of the sewers in time.'

Vivian huffily resumed her seat and sipped her G and T as though it was lemon juice.

Church furniture was now the last thing on Mr Becker's mind. 'And isn't it odd how all the local builders have been cut out of the contract?'

'Yeah, now why would they do that?' Winston asked ironically.

The bookseller shrugged. 'Perhaps there's something in the plans a mere British brickie would not be allowed to see in case he understood it.'

'Well, what about Miss Zelinski? – She's straight. Did our extension last year. Refunded a couple of hundred because they didn't need to make a saddle connection to some pipe. She wouldn't go along with any scam. That's probably why she was cut out.'

The bookseller replaced his glasses to give the gathering an objective look. 'Pity Niblock isn't here. He may be the quiet sort, but he's got a nose for these things.'

Vivian Cupit was unable to sulk any longer. 'I always thought his nose was too turned up to notice the tribulations of mere mortals like us.'

Monty Golden, the bespoke tailor, would have resented anything that came out of the woman's mouth unless it was her last gasp. 'Preston's a gentleman and he keeps himself to himself! Why would he waste his time here? His business comes through recommendation. He doesn't need a shop to stay solvent, unlike some people who wouldn't recognise a French seam unless they tacked their fingers to it!'

Vivian Cupit went bright pink and let out a gasp of outrage.

'Hey, steady!' called Winston. 'There's no point in fighting each other.'

Bored by the machinations of the shopkeepers and her clients, Miss Priddle glanced at her watch. 'Shame about his wife. Looks as though I'll have to wait for that pearl choker now.'

'Pearls for grief,' Monty Golden muttered.

'Well he's certainly had that.'

Mercy Cuffe had already been nursing her own doubts for some time and could keep them to herself no longer. 'That fire. You don't think? I mean…?'

'Deliberate? Probably.' Miss Priddle pulled out a silver note pad and consulted it. 'Fire discovered 1607. Fire service arrived 1614. Merryweather's gutted 1629,' she read as though it were simple arithmetic.

'Do you really think that it was arson?'

'Why else is there going to be an inquest.'

'Then why did the contractors clear the site?'

'Probably because there was going to be an inquest.'

The gathering fell silent. The manager of a small supermarket became uneasy at the implication and left. His store was part of a chain and could relocate.

Mr Singh, the shoemaker, didn't like the connotation either. 'That means anyone one of us here could be at risk.'

'Only if you get in their way.' Miss Priddle tapped her pearlised lips with her gold fountain pen. 'It would be interesting to see the contracts for Palace Parade. This place isn't being constructed to bump up the dividends of shareholders.'

'Why not?'

'Julius Tucker the third never floated Gideon Enterprizes.'

It would be another hour before the smell of traffic was wafted from the coast road and, as though scattered with sequins, the gently rippling sea sparkled in the morning sun. Preston Niblock put down his suitcase to lean on the promenade wall. He had often stood there with Deirdre to watch the sun setting over the headland and the ships passing like pieces on a glittering draughtboard.

A pier dotted with fishermen straggled out into the benign swell, coming to a full stop where some ferry had dashed away the pavilion at the end of it. And the sea walls were higher – large stone blocks indicating the height of public anxiety. Below was the dull clatter of pebbles in the outgoing swell and the smell of decomposing seaweed. Moltonford seemed a thousand miles away, not thirty. The jeweller even stopped thinking about the gems and precious metals sitting in his safe. Though he now ceased to value the materials of his trade, the unfinished jewellery of several clients lay accusingly amongst them. But this was not the time to wonder what stone to set at the centre of Lady Angela's pendant, or about reclaiming the precious filings from the bench apron. Until his hand stopped shaking, filigree falderals, and grain settings were beyond him anyway.

Preston picked up his suitcase and strolled down to Rosedale Guest House. For the first time, he wondered why it was called that when the landlady preferred to have clematis overgrowing the porch. Preston suspected that his sudden desire to analyse everything was a symptom of shock wearing off. Or perhaps he was at last admitting to himself that he was no more than the sum of his own expectations. Without Deirdre to discreetly boss around, life from now on was going to be lamentably empty.

The widower rang the doorbell and braced himself to face yet more condolences.

That evening, if someone had asked him what he had been doing all day he wouldn't have been able to tell them, only that he had the vague recollection of eating, walking and watching some ancient film on television where the star wore pearls the size of mothballs. All he wanted to do was rest. Then the dreaded moment, bedtime, arrived. Having hardly slept for weeks, Preston knew he would only lay awake under Rosedale's rose duvet, listening to ships pass in the night and counting the lights garlanding the promenade. So used to seeing across Moltonford's valley to the council flats and listening to building activity that never stopped, the darkness beyond the sea front was like a deep chasm.

He dutifully brushed his teeth, pulled on his pyjamas, and laid his head on the polycotton pillow to while away yet another sleepless night. The next thing Preston remembered with any clarity was the garnet hands on his travel clock telling him that it was half past ten. As the sunlight came round to penetrate the curtains, the landlady brought in a tray. Not knowing where his dreams had taken him that night, he had the watery feeling that this painful episode of his life had been shed like an ugly scab. Even the mirror revealed a reasonably alert middle-aged man who could have increased his weight by a few pounds and still been able to button his waistcoat.

After a full breakfast, Preston Niblock put on a light suit to make the most of the sun before another weather depression reared its ugly grey head.

He walked along the promenade and beyond to the rough path that wended its way down to the rock-strewn shore to watch fossil hunters busily chipping away at the shale. They always turned up ammonites, and occasionally somebody found that fly in amber or rare fish.

The jeweller turned over a small chalcedony pebble with his toe. Deirdre used to collect carnelian, agate, and quartz by the bucket load to polish in her wind driven machine that kept the neighbourhood awake when she forgot to put the brake on. Then she gave the stones away. Some women served in charity shops or visited the elderly. Deirdre polished pebbles and gave them away. If they had been together for another thirty-five years, Preston still wouldn't have understood her. A pang of guilt reminded him how he had insisted that she need not work, even in the shop. Although married to a master jeweller for most of her life, Deirdre never learnt to tell pearls from plastic poppets, or gold from copper. However much Preston loved her, she could have put him out of business within a week. So Deirdre regularly baked enough food to feed a troupe of boy scouts. Most of the rolls, pies and cakes ended up at bazaars, with neighbours and in the plastic bags of the down and outs in the park.

Preston summoned the strength to put his guilt back in its box and wandered over to the pebbles glistening in the outgoing tide.

Suddenly there was foam splashing over his shoes. He sprang back and brushed the water from his trousers. Someone chuckled.

'You need wellies around here. Pools of water everywhere,' said a short, stout young woman with a puckish smile.

'I'm foreign to this part of the beach. Usually keep to the promenade.'

'You don't sound that foreign?'

'I come from Moltonford.'

At the town's name, the palaeontologist involuntarily blurted out a laugh loud enough to frighten a herring gull from its perch on a breakwater. Preston wasn't sure what was so funny about his town, apart from the eccentric sculptures on traffic islands and pink and cream public amenities.

'You know it well then?'

She took a quick breath from an inhaler. 'Sorry. Only ever went there to buy the odd tool from Pilkington's – Is he still trading?'

'Retired two years ago. Both of his sons moved to Europe so he sold the business.'

'Shame. Don't suppose many specialist shops will last long when that shopping mall opens.'

Until then, the jeweller hadn't really given it any thought. 'You're probably right.'

The young woman started to giggle again. 'Bet they're getting on with it pretty sharpish?'

Preston's innate curiosity was aroused for the first time since the funeral. 'As a matter of fact, they are building at quite a lick.'

'They must know about it then. Have to with a building that size. Depends how far down they were able to sink the foundations, I suppose. But then, I'm a palaeontologist, not an architect. By the way, my name's Coral.'

'Mine is Preston.'

'After the town?'

'Born there to parents of small imagination.'

'That's lucky.'

'Lucky?'

'My parents are consultants on tacky films about rampaging dinosaurs – promote every daft dino DNA theory that reaches the cinema. They were dotty enough to have christened me Sally Sauropod instead.'

'Mine thought that a trip to the cinema warranted exorcism.'

'What did you watch when you managed to escape, then?'

'Harryhausen films about rampaging dinosaurs.' Preston glanced down at the fossil she was in the process of cleaning up. It looked like just another ammonite to him. 'Now it seems people get more pleasure from tacky shopping centres.'

Coral stopped giggling to herself. 'You sure it's going to be that tacky?'

'When it has destroyed all the opposition it can be as crass as it wants because everyone will have forgotten what quality is and how little they used to pay for goods.'

The palaeontologist opened her eyes wide. 'Ooh, there speaks the voice of deep loathing.'

As he hadn't yet come around to blaming it for Deirdre's death, Preston wondered why he suddenly hated the idea of Palace Parade so much. 'Maybe, but I can't see what's so funny about it? I doubt if they unearthed many good jokes during the excavation.'

'If they dig down deep enough, no one would do much laughing.'

Preston was unable to stand it any longer. 'Would you share the joke if I buy you a coffee in that café up there?'

Coral beamed. 'Why not. This can be thirsty work.' She gathered up her small collection of finds in a soggy raffia basket and led the way.

The palaeontologist was obviously a regular and her doughnut and coke arrived as they went to a table by the window.

She slurped down a few mouthfuls then took another breath from her inhaler. 'You know about the River Nox, don't you?'

Preston had never paid it much attention as its water rose some miles away from Moltonford. 'Yes?'

'It runs under your town.'

He hadn't known that. 'I thought its source was in the range of hills over fifty miles away?'

'The drainage basin is, then the river meanders through the bedrock. Guess where to?'

It didn't need somebody as sharp as Preston to work that out. 'You mean ... it will run directly under the new shopping mall?'

Preston's anxiety only made the scenario seem funnier to Coral. She continued to chortle, despite a mouthful of jam doughnut. 'Better than that. I've seen these old charts. The whole of your region – the downs, and Millington Hill – was made by earth movements that caused the rock to fold.'

Rocks on this scale were beyond the jeweller's comprehension. 'Not volcanic, surely?'

Coral laughed. 'God no, but the limestone is ancient and impermeable. During the Cretaceous, when it was more soluble, the run off gouged out a large network of caves.'

'I didn't know that.'

'It would be impossible to sink enough bores to map out their extent. We can only guess by the number of ancient artesian wells. Now most of those have disappeared since the water pressure dropped.'

Preston took a thoughtful sip of his coffee. 'I've lived in Moltonford most of my life and wouldn't have guessed it. Now Preston sounds a safer place.'

'Oh, it gets better.'

'Better?'

'You keen on shopping?'

It was an odd question to slip into a discussion about geology. 'What's that got to do with limestone caves?'

'The centre of Moltonford sits over a bloody huge one. So I hope they don't build any heavy turrets on Palace Parade.'

'But, the borough surveyor-' Preston stopped himself before he stated the obvious.

'Well, that's what the charts said when I saw them last. A year ago I wanted to find the location of this fossil bed worked by the Victorians, but suddenly no one's allowed to look at them any more. Could be cutbacks in library funding, but then, show me sixpence and I'd believe in the tooth fairy.'

Preston Niblock was beginning to wish he hadn't dispensed with his security blanket of religious belief so finally. The idea of some almighty deity watching, ready to punish miscreants wasn't perhaps such a bad idea after all. 'Oh dear God.'

Coral swallowed the rest of her doughnut. 'Well, when it all comes out, somebody's certainly not going to get to Heaven.'

The jeweller shook his head. Being thirty years older, he could no longer deny cruel reality. 'If it gets out.'

Conrad Makepeace looked in the rear view mirror to straighten his tie and comb back his thinning hair before stepping out of the car, ready to face any members of the press at the inquest.

Fortunately there was only one disinterested looking young woman who obviously aspired to report on more action than this. What might have previously led to a murder charge had now been relegated to a domestic tragedy, so the local newspaper had no doubt found a somersaulting guinea pig or rude vegetable to lavish copy on instead.

The councillor waited while the coroner and his officer bustled in, and then joined the other witnesses, glad that Preston Niblock was still away. The last thing the jeweller needed to hear was the gruesome details of his wife's death.

***

Alice clapped her hands and went spinning around the church hall like a lopsided whirling dervish, much to the disapproval of Mrs Roy who preferred Jesus to be worshipped a little more sedately.

Mabel caught her friend's arm. 'No, no, Alice. It's not a waltz, it's a hymn.'

The rest of the congregation were doing their best to cough in time to some irrelevant downbeat and Hector was braying inaudible obscenities to the tune.

Mrs Roy turned accusingly to the piano accompanist. 'This is impossible! What is wrong with them today?'

'It was fish cakes for lunch, Mrs Roy. They don't like fish cakes, much prefer fish fingers.' The old lady in the huge rouched hat smiled toothily without missing a note, as well as hitting quite a few of the right ones.

'What rubbish. How is it possible to show charity to these people?'

'Just think of Jesus, dear.'

Mrs Roy's eyes narrowed and her bosom heaved at the ingratitude of the ancient vagrants she had saved from the streets. Not even the thought of female bishops could fill her with such virtuous indignation. There was an order to all things and some almighty cue kept snookering them out of position.

'Smile dear,' said the smile under the hat. 'Jesus is watching you.'

***

The animal rights activist was a tiny young woman wearing an embroidered cap and braided hair extensions. The sleeves of her antique jacket fell over her hands and the mirrors on her long fringed skirt glittered in an unnecessary spotlight.

'Us, your Honour? No, we don't believe in violent protest. We believe in what Ghandi said. Our protests reflect the dignity of life and the way it interrelates-'

'Yes, Ms Tindal,' interrupted the coroner. 'We all know what Ghandi said. Just tell us if you know of anyone in the Animal Rights Movement who might have felt strongly enough to harm a butcher, namely Mr Merryweather?'

The small pinched face first mouthed the words before it dared utter them. 'No one that we know. Mr Merryweather led the fight against the redevelopment. After he had gone, there was no one to stop the bulldozers ripping the heart out of Moltonford.'

'You mean the park?'

'Yes your honour. It was the lungs of this town and now it will suffocate-'

'Thank you Ms Tindal.'

An usher gently escorted the animal rights activist from the witness's chair as though she was liable to flutter up to the balcony and throw down leaflets about saving the whale.

Sub Officer Yeoman took her place.

He explained that Fire Prevention had enough suspicions to recommend an investigation, but after the site was bulldozed they became academic.

The coroner resented being robbed of the chance to find reliable evidence and wasn't going to let the matter go easily. 'Tell me, is there any way of starting such a fire without leaving a trace?'

The sub officer's eyes momentarily glazed as though his reply would be broadcast nationwide for every arsonist to hear.

The coroner added, 'Of course, any members of the media will exercise discretion and not report your answer.'

The disinterested, solitary trainee from the local newspaper's sports desk continued to chew her pencil, unaware that her lewd doodles were being taken as a threat to the legal

38

process. The usher discreetly reached over and confiscated the frayed writing implement.

At last having the chance to air his suspicions, the sub officer's face lit up. 'There were several thermostats in the basement and, as the room was reasonably airtight, it would have been possible to release pure oxygen or any other flammable gas into the void.'

The coroner waited for the punch line. 'Yes?'

'Pure oxygen is very flammable, Sir. A spark from any of the thermostats could have ignited it.'

The coroner paused. 'Thank you Sub Officer Yeoman.' Over half moon glasses his glance swept the room. 'Is Mr Conrad Makepeace here?'

Everyone in the packed hall held their breath and from a privileged seat in the balcony, Neville Grablatt looked down at the thinning silver hair as his adversary took the witness chair.

'Mr Makepeace, I understand you had some communication with one of the deceased before this incident?'

'That is correct Sir.'

'Could you tell us the nature of it?'

Councillor Makepeace put on his glasses and referred to several letters. 'I received my first communication from Mr Merryweather on the 4th of November. He complained that he had been under pressure to sell his property to a company called Gideon Enterprizes. Despite several approaches he declined, though many other residents did accept the offer. Later, the borough engineer sent letters to everyone still with property in the street stating that, as the houses were so run down, they would be demolished to make way for a new development, not specified. Mr Merryweather was angry because his premises had always been well maintained, and had stood on the same site for over two hundred years.'

'This actually being the business he inherited from his wife's father?'

'That is correct.'

'Please carry on.'

'Mr Merryweather had encouraged the remaining residents in Victoria Street to resist the compulsory purchase order and asked me to look into the matter. I did so, yet was unable to find any report by the borough engineer or planning office that explained their correspondence.'

'Was there no record of the letters being sent from council offices?'

Conrad Makepeace removed his spectacles. 'None Sir.'

'Can you say where the letters might have originated from?'

'Paper with Moltonford Corporation letter heading would be easy enough to come by.'

'Do you have any reason to believe that Gideon Enterprizes was involved in this matter?'

'All my letters to them were ignored.'

'Where were the threatening letters to Mr Merryweather posted?'

'Unfortunately all his correspondence when up in the fire. I have no envelopes and only photocopies.'

The last line of enquiry cut, the coroner sat back. As he glanced up, the large, grinning face of Neville Grablatt seemed to rise like a malevolent moon over the balcony balustrade.

***

Relegated to the garden for bad behaviour, Hector, Alice and Mabel took their plastic chairs to a bushy magnolia and clustered beneath it like plotting magpies.

'Not like park,' rumbled Hector, thinking of the goodies that Deirdre Niblock used to regularly bring them. 'Where's Jenny?'

'I keep telling you, she's gone,' scolded Mabel.

Alice sighed. 'Why can't we dance any more?'

'We were wearing out the parquet paved with charity.'

The other two ignored Mabel when she talked like that. It also made do-gooders suspect that she wasn't quite what she seemed.

'Merryweather! Sausage!' Hector suddenly blurted out. 'In bun! Mustard!'

'Only on Sundays,' Alice reminded him. 'Only on Mondays.'

'Not since plumbers.'

'No, not since the plumbers.'

Mabel nodded. 'They should have fitted sprinklers.'

Alice was momentarily lucid. 'What were they fitting in his basement then?'

'No idea, but it wasn't sprinklers.'

'No, I suppose not. Burnt down the same day, didn't he.'

'Yes Alice. Poor Mr Merryweather and Mrs Niblock burnt down the same day.'

Much to her irritation, Miss Priddle scratched her nail varnish on a staple as she pulled out the brashly coloured brochure from its envelope. She read the Gideon Enterprizes promotion with a mixture of distaste for its simplistic hype, and outrage at the enclosed list of proposed ground rents for Palace Parade. The cartoon crown sitting at the top of the page should have been a tin hat, because there were going to be some pretty annoyed shopkeepers in Moltonford. None of them would be able to afford Gideon's charges, even if they took out a second mortgage and sold the family silver. As well as the craft workers and bespoke goods outlets she had agreed to represent, this was also going to hit the small industrial units. Preventing so many businesses from going under would tax even her ingenuity.

Large companies came in many sizes and shapes. Those controlled by only one person were the most difficult to deal with. You could lop the occasional head off multi-headed monsters without the others realising what had happened. One person capable of managing a multi-billion dollar empire was instinctively programmed to know everything about their business, from when to seize and asset strip competitors to how many paper clips went missing from his secretary's desk. Getting past the Cerberus that guarded Gideon's gate was going to be a challenge.

The next meeting of Miss Priddle's clients in the small church hall was subdued. The gathering of shopkeepers and craftspeople now had no Grablatt to shout at, and knew that virtuous rage would not prevent their businesses from bleeding to death. Mercy Cuffe was close to tears and her indomitable brother at last lost for words.

The accountant took an envelope from her briefcase and tried to sound matter of fact. 'Of course, there is this goodwill promise of one sizeable unit to act as an outlet for several businesses. It would at least afford a collective presence in the mall while you retain your original premises.'

Monty Golden shrugged. 'Where would be the point? However large it is, it couldn't carry the stock of everyone here, let alone display it.'

'And it's tucked right by the Victoria Square entrance,' sneered Vivian Cupit.

'Nevertheless, I am recommending that you allow me to take up the option so they won't have the excuse to rent it out to someone else.'

Monty Golden couldn't see the point, yet deferred to her clinical reasoning. 'You're the brains.'

Aware of the bespoke tailor's business acumen, Miss Priddle doubted that he meant it. 'Thank you.'

Ever the optimist, Vicky Wade asked, 'Can you see a way of making this work for my pottery?'

The accountant neatly folded the letter and replaced it in her briefcase. 'No prospect is totally hopeless, though I would advise those able and willing to take any compensation move their businesses. From now on, it will be an uphill struggle for all the specialist shops in Moltonford, but...'

It was unlike Miss Priddle to hesitate, so the potter prompted, 'But?'

Mental cogs had started turning. However, even this mathematician needed time to calculate one of her Machiavellian schemes. 'I will have to study the small print of the contract a little more closely. From an initial reading, it appears to contain guarantees of tenure and rent, as well as generous storage space directly below the premises.'

'That's because they don't expect us to take it up,' said Mr Becker. 'How could we manage to fit a bookseller, potter, electrical goods, health foods, clothes, shoe maker, and jeweller all into one unit?

The jeweller he had actually been referring to was Lucy Tribble from the industrial co-operative, though Vivian Cupit cut in rather nastily, 'Well, I can't see Mr Niblock taking up any space. They say his mind isn't what it used to be after what happened to his wife.'

'That was uncalled for!' snapped Sonia, wishing she could tip her touchy sister into the footings of Palace Parade and let them concrete her over, though the acid would have probably seeped through the hardcore.

Miss Priddle snapped shut the catches on her briefcase with a click that resonated about the timber roof void. 'If anything constructive is going to come of this there must be no disagreements. I've seen too many businesses fold because partners fall out.' The tone was not so much schoolmarmish, but Madam Speaker.

'Hear, hear,' Mercy Cuffe muttered into the intimidated silence.

The accountant expected nothing to be resolved that evening. Ideas fluttered through her mind. Those without plausible business portfolios tucked under their wings were quickly shot down.

As the gathering morosely dribbled out to late dinners and the pub, Miss Priddle repaired her lipstick. In her mirror she noticed a butterfly standing between the rows of stacking chairs.

'Mrs Singh, I never saw you in the audience?'

Despite her elegant saris, the wife of the shoemaker only made a point of being noticed when it was convenient.

'I do not wish to detain you, Miss Priddle.'

The accountant laughed. 'I'm pretty sure you can't have anything less constructive to offer than the others. What can I do for you?'

The breeze from the open door seemed to waft Mrs Singh forward. 'In my home village my grandfather used to own a large store. As it was the only store, he had to sell everything. Some things were not always available when people travelled from outlying districts to purchase their goods. It was often months before they were able to return. Had he known exactly what they needed, he could have had it waiting for them.

'My grandfather's brother used to send him books from the United States. Many of them were very old. One day something arrived which gave him an idea. An idea that has worked in different ways, and different places, over and over again.'

***

Preston Niblock read the article once more. If he had stayed away another week it would have given Fran time to gather up all the newspapers in the neighbourhood and incinerate them. He hadn't told her of his intention to return for fear of coming back to a house filled with flowers. Preston had never managed to pluck up the courage to let his sister-in-law know that carnations made him sneeze. How could you tell the owner of a garden centre something like that?

Once again he read the coroner's conclusion. 'Frank Merryweather and Deirdre Niblock met their deaths in a fire, the causes of which were suspicious, though without sufficient grounds to recommend further investigation, I must therefore return a verdict of unlawful killing.'

Deirdre murdered? As well as illogical guilt, Preston's mind was now seared with rage.

In the days that followed he kept the closed sign on the shop door and sat in his garret workroom, idly trying to play shove halfpenny on his bench pin with cabochons and soldering the swarf of precious metals into bizarre doodles. Then he used a blank of platinum to chase the image of a skull and grain set scrolls of diamonds and sapphires over its surface. He would have pierced Satan's outline in gold but didn't have the right star rubies for the eyes and suddenly felt hungry.

The jeweller went downstairs to make a sandwich with dry bread. Then he sat brooding behind drawn curtains and ignored it.

Somebody turned the keys in the locks of the shop door. He ignored that as well.

Fran, not having heard from him, had a hunch that he had returned days ago.

Seeing Preston's mug of cold coffee, she put on the kettle. 'You've read the paper then?'

He continued to stare at the wallpaper. 'Why would anyone want to kill Deirdre?'

'They probably only intended to burn down Merryweather's.'

Preston often found his wife's family unsettlingly practical when they should have been passionate. 'She was your sister?'

'If I knew who was responsible I would commit murder, but I don't, and am never likely to.' She pushed a plate of biscuits in front of her brother-in-law then sat down to face him. 'Preston?'

'Yes?'

'Are you sure you want to stay in Moltonford?'

'Why shouldn't I?'

'It's not going to be much of a place for small businesses from now on. You could afford to move to the coast, retire, or start that small museum you wanted.'

He looked vacantly at the tea service as though it was about to vote on his sanity. 'I have to know why Deirdre died.'

'Preston..?'

'Would you move?'

Fran shrugged. 'My business won't suffer. Given the way they'll heat the place, they can't have a garden centre in the shopping mall.' Fran threw open the curtains then poured their tea. 'You'll have to decide one way or the other. People are starting to enquire about their heirlooms.'

Preston hadn't given closing the shop much thought. It was a decision he might have drifted into before he realised that Deirdre had been murdered.

Cold logic joined hands with his guilt. 'No. Whoever was responsible for her death is probably connected with Gideon Enterprizes, and I'll be damned before I allow some corrupt speculator to put me out of business!'

Fran lowered her cup in surprise. She had never heard so much conviction in his tone. Although sharp-witted, her brother-in-law had always appeared mild mannered. Now some metamorphosis was taking place, but not one liable to flutter off on pretty wings and sip nectar from the buttercups.

CHAPTER 12

Palace Parade stretched from the town hall, right through the centre of Moltonford and to the small square commemorating Queen Victoria at the other. When it was closed it effectively cut off access from one side of the town to the other.

True to its royal pretensions, the contractor had cast preformed Hellenistic pillars for its grand front entrance and façade, though they owed more to Walt Disney than Palladian pretensions. Supported by the load bearing outside columns, five levels of cantilevered gallery ran the length of the mall. This allowed in enough sunlight from the six storey high glass ceiling to illuminate the mall's simulated marble and mosaic floor. That was all the customers would be allowed to see of the great outdoors. Even the vast store windows facing the High Street were filled with displays backed by screens that blocked out daylight. At night the Moltonford ghosts, whose haunts the monstrosity had displaced, would only have the safety lights to find their way around, apart from Molly MacGlagen the axe murderess, who had committed her deeds by candlelight and always had a match handy.

It was opening day. Palace Parade was festooned with bunting and balloons, much of it in places only hydraulic platforms and the surviving pigeons could reach. All that was left of the old High Street was two fast food outlets, half a dozen estate agents, and a forecourt in cream and red brick from which the customers could be enticed into the major stores. Neatly dotted with flower containers, it made a promise of the antiseptic interior.

On the other side of the wide, welcoming glass doors escalators rotated like jewelled treadmills and see-through lifts ascended and descended with no visible means of support.

Everyone in Moltonford with a credit card and car boot was thronging around the steps of the town hall where Neville Grablatt and a star from a television soap out-performed the town's dowdy little mayor. The poor man had only been voted into the position because he never got in anyone's way or upstaged the real stars. If it hadn't been for his chain of office, he would have been mistaken for Grablatt's lunch.

After the menacingly ebullient councillor had finished his oration to Gideon's commercial vision, the mousy mayor uttered a few piping words. Then the Botoxed soap star tottered down the High Street on five inch heels, ready to snip the pink tape across the entrance to consumer heaven after the parade.

A huge net burst asunder and excited children chased after the released balloons that hadn't floated up to further alarm the much harassed pigeons. Few people bothered to read the small print on them, just below the cartoon crown, and probably wouldn't have known what Gideon Enterprizes was anyway, despite Grablatt's eulogy. The only thing Moltonford seemed interested in was shopping; for many the ideal substitute for sex. It may have been more expensive, but you always came out with something to show for it other than pregnancy or some noxious disease.

Then the majorettes arrived. Exhilarated by their success in a baton twirling competition, they spun, twisted, skipped, and kazooed for the milling crowds, clearing the way for the main attraction, floats of every nation. Well, nations north of the equator with the income and a similar appetite to shop. Stars and Stripes led the procession and onlookers grabbed the proffered beefburgers and hot dogs from huge two-legged, foam rubber buns.

On the French float paraded fashion plate models with coat hanger shoulders in off-the-peg clothes that would be available to the public in only a matter of moments from the largest store. Holland was laden with cheeses that had little in common with Dutch cows, and cereals that had everything to do with genetically manipulated soya, maize, and sugar. Then there was a flotilla of smaller floats filled with clothes, groceries, more clothes, shoes, and even more clothes.

Miss Priddle was sitting at the window of her first floor office with Toni Zelinski watching in contemptuous amazement.

No one knew Miss Priddle's first name. She guarded it as though it was even more unlikely than her surname. Whatever else she might have been, the accountant was not a Priddle. She was an Athena of the ledger, the goddess who could stand before the tide of outgoing expenditure and make it flow back into its original budget. Many a suicidal businessman owed his sanity to her inventive - and totally plausible - way of presenting accounts to the Inland Revenue. She had thrown life belts to shopkeepers mired down in receipts, and found obscure items of legitimate expenditure that turned around the profits of several small businesses. Names wended their way from the City to discreetly ask her to unravel unfortunate commitments they made in the flush of yuppiedom, and the managers of international firms surreptitiously faxed her their accounts to find out who had been embezzling the tea money.

No one was sure what planet Miss Priddle had arrived from, or to what she owed her phenomenal capacity for preventing people from being suffocated by their own spreadsheets. Because her hobby was making herself look like a model who fell off the catwalk some time in the seventies, her occupation seemed all the more remarkable. When her clients had an accountant who could save their businesses, they weren't going to wonder too much at the tightness of her skirt, height of her heels or how much lip-gloss she used.

Sipping wine, the accountant and civil engineer peered over the flower box to wonder as float upon cumbersome float appeared from nowhere.

'I wonder where they had all those parked?' mused Miss Priddle.

'Probably that set-aside field on Butt's farm.'

'The wretched man hasn't sold the land to Gideon has he? I don't think I could cope with more than one procession like this in a lifetime.'

'Don't worry, it's too far out. The field turns into a bog after a shower and it wouldn't be worth draining for a car park. They need land in the town centre.' Toni noticed the next set of floats approaching. 'Oh my God. This must be the seasons.'

Spring just managed to stop short of infringing Disney copyright, although the suspended polystyrene centaurs and blue-haired sprites were a risky cross between My Little Pony and Fantasia. Dolls and toys for babies bounced from a canopy of billowing, parachute like clouds and media related mechanoids for teenagers chased each other with alien weaponry to tinny sound effects on the rolling daisy covered hillocks below.

Toni Zelinski was more interested in autumn's castle than why the float had managed to arrive before summer. It shouldn't have been possible to balance the top-heavy construction on the truck's narrow base, let alone have a dozen knights in full armour perching on the battlements. Her gaze eagerly followed it like a spectator at Le Mans anticipating a pile up. The fact that the castle was advertising kitchen utensils quite escaped her. The last place she expected to see a saucepan was on the head of a Norman knight.

Summer, rushing to catch up, was festooned with so many billowing drapes that the point of the spectacle was mostly obscured. Tony Zelinski and Miss Priddle decided that it had something to do with fashion. As the accountant had her own firm ideas about dress and the civil engineer was more used to boots and safety helmets than frocks, they felt no sympathy for the models being strangled by their own backdrop.

Winter predictably had a ski slope crowded with the members of a sports club demonstrating how you too could have bodies like them if you exercised with their selection of equipment.

Miss Priddle stifled a yawn. 'This is going on forever.'

Toni noticed a new wonder. 'Oh look, a Jacuzzi on wheels.'

'What's that supposed to represent? Effluent control?'

The builder had something else on her mind. 'Wonder how they managed to plumb it in?'

The accountant's priorities were slightly different. 'I wonder if that blond beefcake is wearing knickers?'

'Given the height of those bubbles, he needs scuba gear.'

'They left out Russia.'

'Vodka and the Mafia?'

Miss Priddle reached over the window box and caught a balloon. She tapped the small print beneath PALACE PARADE 'That's the closest we're likely to get to Gideon Enterprizes.'

'Not even an address I can send my hate mail to. At least being just across the road from them won't do your business any harm.'

Miss Priddle burst the balloon with a sharp scarlet nail and scared the pigeons roosting in the guttering above. 'This shifty estate agent from out of town has an "important client" who wants to make me an offer for the place.'

'Just as well you own the freehold.'

'Now why on earth would Gideon need this side of the street as well?'

'Because property values will be soaring in a matter of minutes?'

'I doubt it.'

'You're right. No other business would stand a chance. The rest of the town centre will only be fit for charity shops and estate agents by the end of the year.' Toni took a sip of her sherry. 'Still prefer to see the old park there instead of a wall of glass.'

'At least it will give the local yobbos something to amuse themselves with.'

Toni Zelinski shook her head. 'Not that stuff. It's not your regular laminate or toughened glass. Even I wouldn't have been able to supply it if they had given me the contract.'

'You know anything about the construction company?'

The builder shook her head. 'Mystery to me. American architect, Hungarian contractor - civil engineer probably came from Mars.'

'Why's that?'

'It was a bloody funny way to put up a place that size.'

'What do you mean?'

'Everything hangs from the outside columns.'

'Shouldn't it then?'

'A place with those overheads needs to maximise its floor space. The complex could have contained stores on several levels. Instead, it has those narrow galleries of boutiques you could hardly turn a pig in. They make the building look like a gutted liner.'

'Oh, they won't be losing out. Add to the exemption from rates, no need to pay ground rent for five years, and the fact they only had to fork out for building the place and they're laughing.'

'No kidding?'

'Now there are some books I would like to go over. Neville Grablatt has all the answers, but they aren't going to be published in the local council's newsletter.'

At last the soap star dutifully cut the scarlet ribbon and. as the large glass doors to Palace Parade opened, another net of balloons were released, along with some rather disorientated doves that zeroed in to the pigeons returning to Miss Priddle's roof with outraged territorial cooing.

She closed the window.

The Mayor's party quickly stepped aside as a stampede of shoppers rushed forward to be first at the special offers.

At every corner inside Palace Parade stood lithe young people wearing comedy crowns and garish uniforms plugged into welcome mode. They handed out commemorative pens, lollipops, and fizzy drinks. Throughout the heart of the complex the escalators criss-crossing to different galleries framed a fountain dancing to a selection of mind deadening Musak.

Quickly overcoming their awe at this cathedral to consumerism, people began to search for discounts. Customers who counted the pennies when buying baked beans suddenly found the money for frilly blouses that would only be worn once, monumental candles for the patio, and aftershave guaranteed to attract every airhostess from Florida to Singapore.

The shopping frenzy eventually died down when some residual logic told everyone that the mall would be open the next day as well, and the day after that and so on, until all the world's special offers dried up.

Some stores had a sameness about them, like familiar tunes played in a different key. If one had petit four boxed in cellophane, another would have the same confectionery in glass trays with a spray of silk violets costing twice as much. Perfumes for every occasion and person, male, female, and pampered pet, were also priced according to container. No one seemed to mind. The point of having an expensive looking bottle on your dressing table was that visiting friends retrieving their coats from the bedroom after dining on your cordon bleu crab paté would realise what an affluent and discriminating acquaintance you were. The fact that the selfsame product could be bought in half litre bottles in one of the large chemists for the same price would escape their attention because they weren't going to admit that they shopped in such a downmarket outlet.

The Tots 'n Tinies store sold every media related toy parents dreaded as soon as the film appeared. Overpriced moulded rubber cartoon characters were one thing - fiendish plastic engines that spat pellets, shot out blades and kung-fued the cat without warning, were quite another. Life in the nursery was already hazardous enough.

The Tots 'n Tinies imprint published alien, brain-sucking monsters for the semi-literate mind. If the tots were too tiny to revel in the adventures of the World Destroying Demon of Mars, they could always read about the inane antics of little fluffy animals running around in frilly bonnets, patchwork waistcoats, and pinnies. And for those parents who couldn't read, there were sticky transfers of expressions they could help their offspring fix to the right face.

The larger stores appeared to have found a mythical Far Eastern island where the inhabitants lived side by side with grinning turtles, large bland bears in straw hats, and a whole range of other cute animals they were impelled to replicate wood, straw, stone, and metal. The ornaments sat, perched or crouched beside small porcelain houses with filigree thatched roofs and twisting chimneys, and notebooks of handmade paper decorated with gold scrolls. After the senses had been desensitised by display upon display of these gewgaws the price didn't seem to matter.

Embroidered linen sheets to match the wallpaper, wallpaper to match the curtains; everything had its place on the display shelves. It would all be rotated once in a while to give more useless items room. Palace Parade may not have had a feel for the necessities of life, but it certainly had the knack of making people wonder how they could have existed for so long without an exotic wooden salad bowl, onyx candlestick, or inflatable sandpit.

That evening Preston Niblock watched from his garret workroom as a spotlight on the roof of Palace Parade projected the silhouette of that dreadful crown into the sky.

He put on his coat and strolled down to the Victoria Square end of the High Street. From there the shopping mall resembled a monstrous glass serpent that had just swallowed the town. The inadequate car parks were filled with the honking and abuse of those trying to escape from its belly.

'My God,' he murmured to himself as though noticing Palace Parade for the first time. 'It's six storeys high.'

The jeweller felt a chill breeze, pulled up his collar and walked back home.

CHAPTER 13

One of the secondary entrances to Palace Parade opened onto the small square that was all that was left of Victoria Park and faced the gates of Fran's garden centre. Having bought their plastic flowerpots, potting compost, and trellises in the shopping mall, people were fortunately fired with enough ambition for something other than plastic flowers.

Before padlocking the main gates the next day, Fran thanked goodness for the damage the central heating in Palace Parade would have done to bedding plants and started to tally up the day's takings. Predictably, compost and garden tools were down. Plants had been going as soon as she received new stock. That was the way she preferred it. Flowers were shelf worthy for a limited period, compost only matured with age. When Fran thought about the rapid decline of the other local businesses she felt a little guilty, and wondered why the planners of the shopping mall had allowed her to survive. Unfortunately there was a reason. It was standing in the greenhouse outside her office door.

The professional looking young man with a smart suit and flash mobile probably had too many diplomas to be a regular estate agent. As soon as Fran realised the purpose of his visit she recalled that Frank Merryweather's troubles had started with a letter from some anonymous client offering to buy him out.

Although tough when handling business matters, the appearance of this hardly weaned executive made Fran's blood run cold.

Her staff had just left so she locked the office door to come out into the fuchsia house to meet him, only to realise that she was now too far from the panic button. Though he was unlikely to give her reason to hit it, the option would have been a comfort.

Of course, this young man's client was prepared to give her a good price for such a favourably situated site, and shares in the development planned for it.

Fran's response was immediate. 'The rest of Moltonford's been concreted over. It doesn't need any more development.'

The young man was momentarily disconcerted by the way the red-haired woman lowered her head as though about to charge. He hadn't been briefed to deal with this degree of recalcitrance. It looked as though the menacing aura he had spent hours perfecting in front of the executive washroom mirror would at last have its use.

'You'll never get another offer like this. You could retire and live comfortably for the rest of your life.'

'I'm used to working. My family prefers to work until they die. This business has been good to me, and I'm keeping it. Anyway, how can you be so sure you'd get the planning permission to build on it?'

The young man's smile was humourless and sinister, as though some demonic entity was preparing to break through his bland, pale skin. Planning permission was obviously no problem. 'You've a very long perimeter here. Must be difficult, keeping out intruders?'

'Just the squirrels, and they're only here because they were evicted from Victoria Park. So what is it your client wants to build on this site?'

If Preston Niblock hadn't put on crepe soled shoes for the first time in his life they would have heard him come in. 'How about another car park?'

They turned to see the master jeweller lounging against the frame of the greenhouse door.

He hadn't been part of the young man's equation. In fact, he had been given to believe that Preston Niblock was so overcome with grief he refused to leave his house. But there he stood, tie-less, slightly dishevelled, and nonchalantly swinging a carrier bag as though he had just been deadheading the roses with an automatic pistol.

The visitor frowned. 'What makes you say that?'

Preston strolled in. 'Oh come on, as long as the industrial units in Archway Road refuse to part with their premises, and nobody in the streets facing the mall will sell up, it's obvious. There's no room in Palace Parade for cars and Gideon Enterprizes isn't going to use valuable shop floor space for parking.'

Having the advantage snatched away from his well-manicured grasp, the visitor suddenly sounded older. 'Who are you?'

'You know who I am. My name is Niblock, Preston Niblock. Your client will certainly remember the name. My wife was "unlawfully killed" when Frank Merryweather's shop burnt down.'

Fran marvelled at the hardening of her brother-in-law's manner. It looked as though he was about to make up for a lifetime of being mild and meticulous.

'What are you saying?' Though the young man sounded threatening, he stepped back, knocking over a Dollar Princess standard as the jeweller approached.

'I am saying that, if I ever discover who was responsible for my wife's death, I will destroy them. And if so much as a lit cigarette end falls onto a packet of petunia seeds I shall go to the relevant authorities with a few surprising geological facts.'

The young man hesitated. 'What are you talking about?'

'You don't need to know. Just tell your boss. Now get out!'

Trying to stay cool, the interloper picked up his briefcase and wended his way through the Campanella and Lena Daulton to the entrance. Fran and Preston watched in silence as he drove off.

'What was all that about?' she asked.

Preston smiled. 'I've suddenly developed an appetite.' He pulled a package from the carrier bag. 'You do like fish and chips don't you?'

***

A couple of days later, when Ben returned in his lorry from Italy at 10 o'clock in the evening, the garden centre car park was suddenly floodlit and two huge Alsatians hurtled at the perimeter fence. Then he noticed the razor wire that a Russian vine was about to colonise. Even the family home next door to the garden centre was equipped with automatic sensors, and as he opened the front gate he was once again lit up like an ice show.

Not daring to find out what would happen if he unlocked the front door, Ben rang the bell. His eldest son and two grandchildren who were on the way out let him in.

'What the hell's going on?'

'Mum's had an odd visitor, but Uncle Preston saw him off. How was Italy?'

'Still on the right side of the Alps.'

'Great. See you.'

Late for bed, Josey and Jim were bustled away to the car.

'Preston? Saw off..?' The lorry driver just managed to stop the door slamming before he went inside.

After eight hours on the road he didn't really want to unravel the reason why his home had been fitted with enough

surveillance to deter a small army. By the time Fran had
explained, he realised he was older than he wanted to admit.

She poured some wine and went out to throw together a
stir-fry. 'Sorry, should have warned you, but Preston insisted
on doing it right away!' Fran called from the kitchen.

'Could this bloke be something to do with the company that
tried to buy out Merryweather's?'

'Wouldn't be surprised. Preston knows something else but
isn't telling me.'

Ben tossed his lorry keys onto the sideboard and pulled off
his T-shirt and jeans. 'No rice for me, love. I'm trying to lose
weight.'

Fran peered through the serving hatch. 'My God, with a gut
like that you should stop eating at motorway café s. And Ben...'

'What?'

'Draw the curtains, you're scaring the dogs.'

Ben had been on the verge of asking if she wanted him to
stay on for the rest of the week, then changed his mind. He
would probably only end up preparing meals for the resident
security team.

'Where did you get those animals?'

'One of Preston's customers supplies the police with
Alsatians. Apparently these two couldn't quite get the hang of
it.'

Ben paled. 'How do you mean?'

'Word blindness.'

'What? You mean they're dyslexic?'

'No. Couldn't understand what "LET GO!" meant.'

'What?'

Fran's face appeared at the hatch again. 'Only joking. Want
mangetout?'

Given her occupation, the civil engineer had fought her way through wilder pastures than Preston Niblock's garden, though had never been invited to take afternoon tea in knee high grass, buttercups and dandelions.

'Of course, my husband thinks I should give up the business, but I employ too many people. They are dependent on Zelinski's, and jobs in the building industry are no longer guaranteed.'

Preston took plates from the tray and arranged them on the garden table. 'I didn't realise how bad things had become.'

'Nobody expected you to being paying much attention.' Toni Zelinski opened one of the napkins Deirdre had kept for special occasions, and took a cress sandwich. 'The small maintenance jobs always used to tide us over. Now the centre of Moltonford is under concrete the older buildings aren't there any more. When we've completed that extension for John Street School, there's nothing else apart from roads, and I don't have the contacts. I could always ply for work up North but moving the plant that distance wouldn't be economic. To keep a dozen of the men employed I loaned them to a contractor putting up offices in Docklands. Leaves me with a skeleton crew and yard full of cranes, excavators, and dump trucks.'

'Could you loan them out?'

'Not to the piss artists in this area who undercut us and build at an angle.'

Despite his own ills, Preston felt illogically responsible. 'I don't know what to say. I thought about giving up my business. People still bring their jewellery in and want new work, though. It might be sympathy of course.'

'Your jewellery is superb. As long as people have money in their wallets there will always be a mistress to buy it for.'

'Toni, you are becoming cynical.' Preston scolded his tongue on his tea. 'I don't know how Deirdre managed to drink hers so hot?'

'She was always too busy to wait for it to cool.'

Though not meant as a criticism, the remark reminded him of his wife's determination to keep herself occupied.

Preston replaced the cup on the tray. 'I assume you have spoken to Miss Priddle about your problems?'

'Priddy has gone into one of her mysterious phases.'

'Oh no.' Preston remembered what had happened the last time the accountant had worn her crocodile smile. A copy of the export ledger of a major manufacturer trying to asset strip one of her clients mysteriously ended up in the hands of the Customs. Unable to pay up the VAT, they were bankrupted. It ran in the newspapers for weeks. He laughed. 'That should be worth staying around for.'

'You did know that some of the shops and small manufactures in the town centre have engaged her to look after their businesses?'

'Mr Becker told me. She persuaded him to expand his imprint.'

'With only one outlet? How would he sell his books? And on church furniture?'

'The Internet. God's probably got his own website to publicise stone tablets and the home addresses of evolutionists.'

Toni Zelinski realised. 'Of course. Priddy has taken to the Internet like a ferret takes to holes.'

'Come on, I know you two are the best of friends.'

'Until she digs me out of the shit, I reserve the right to abuse her.'

'I heard she has also taken the option on that unit in the mall local businesses were offered?'

Toni Zelinski shrugged. 'I don't know why. At least they didn't want a deposit. Something about goodwill. Only know there isn't enough storage space for a bulldozer and backhoe loader.'

'Ever thought about hiring them out as children's rides?'

The civil engineer cast Preston a pitying look, so he turned his attention to the overgrown flowerbeds and rockery wearing campanula like a tea cosy. If he hadn't been so worried about Deirdre over exerting herself, she would have probably kept the ground elder and brambles in check.

'I should really do something about this place. There could be half a dozen travellers camping in there for all I know.'

Toni was surprised at someone as meticulous as the jeweller allowing the garden get into such a state but then, before Deirdre's death, it would never have occurred to him to wear embroidered waistcoats or a neck scarf instead of a tie.

'Marvellous for the wildlife.'

Preston gave a small laugh. 'Nothing dare nest here. The neighbourhood cats use it as a singles club. There was a laburnum somewhere out there. That became their trapeze and scenting post.'

'Can't see it?'

'At the back of those nettles. Brambles swallowed it up. Now the cats use the magnolia. Don't have a gardener on your books do you?'

Toni swung her foot through the long grass and buttercups under the table. 'Yes, qualified landscaper. Mowing lawns at the moment. How long do you want her for?'

'How long do you think?'

She tried to lie. 'Day with a rotavator, three to dig in compost and two more to plant, I should think. I could do it for two hundred and fifty.'

'Oh come on Toni, this is Amazonian rain forest.'

'I underpay appallingly and I've no doubt your sister-in-law will throw in a few plants.'

'I'm all right. Stop feeling sorry for me.'

'I'm not. When do you want it done?'

'Before the anaconda finds its way out.'

After double yellow lines were painted on the roads surrounding their premises, the two medium sized supermarkets on either side of Moltonford were the first to notice the drop in trade. They could match the Palace Parade food hall prices on a whole range of goods, from spaghetti to disinfectant, but not the soporific environment that made the customers feel as though they were floating down the aisles. They would have had to pump a powerful narcotic into the air to achieve the same mind deadening effect. So within months the owners of the supermarket chains cut their losses, moved the stock to other stores, and boarded up the single storey buildings, hoping that someone might decide to convert them into restaurants or day care centres.

Next to leave were the delicatessen and three bakers. Bread could be bought in the food hall for half their price alongside temptingly lit packets of ten mean little scones at a generous discount. And when all the bakers had gone out of business, or become sandwich bars for the office trade, nobody would remember what freshly baked bread tasted like anyway. Even the cool, clinical air wafted from the cooked meat counter in Palace Parade's food hall was now preferred to the smell of the old delicatessen, once thought aromatic and sensual.

The High Street barrow owned by a local grower of organic vegetables was also swept away in the drive to tidy up Moltonford. Not easily beaten, he offered his produce to the food hall. Their management decided that its natural taste would damage the sales of their own imported, under-ripe fruit, and homogeneously shaped vegetables. So they told him to wash his produce. The grower told them what to do with their cabinets of antiseptic food.

Mr Becker managed to hang on because he had contracts to supply textbooks to several schools. Three other bookshops, having to compete with the stacks of discounted titles in the shopping mall, disappeared within six months. A florist, stationer, aquarium supplier, and furniture store also never saw out the year.

***

Mabel, Alice, and Hector carefully pulled back the branches of the hostel hedge. They slipped out into the street, wending their way through the mid morning traffic lined up to make sure of a place in the limited space of Palace Parade's car park. As long as they were back for lunch and the Bible reading, the dreaded Mrs Roy wouldn't miss them.

Well scrubbed and in new second-hand clothes, they were taken for regular senior citizens coming to queue for their pensions at the Post Office counter in the Palace Parade supermarket.

Once inside the gleaming interior of escalators, galleries, and fountains they scuttled about like gerbils in a new cage. Nothing escaped their scrutiny, from the genealogical scrolls being sold on an ornate barrow in the main mall, to the special offer on Alice's favourite chocolate biscuits in the cathedral sized food hall. Free samples were tasted or pocketed until Alice's coat sagged with hazelnut ice cream, tins of tuna and perfumed bleach. Mabel was more discriminating and allowed a cosmetic artist to demonstrate how to make up the worldly worn features of the older woman. When she had finished, Hector panicked at the transformation of his friend's face and had to be brought a chair and cup of tea.

Then the companions watched a woman wearing an alarming patchwork smock showing a small crowd how to transform that ancient, unwanted piece of furniture Auntie Mavis left you in her will, to spite you for never visiting her, into a conversation piece guaranteed to astound your friends and frighten the budgie. From out of plastic stacking crates, wonderwoman produced acrylic sprays, gold leaf, rolls of car upholstery fabric, brushes to varnish appliquéd sunflowers, and paint to make wild loops over every surface she hadn't tacked simulated leather to.

As he watched, Hector's mind retreated to chase candyfloss fantasies in the disorganised furniture of what was left of his brain. Alice and Mabel had to ease him away like a mesmerised chicken being presented with a straight line. Episodes like that frequently ended with an eruption of 7.5 on the Richter scale.

Security cameras had already picked out the eccentric companions. As they had not caused mayhem or lifted anything other than free samples, their pictures were merely placed on file.

It was Alice who noticed that the gold and marble clock suspended under a huge crown was about to strike twelve. In a matter of minutes they would all turn into pumpkins, and Gospel Gertie give their dinner to the hostel cats. Clutching their booty, they darted about, trying to find the main doors. Mabel suddenly noticed her reflection in a store mirror and stood transfixed by the sight of the strange woman looking back at her.

'I can't go to dinner like this!' she wailed, then darted to the nearest fountain, took out a free sample of soap and a flannel and washed the make-up from her face.

Dinner was fish cakes again. If Hector, Alice, and Mabel had known that they would have stayed in the mall and scrounged more Swiss rolls.

Confined to the hostel by a council willing to subsidise someone else to keep them off the street, life was tasteless and tedious. The other inmates were either too elderly or too infirm to fight back and their old stamping grounds had also been concreted over. They were resigned to their enforced domesticity, even at the cost of having their souls saved by the evangelical Mrs Roy.

But the trio from Victoria Park had tasted the forbidden pleasures of the mall. From then on the sweet music played over its sound system would call like a siren, luring them into a cornucopia of free samples, seats by the fountains, and a selection of half smoked cigarettes security had made customers stub out at the main entrance.

CHAPTER 16

Preston increased his grip on the rope from which his life depended and watched the beam of his helmet light disappear down into the gloom.

'I thought you said it was only a short way?' he called.

A voice husky with a tobacco abuse echoed up, 'Don't you worry, Mr Niblock. Once we're out of this chimney we drop straight into the adjoining cave.'

'Drop! You never said anything about dropping!'

'I meant slide down. Don't you worry.'

If Arnold Mold said, 'Don't you worry,' once more, the jeweller knew he would freeze and end up suspended forever in that rock chimney like the fly in the amber he had promised the caver's wife. He hadn't panicked so far because the breeze circulating through the network of caves was oddly reassuring. As daylight disappeared he knew they were tempting bats the size of vultures, and troglodyte rodents with teeth like ripsaws.

Preston closed his eyes and pulled himself together. He carefully slackened his grip on the harness release and slowly slid into the Cretaceous blackness. His borrowed boots eventually reached a ledge he could thankfully rest on.

'How far now?'

'You're there.'

The jeweller looked down to see a surprisingly even floor two metres below him. Though his legs were still trembling, he lowered himself down, released the harness and followed his guide over boulders and under stalactites to the other end of the long cave.

After they had crushed themselves through a narrow entrance, Preston began to worry about how they were going to find their way out.

Then Arnold turned a powerful torch onto a vast ceiling that domed away into a cavernous darkness, which almost roared back. 'Only got to shin down that rock face over there and you're on the old river bed.'

'I can't hear the river?'

'Oh it's there all right. The level's gone down so much we'll have to walk on a tad to reach it.'

There was no other sound apart from the panting of a nervous master jeweller.

'You ain't used to this sort of thing are you, Mr Niblock?'

'The nearest I've ever come to geology is polishing slivers of it and setting them in a collet.'

'Ah, you've missed a lot.'

At that moment, it was fortunately too dark to tell just how much.

They negotiated the rest of the way over the ancient bed of the Nox.

The cave was shaped like a long scoop, at the bottom of which ran the river, not vigorously, but very deep. Somewhere in the distant gloom there was the turbulent sucking and churning of water.

The cave floor, smoothed by the river, was strewn with boulders brought in by the ancient torrent, and an irregular curtain of stalactites ran the length of the chamber, though they had millennia to go before they closed with their embryo stalagmites. Preston cast a worried glance at the crack the minerals had seeped through.

'Millions of tons of water used to gush through here every minute,' explained Arnold Mold. 'It carved out caves in the limestone - hundreds of them - and rises in umpteen different places. This tributary comes out at Bald Wendy.'

Preston was too awed by the cretaceous cathedral to fully register what the caver was saying. 'Tributary at Bald Wendy?'

'Yes. This one feeds the Coney Canal.'

'I didn't know that?'

'Well you wouldn't. A gate was installed over a hundred and fifty years ago. The water level sank and willows covered the entrance.'

Preston pointed to the distant gloom where the water sounded as though it was being churned by an overactive sink plunger. 'What's over there?'

'Another cave. Dangerous place that. Behaves like a sump. When sommat's dragged down there it don't come up again.'

Exhausted, Preston sat on a water worn boulder. 'Can we have that tea now?'

Arnold pulled the flask from his knapsack and poured the strange looking liquid into two beakers. 'Early Victorians used to have boat races through here. Started at Millington Hill, then turned into this tributary. The first crew to reach Bald Wendy were given a sovereign each.'

'Millington Hill?'

'River Nox used to rise there, but it was built over at the turn of the century. Hell of a surprise waiting for the contractor who demolishes that old factory.'

'Daft place to build one.'

'They thought the river would power the turbines. Hadn't counted on the water level dropping.'

After all the years he had been supplying Arnold Mold's wife with amber, Preston wondered why he hadn't shown more interest in some of his customers and their eccentric interests. When the market gardener first told him about the joys of caving, the jeweller hadn't envisioned taking any neck-breaking journeys into the Earth's crust.

'I didn't know any of this, especially about the boat races.'

'Ain't common knowledge. One year the teams were caught in a flash flood. Only one boat made it out, there was no hope of recovering the bodies of the others from that sump over there, so's they put gates over the entrances to let it be their grave.'

The jeweller didn't have a superstitious nature. However, so deep in the gloom, it was easy to waiver. 'Surely no ordinary downpour could have flooded a place this size?'

Arnold pointed to a water line on the nearest rock face high above them. 'Water table's gone down no end. Could never happen again.'

His knees no longer trembling, Preston got up and made his way to the river's edge.

'You'm be careful,' Arnold called after him. That's slippy down there.'

Despite the warning, the river looked languid, fatigued by its journey through the limestone hill, though it was still wide and deep enough to take boats. The water gently slurped against the far rock wall and filled the cave with a pleasant breeze.

Arnold joined him. 'You want to see that chimney now?'

Yes, of course. That was what Preston had risked his neck and an embarrassing bowel movement for. He followed the wiry old man up and along the cave until they came to a regular shaped hole in the ceiling. So that was the secret way down from Moltonford's Victoria Park. No wonder the area was cleared before anyone could rediscover it.

'There was a manhole cover in the boathouse. Bolted from underneath so's no one could fall down it. Cavers tried to find another way in. Wouldn't tell them about mine though. Didn't want all them bodies traipsing over my land. That's why I had the grating made and keep it padlocked. No one's bothered to enquire about it for years now. Reckon they forgot it existed.'

'Aren't you worried I might say something?'

'Nah. Whatever you're down here for, you don't want anyone else to know about it. And my wife would never forgive me if she didn't get that piece of amber. Make her collection complete that will.'

Preston stared absently at the ceiling. 'I know. She should keep it in a more secure place than the mantelpiece.'

'No good talking to her. The woman won't be told about things. She still takes oil lamps into the barn. Bloody thing will burn down one day.'

Arnold rambled on as Preston continued to stare. Only a matter of metres above his head sat a concrete conglomeration weighing a million tons. Here and there the cave roof touched the floor with the odd stalactite and stalagmite. It had no other support. There was just a huge stretch of Cretaceous rock linking molecules across a span that would have given Brunel pause.

'Is it still possible to get in here from Bald Wendy, Arnold?'

'Probably. That gate must be well and truly rusted in after all this time.' The potholer paused. 'You'm thinking about trying it then?'

Preston would have trusted the retired market gardener with his life, but was painfully aware of what could happen to someone who threatened the existence of Palace Parade.

He laughed. 'Just a thought.'

Mr Singh and Monty Golden looked across the street at each other through their shop windows. Lately they had little else to do but gaze out and wonder when the next person would appear in Canning Road, perhaps take a cursory glance at the quaint shops, then pass on down to the six-storeyed Palace Parade at the bottom of the hill. The neighbouring camera repair shop had already cut its losses and moved to another town before trade disappeared altogether. Perhaps they shouldn't have dismissed Miss Priddle's idea of taking an option on the mall unit so quickly; anything was better than financially bleeding to death. If it weren't for the compensation from the council, the remaining shops would have closed months ago. That money wouldn't last forever.

Two streets away Mr Becker was at his PC, indexing the final draft of his book on church corbels and saving it to disc. He had been looking for an excuse to publish his tome for a year. Now he had a reasonable estimate from a printer, a website, and good accountant. If it was the last business venture he ever launched, at least he would go out with some style.

In Archway Road, notice of closure for redevelopment had been given to the craft co-operative, and new premises allocated in the middle of a council estate where the residents depended on charity shops for their fancy goods.

The Electronauts were a small company who designed and assembled electronic goods such as radios, CD players, pocket televisions, and mobile phones, but mainly computers. It was run by intense young people who, many suspected, got their entertainment from hacking into national defence systems. They kept themselves to themselves and, as long as the military police didn't come knocking at their shutters, the other businesses in Archway Road never bothered them.

The Electronauts were also good at retrieving vital information from discs that had gone into error or been erased. Although Miss Priddle was capable of creating the occasional serpentine program to run rings around the Inland Revenue, she had availed herself of their services several times. Fortunately their expertise never ran to understanding the figures she had been juggling. Rumour had it that the computer experts had also lifted sensitive technology to create a transmitter that could pulse readable signals through mountains, and that a certain civil engineer had bought the prototype they constructed. Few who knew Toni Zelinski believed it - for long.

Ron Acton, the owner of the Kitchen Collection, was doing a final tally of his stock. He employed half a dozen metal workers and electricians to design, press and assemble stylish kettles, toasters, hotplates, small conventional ovens and lamps. They had an agreement with him to take time off when business was slack in exchange for a percentage of the profits when it picked up.

The Kitchen Collection's sturdy products could easily outlive the cheap ones sold in the major stores. Now all roads led to Palace Parade, few people stopped any more. There was nothing left to do but mothball the stock and look for new premises.

Though Vicky Wade kept her regular customers from out of town, to stay solvent she needed to sell a kiln full of mugs, cups, and saucers every week. Now, not even porcelain fridge magnets were moving.

The large music store in Palace Parade robbed Winston and Mercy Cuffe's Riotous Records shop of virtually all trade, bar those specialist labels not mainstream enough for major outlets to stock. The blanket of soporific music that enveloped people as soon as they set foot in the shopping centre effectively erased the desire for anything challenging or different. From reggae to Verdi, music had to be filleted and left with only the recognisable bits. The once popular stock of the Cuffe's was now too raw and had to compete with online pirates.

Sonia and Vivian Cupit were on the verge of breaking up their business partnership. Their stock of children's clothes had already been divided between them and stored until they either started up somewhere else, or took jobs on the checkouts in Palace Parade. So many customers were flooding into the shopping centre from outside Moltonford staff of any age were welcome.

As soon as the vans loaded with pottery, electrical goods, and kitchenware left, the plant moved in to demolish the Archway Road industrial units. There was no point in anyone taking up the offer of new premises in the middle of the council estate, so sympathetic friends stored as much stock as they could in attics, back bedrooms, and sheds. One of the shops in the mall offered a knock down price for the kitchenware and electrical goods, but that was like the fox going back for the eggs after raiding the chicken coup, and Ron Acton declined.

Ever the optimist, Vicky Wade set up the kiln in her shed and pottery wheel in her kitchen from where she continued to produce fancy vases until every shelf, mantelpiece, and relation's sideboard groaned.

Little Lucy Tribble had used a bench in Vicky's showroom. She had been making bead jewellery for longer than any of the others could remember. The only other outlet for her ropes of pearls, plated bugles, and strings of coral used to be a knitwear shop. That had also gone out of business. So at last Preston Niblock did what Deirdre had been asking for years, and set up a display of Lucy's work in his window, and then he invited her to sit behind the counter and sell it. This saved him from having to be there: after so much consoling over his wife's death he had sympathy fatigue and was finding it difficult to face the general public. Anyone who needed to see if he was becoming as eccentric as rumour had it could always come up to his workroom.

As the businesses in the streets radiating from Moltonford's centre continued to relocate or close, all the yellow lines surreptitiously disappeared. This opened up more parking space for people desperate to immerse themselves in the wrap-around shopping experience as though Palace Parade was a free theme park.

Customers basked in the gleam of affluence reflected from the chrome balustrades, and luxuriated in the perfumed air. They didn't notice the narrow windows through which a security team made sure no one wandered too erratically, bunched suspiciously, or paddled in the fountains. School truants looking for anonymity in the bustle of bodies, were discreetly picked off by young people in uniforms resembling those worn in hamburger restaurants. Instead of being offered fast food, they were delivered to a small unfurnished room, suitably intimidating, to await the relevant authorities. Even professional shoplifters were unable to pinpoint the location of cameras watching for wandering fingers or the odd bulge.

Some local residents resented having to queue in a huge food hall for a pint of milk. Many more joined the compulsive purchasers and cruised the shelves like barracuda shopping for the whole shoal.

The only break in the mall's sweep of radiant store fronts was one blacked out window. On its door, in the exact handwriting of Miss Priddle, was a brief declaration: - 'These premises have been reserved for the resident shopkeepers of Moltonford.' She intended the window to remain blacked out, like a gap in the smile of a catwalk queen, for as long as was contractually permissible.

***

One morning, customers waiting for Palace Parade to open were diverted by the spectacle of a limousine with clouded windows sweeping across the pedestrian area to the main entrance.

From a following car stepped four sharply dressed men in dark glasses. They surrounded the limousine as an elderly man with a Kashmir coat draped over his shoulders like peer's ermine, stepped out. He was tall, tanned, and with a head of immaculate hair too brown to be his. Some of the watching crowd fancied they had seen him in Hollywood films.

The visitor ignored the buzz of excitement and swept inside Palace Parade as though he owned it. A minute later a large councillor with a hippo smile followed his entourage. Most of the crowd did recognise him.

CHAPTER 18

Preston Niblock dodged people who were mindlessly meandering as though their self-awareness had been surrendered at the entrance of Palace Parade. He wondered if he would ever manage to get to the other end of the mall without craving a burrow to dart down. The mobiles of plastic prisms hanging from the galleries seemed to mock the jeweller with their rainbow refractions and the flamboyant, crown shaped, chandeliers reminded him of the apprentice days when he had to set buckets of paste diamonds until his retinas were numb.

Today he had made an effort at smartness, yet shafts of sunlight from the high ceiling perversely picked out every item of casual clothing he had for months been fighting off the urge to wear. If he was becoming slovenly, he would at least have the good taste to do it by degrees.

Preston pulled out his brass fob watch, having left the gold one at home for safety's sake. There were only five minutes before his appointment. What insane whim had tempted him into the place? The jeweller hated soothing Musak, fluorescent lights, and shopping trolleys. It was the same whim that had persuaded him to buy a ticket for the National Lottery to prove to himself what a waste of money it was. So he felt obliged to walk through the mall at least once before being qualified to declare it was a dreadful idea.

Those shoppers who still had a few molecules plugged into reality cast suspicious looks at Preston's smart overcoat as they trundled past to buy a pretty porcelain shepherdess or month's groceries. Deirdre would have loved Palace Parade. The jeweller's heart sank at the thought, and guilt once more descended. As soon as he reached the Victoria Square entrance, he dashed out to the sanctuary of Fran's garden centre.

Miss Priddle was already waiting for him at a table in the café.

'Sorry I'm late. Conrad Makepeace bought in his wife's cameo to reset and we had trouble finding a collet. Then I decided to stroll through the mall and lost all sense of time.'

Toni Zelinski was right; the accountant did have an unnervingly enigmatic smile. 'How did you like it?'

Hot, and trying not to sound bothered, Preston took off his coat and placed it on the back of his chair. 'How did you know it was the first time I've been in there?'

'You have the aura of the recently blooded.'

He had never looked upon shopping as a blood sport until Palace Parade. Not wanting to admit that it had made him lose his appetite, he asked half-heartedly, 'Shall we order a sandwich?'

'I'd prefer to go somewhere more private.'

Preston remembered the accountant's red sports car. 'How far?'

She swallowed her coffee. 'Only take ten minutes.'

Given the way she drove, that could have been Land's End.

Fran saw them heading towards the car park and was intrigued. 'Want me to make us some lunch later?' she called to Preston.

He turned and shrugged.

The jeweller had forgotten the last time he had visited Millington Hill with Deirdre. It must have been at least twenty years ago, just before the cat's-eyes started to trigger multiple images and he sold the car for fear of running down a real cat. The view across the downs seemed somehow tidier and the gliding club had disappeared, leaving less trace in the topsoil than an Iron Age settlement. In the distance Preston could make out some crop circles. They looked more like the work of an out of control tractor than aliens. He peered over the railing at a very long drop. Either Millington Hill had grown since he was last there or he had shrank.

The accountant teased a strategic curl of her coiffure into place. He wondered what anti-gravity technology made it stay up in the stiff breeze. 'You come here often?'

Her car apparently tackled the gradient quite frequently. 'I like the fresh air.' Miss Priddle turned her crystal gaze on him. 'I have a proposition to put to you.'

Preston wasn't used to mysterious proposals from elegant women with the expertise to bankrupt major companies, and he tried not to sound surprised. 'As long as it doesn't involve the combustion engine or biology, I'm listening.'

'You might have heard that I am managing the financial affairs of several local businesses?'

Heard? Her demands were the talk of the Palace Parade Development Committee meetings and local newspapers, and had no doubt persuaded a few Gideon executives to try to uncover some dirt on the accountant. Preston was too much of a gentleman to guess how many amorous liaisons they would find.

'I've never used an accountant myself.'

Especially Miss Priddle. Deirdre had been so scared of the woman she would never join Toni Zelinski when she arranged to have coffee with her.

'I'm sure your ledger is a work of art and my modest services would not be able to improve on it.'

He was beginning to see his late wife's point of view. 'Thank you.'

'I would just like your assistance in a small matter.'

The jeweller leaned on the railing and, trying not to give himself vertigo, gazed out non-committally at the sunlit landscape. 'Really?'

'I have formulated a solution that would allow most of my clients to - at least - avoid insolvency.' She noticed his expression harden. 'Is something wrong?'

'You're speaking like an accountant.'

'Sorry.' Miss Priddle modified her approach. 'For my idea to work, I need the co-operation of someone they trust. Accountants have the unfortunate reputation of being only interested in their fees.'

'And you're not?'

'If these businesses fail, mine could follow.'

Preston didn't believe her for a second. This woman kept books for other accountants. 'And, to save your clients from insolvency, you need me to put this formula to them?'

'Let me show you.'

As his stomach had only just settled down from the last journey, Preston was reluctant to experience the G force of her driving yet again. 'Is it as private as this?'

Miss Priddle's enigmatic smile faded for a moment as an unsettling thought crossed her mind. 'No. They surely wouldn't have bugged the place.'

Even more apprehensive, the jeweller once again allowed himself to be swept away in a sports car that could have provoked road rage in a sedated sloth.

The last place he expected to find himself was back in was Palace Parade; one visit a year would have been quite sufficient for him. At least the premises Miss Priddle led him into were shuttered from the brash mall lights and totally empty. Inside, the drone of mindless shopping was deadened.

She put on the lights so he could see the dimensions of the unit.

'The ground space should have been larger, but it was decided that the premises at the Victoria Square end be allocated to a sportswear business. Without a co-operative willing to move stock in right away I was unable to object. Unfortunately, the contract for these premises stipulates a café.'

'What good would a café be to a dozen shops that retail books, kettles, and records? You'd be selling music to go bankrupt to.'

'The Cuffes have an idea, but I'll come to that later.' Miss Priddle went to the solitary table at the centre of the large room. She pulled a contract from her briefcase as though she hadn't already analysed the contents and committed them to memory. 'The conditions allow a limited area to be given over to the sale of goods. If we use the wall facing the kitchen there should be enough room for a display area.'

'What about the floor space? Line dancing perhaps?'

'Must be chairs and tables only. Something to do with health and safety.'

'And the back wall?' Preston was about to suggest a rifle range. He detected a tightening in her tone and decided not to push his luck.

'The door there leads to the stockroom lift - it is a very large stockroom.' Miss Priddle suddenly replaced the contract in her briefcase. 'Fancy a coffee?'

'Prefer an aspirin.'

Once again Preston was whisked away, this time to the accountant's favourite restaurant where there were certainly no bugs of any description.

'I hope your sister-in-law isn't expecting you back for lunch? Would you like to phone her on my mobile?'

He backed away from the infernal device as though a tarantula wanted to whisper in his ear. 'It's not a regular thing. We're just... looking out for each other,' he explained.

'Really?' The woman had the acumen to not only read between lines, but translate the air in any other spaces as well. 'You'll have to tell me about it one day.'

'Now look Miss Priddle-' but after his hectic morning, Preston suddenly lost the will to argue.

Then her tone changed. 'There is something in the conditions that Gideon Enterprize's brilliant lawyers forgot to cover.'

'You mean, they don't want a pound of flesh from everyone they put out of business as well?'

'Along the back wall there will be a display counter.'

'That's a long wall.'

'With several people serving.'

'Serving what?'

'Goods.'

'What goods?'

'Ones they see in a catalogue.'

'Catalogue?'

'Products that can undercut their poorer quality equivalents in all the other stores. The novelty of buying goods over the Internet, having to pay postage and then return them when they're not what the pretty promotions said they were, will wear off soon enough. Customers will still want to look around for a good deal, and they won't find them in Palace Parade once they have a monopoly.'

So that was her game.

Preston sat back and tried not to admire her. 'There are much larger catalogue outlets that could outgun you.'

'Not in this town, and certainly not in Palace Parade.'

'Why not?'

'The other stores wouldn't tolerate the competition.'

'So what makes yours so special?'

'I have a watertight contract.'

'You'd never get away with it.'

'Oh, yes we will. Gideon was so busy trying to prevent us setting up an effective business, they totally forgot about the catalogue clause.'

'So that thing you've been waving about isn't the real contract?'

'That's safe in the bank vault of my solicitors.'

Preston wouldn't have wanted to blunder into them in a dark courtroom. 'And what else?'

For a moment Miss Priddle was fazed. 'What do you mean?'

'My wife was probably murdered, my sister-in-law has received a visit from a mysterious young man wanting to buy her out with menaces, and the industrial units in Archway Road are not being renovated, but demolished to make way for a multi storey car park. So there must be something else. You'd disappoint me if there wasn't.'

Perhaps Preston Niblock was even sharper than popular rumour had it.

'Ah, later perhaps.'

The office's carpet had a pile deep enough to make rabbits feel secure. Unfortunately it didn't do as much for the large councillor sweltering in the excessive central heating.

'Warm, Grablatt?' barked a voice from the other side of a wide desk.

'I'm not used to the Nevada climate, Mr Tucker.' The councillor daren't sound too rebellious. However profitable his dealings with Gideon to date, these people were still an unknown quantity.

Julius Tucker the third came from a long line of entrepreneurs, the American equivalent of royalty, and resembled an elderly film star despite the fact his voice was harsh enough to make even his bodyguards flinch behind their shades.

'You know why I'm here, don't you Grablatt?'

As far as Neville Grablatt knew, nothing had gone wrong so he could only guess. 'The coroner said it was unlawful killing that couldn't be proved, and Conrad Makepeace has run out of ideas.'

Tucker thudded the desk blotter with a crystal paperweight. 'Ever heard of a man called Niblock?'

Grablatt hadn't been expecting that. Without invitation, he sank into a chair. 'Yes, of course. He's the jeweller who lost his wife. What on earth has Preston Niblock got to do with Palace Parade? He wasn't even at the inquest.'

'Preston Niblock has got everything to do with Palace Parade.'

'How?'

'He knows about geology.'

'Geolo-' Grablatt stopped. 'Dear God! It's not possible!'

The tycoon turned to his henchmen. 'Out, you two.'

They left as though relieved not to have to hear the conversation.

'He knows!' Tucker told Grablatt. 'And we need to know how he knows.'

The councillor fished inside his pocket for a handkerchief to mop the perspiration from his face. 'It's not possible. The entrance in the park leading down to the cave was the first thing we dealt with. It's been sealed with hardcore. Any maps still in existence have been tracked down, and nobody is old enough to remember the boat races to Bald Wendy.'

'Well he's found out, Grablatt. All he need do now is have a quiet word with your Mr Makepeace.'

'No, I can't believe it.'

Julius Tucker the third leant forward on his desk like a well-manicured gargoyle. 'What is this Niblock like?'

'A quiet, mousy little man. Never known him cause trouble. Even if he did know, what reason would he have to-?'

'Would anyone miss him?' Tucker interrupted.

Neville Grablatt stopped mopping his face and gazed at him. The thought may have easily crossed the councillor's mind. It was disconcerting to hear it coming from the multi billionaire. 'Of course people would miss him. Everyone in Moltonford knows the man after he lost his wife in that "horrible accident".'

'What about his sister-in-law?'

'The garden centre? That's ringed with razor wire and security lights, has two rabid dogs guarding the grounds, and direct line to the police.'

Tucker lurched from his chair and began to patrol the room. That made Grablatt sweat even more.

'Is this Niblock open to suggestion?'

'What sort of suggestion?'

'You know. Keep quiet or things might happen?'

Against his better judgement, Grablatt chuckled. 'The man's not a fool. If he does have information like that, he's not going to keep the proof tucked in his sock drawer. And he may not be easily intimidated.'

'So I understand.' Tucker did another circuit of the office. 'So how much will it take to buy him?'

Grablatt shrugged. 'How long do you expect him to keep quiet for?'

'Another five years and Palace Parade will have served its purpose, then we can sell the place.'

'Hmm, five years of silence. And expecting him not to say anything when the sale goes through. Couple of million I should think.'

'Dollars?'

'Pounds. You must gross that in a week. Just trick him into some deal so he'll be as guilty as everyone else if it all comes out.'

Tucker at last finished his tour of the expensive paintings and crashed back into his seat. 'You're a good man, Grablatt.'

By the time the councillor had reached the main entrance of Palace Parade, he didn't really care what the tycoon thought. All he wanted to do was choke the life out of Preston Niblock. Unfortunately the reading of the master jeweller's will would probably reveal that Palace Parade had been built mostly on thin air.

***

Conrad Makepeace removed his glasses and rubbed his eyes. After viewing the next film roll of local newspapers he would have to call it a day. It would have helped if he knew what he was looking for. Being dogged often had its own reward, though a little inspiration sometimes helped.

The business directories had turned up nothing out of the ordinary on Gideon Enterprizes. In fact, a respectable New England family had founded it and the contractors responsible for building the shopping complex had been disbanded and their workers left the country because their permits had expired.

The councillor tucked the photocopies he had taken into a folder and left the library for the fresh air of a High Street that was now the forecourt of Palace Parade.

As he approached the town hall, he glanced back to see Neville Grablatt striding from the shopping centre. The man's angry demeanour was unlikely to have been caused by a mislabelled tin of pink salmon. Perhaps Conrad Makepeace had been searching in the wrong place.

CHAPTER 20

Preston pointed to the derelict building straddling the tributary that fed Coney Canal. 'It was originally called Auld Windy. The locals corrupted it into Bald Wendy.'

Miss Priddle turned her car onto the track leading to the water mill. 'Rather dismal aspect.'

'Don't suppose they do get many sightseers out here.'

Bald Wendy was three storeys of ungainly brickwork straddling the River Nox tributary on two arches. The narrowest of them housed the much-ravaged undershot wheel; its wooden floats barely attached to the cast iron rims. The wider arch once contained a sluice gate to hold back the head race when the water had been deeper. Now its true course had been diverted to feed the nearby Coney Canal. Overhanging the front entrance was a lucam, the small lookout cabin housing the hoist gear.

The tributary's banks had been raised to increase the water pressure and a flight of steps and ramp led up to the door of the gearing room. In the past, the water mill had no doubt earned its name of Auld Windy because of the winds channelled around the hill the tributary rose from. Now the hillside was clad in ash and weeping willow, and there wasn't even a breeze to dissipate the lingering mist and reveal where the water rose, or even came from.

Miss Priddle switched off the car's engine and climbed out. 'If I break a heel I shall send you an invoice.'

'Believe me, this is the easy route.'

As the accountant was used to playing life's game of poker, she refused to demand why he had brought her there. Despite a tight skirt, she elegantly picked her way down the steep slope to the water's edge. 'This bank needs a hedge trimmer.'

'Doubt if anyone would send a work experience team out to this backwater. It's on the way to nowhere and boats never use it.' Preston pointed to the Coney Canal. 'Any water traffic passes over there.'

'The level's not high enough to drive a mill wheel?'

'That was over a century ago, before the infernal combustion engine.'

She suspected that was a dig at her red sport's car, but let it pass. 'What did it mill?'

'Probably anything when there was the water pressure.'

'Not enough to shell peanuts now. Where is it coming from?'

Preston pointed to the willow-clad hillside. 'Out of there. It's a tributary of the River Nox.'

There was a short silence, and then the accountant turned and looked at him as though he was mental arithmetic. 'But that's...' She pointed vaguely into the distance.

'The main river rises twenty miles away.'

Preston didn't need to say any more. He could see the mathematics of the conundrum being computed behind the shimmering eye shadow.

'In that case, given the general angle at which the river must branch underground...' Her pearlised lips formed an understanding "O".

The jeweller pushed his hands into his pockets and leaned back to trust his insubstantial weight to a weeping willow sapling. His aura of cool was ruined by an overwhelming desire to sneeze. He didn't know where the pollen was coming from and had no intention of admitting that he had hay fever to this woman.

Preston quickly blew his nose and explained, 'About three miles away, on the other side of the downs. Straight under Moltonford.'

'Go on?'

Preston laughed. 'Oh no. Not until you tell me about Gideon Enterprizes.'

Miss Priddle put on the syrupy tone she used for intellectually deficient clients. 'What on earth are you bothered about them for?'

'Don't patronise. I've just had to grow up very suddenly.'

'We all do at some time or other.'

He suspected that Miss Priddle had come into the world clutching a calculus.

She opened her briefcase and was about to delve inside.

'Please don't wave any more sheets of paper under my nose unless you intend me to read them.'

Miss Priddle clicked the catch shut as though crushing a particularly obnoxious insect. 'Gideon Enterprizes is a little more than it seems.'

'Only a little? I was expecting a brontosaurus of an organisation.'

'It's more like a pack of velociraptors.'

'Nasty.'

'Bites chunks out of companies and, before they know it, they've been consumed.'

'Asset stripping?'

'Far from.' Miss Priddle wandered along the bank, her scarlet nails plucking fluffy seeds from reed mace. 'After buying up all the company's shares, Tucker puts in his own executives to control them.'

Preston allowed the sapling to push him upright so he could follow her. 'Is that unusual?'

'No, admirable in many ways.'

Preston wasn't so good at poker. 'Oh come on?'

'You first.'

He sighed and went down to the stand of weeping willows that had colonised the lower hillside. 'Through there is a gate installed by the Victorians,' he called back.

It was an effort for Miss Priddle to catch up in her high heels. 'If this is earth shatteringly scandalous, you might consider keeping your voice down.'

Preston waited until she was within whispering range. 'This tributary has carved out a vast cave under Moltonford.'

She paused. 'How vast?'

'Looks bloody big when you're down there.'

She gave a crystal smile. 'You a potholer? In that waistcoat? You surprise me.'

He ignored her. 'It's larger than Palace Parade.'

'How about under my office?'

'From what this palaeontologist told me, everything on the valley margins, including your office, sits on bedrock but, in its centre, the span of the limestone ceiling is probably no more than a couple of metres.'

The accountant chortled as though someone had given her the freedom of the Stock Exchange. 'Wonderful! Those bastards knowingly built Palace Parade over a bloody great hole in the ground.'

'That's about the size of it.' Preston cast her a circumspect glance. 'What's so wonderful about it? The place could cave in without warning.'

Waving a salutary finger, she teetered back up the bank. 'No, no. They wouldn't have run the risk. That explains what Toni was puzzled about. When they sank the footings they had to spread the load and cantilever the upper floors. That's why they couldn't add another level for parking.' She giggled like a schoolgirl. 'I love you Mr Niblock - will you marry me?'

Preston was beginning to know how Jonah felt. The thought of being engulfed by a calculating killer whale, however elegant, made his savoir-faire reel.

'I must decline. I don't think Deirdre took out so much life insurance because she expected me to marry an accountant.'

'You're a funny man.'

'And you are a tease, Miss Priddle.' He gave a wide, false smile. 'That was my side of the bargain, now what have you got to tell me?'

'You still want to know?'

'Naturally.'

Miss Priddle's enigmatic smile returned. 'Some of these companies Gideon Enterprizes took under its vulture wing...'

'Yes?'

'Own all the stores in Palace Parade, from the food hall to the jewellery boutiques on the sixth floor gallery.'

Preston scrambled out of the willows to join her. 'But - is that allowed?' he whispered earnestly.

'What? A price fixing cartel?'

It was a stupid question. 'No, of course not. But surely they are listed somewhere?'

'Oh yes. Not under Gideon Enterprizes though. It took me days to check out just one of them. The list of decoy companies involved is so labyrinthine it would have given Robert Maxwell a headache.'

'Surely they could make just as much by leasing units to large independent stores?'

'This way they don't have to pay rates or ground rent for five years. They would if they sublet. Hence no major catalogue shop to compete with us. As Gideon doesn't have competition now the local shops have gone out of business, they're able to fix prices.'

'The other major chains must have kicked up?'

She laughed. 'When they decided to leave the town centre and build superstores miles away for the benefit of people with cars, they lost any moral high ground. And the Palace Parade Development Committee has no control over what rent Gideon would ask.'

'People who come to Palace Parade have cars, so Moltonford might as well be an out of town shopping centre. All the residents wanted was a new precinct with a few shops. None of them seriously thought its centre was going to be concreted over for a money-making monstrosity.'

Preston fell quiet until they reached the old mill. 'So what are you going to do about it?'

'Do about what?'

'This cartel of Gideon Enterprize's.'

'What should I do about it?'

'You represent the people being put out of business. Surely you could use what you've learnt to help them?'

Miss Priddle looked at him as though he were a newly evolved life form that had just clambered out of the River Nox. 'Silly boy. With these people you do not play skittles.'

A surge of rage overwhelmed Preston. 'They probably killed my wife, and Frank Merryweather!'

'All the more reason to keep out of firing range.'

'There has got to be something-'

'If I was a government department or local bigwig, perhaps. But, however serpentine you believe me to be, I am not bloody daft.' She returned to her sports car and tossed her briefcase onto the back seat. 'And you will have to keep quiet about it as well. I'll deny everything if you try to start any rumours.'

'What about the cave under Palace Parade?'

'I doubt if there's enough artesian pressure down there to supply Palace Parade with another fountain.' She gave him a demanding look. 'I hope you haven't mentioned this to anyone?'

Preston recalled what he had said to the sinister young man in his sister-in-law's garden centre, and shuddered.

CHAPTER 21

Fran cast a critical glance over the two tables laden with sandwiches and jugs of soft drink then turned her attention to Preston's newly dug borders. She had a cancelled order for tagetes, so they would make a bright splash of orange in the central flowerbed with the magnolia. After knowing Preston Niblock for more than thirty-five years, she still hadn't found out that they made him sneeze even more than carnations.

Fran turned to the young woman removing couch-grass roots from her fork. 'What do you think about a hedge of lavender by the fence?'

The gardener rubbed her nose with a muddy hand. 'Really needs something higher, like philadelphus. They like it damp.'

'Right, I've got a dozen that have escaped their pots.'

'I was thinking more in the line of one.'

'No, no. Just think of that wonderful bank of white wafting a cloud of perfume into every room on an early summer day.' Fran suddenly noticed Preston's wan face. 'Hello Preston. Everything all right?'

'I get hay fever, Fran.'

His sister-in-law was wrong footed for a moment. 'No, you don't.'

'I never said anything before because Deirdre loved her mimosa.'

'Well, I'll be damned.' So that was why he didn't use the garden and let it run riot. With Preston, there was always a logical explanation, however secret he managed to keep it.

He turned to the gardener. 'All I need is something that doesn't chuck pollen into the air like Liberace with the talcum powder.'

'Crazy paving would be nice,' she suggested.

'With concrete tubs of box.'

Fran was beside herself. 'No! No! This garden is sixty feet long and thirty wide. You can't pave it!'

Preston started to laugh.

Fran's eyes narrowed. 'You're both having me on.'

'Just leave out the tagetes and banks of orange blossom.'

'I sometimes wonder what Deirdre saw in you?'

'She liked bald men.'

Preston still wondered how Fran could have been related to his Deirdre; even half-sisters should have had some small thing in common. Assertiveness had been separated from the demure and allocated to each sister without any regard for the consequences. Those being that Ben, giant of a man that he was, often had to load his cab with Italian or French shrubs and hope Customs never mistook them for cannabis, and that Preston had always felt obliged to accompany Deirdre whenever she went further than the next town for fear of her getting lost. The jeweller had to admit that it was refreshing to deal with a woman who knew her cotoneaster from her japonica, even though the only way she could massage a man's ego was with gardening gloves.

Fran thought he was studying her hair, which was now an orangish yellow. 'Don't you like it? Thought it would make a change from streaks.'

Not having enough hair to appreciate the effort others put into theirs, Preston forced a smile. 'It's the same colour gold I recently worked a brooch in.'

Fran took it as a compliment. 'Thank you.'

'Devil of a job matching the solder.'

Mr Becker arrived first, carrying a copy of his volume on church corbels. 'I've started documenting medieval painted screens and choir carvings. Then after that I want to compile a volume of the complete Grinling Gibbons.'

Preston wondered how many church fittings were left. 'I'm not sure my idea will enable you to run to that expense.'

'I know you Niblock, you're the only one fly enough not to have a business about to crash. How do you manage with a shop way up here?'

'I've got a captive clientele.'

'Then why are you so keen to help us?'

'I'll explain everything when the others arrive.'

Within twenty minutes Monty Golden, Mrs Silvestri, Winston and Mercy Cuffe, Vicky Wade, Ron Acton, three of the Electronauts, and Mr Singh had arrived.

And as they were about to start, Sonia Cupit dashed into the garden. 'Sorry I'm late.'

Fran offered her a cool drink. 'You look flustered?'

The clothes designer gave a tight smile. 'It's Vivian. We had a disagreement.' She cast a guilty look at Monty Golden.

Everyone quickly jumped to the wrong conclusion.

The tailor raised his hands. 'Oh no, it's not want you think. With my wife, I wouldn't dare.'

'My sister believes that Mr Golden and me are compromising our standards.' There was an interested silence, so Sonia Cupit was compelled to go on. 'We have agreed to merge our businesses and make off the peg clothes.'

There was a collective intake of breath.

Fran could imagine Sonia's ultra-sensitive sister's reaction. 'And Vivian thinks that's selling out?' She stopped short of telling Sonia that she was well shot of the touchy woman.

Preston was interested. 'That could be useful. The idea I have will need stock, and plenty of it.'

'Your idea?' voices echoed.

He was suddenly reluctant to take all the blame. 'Well, actually it's Miss Priddle's, but I understand her persona is a little too adamantine to fill you with enthusiasm.' Mr Singh's amused smile caught his eye. 'Well no, it's actually Mrs Singh's - Let's just say that it's been bounced backwards and forwards across the world, turned into two major chains, and it never fails to work with the right organisation.'

'Will it save us from bankruptcy?' asked Ron Acton.

'Oh yes, as long as enough businesses take part. Mercy has already agreed to run the café.'

***

It was the first time Miss Priddle's clients had been inside the mall unit Palace Parade Development Committee had insisted it be set aside for them.

Preston pointed out the strategic areas. 'Kitchen, counter, display area and enough room for two small stalls.'

Mrs Silvestri carried enough stock to make a battleship sink past the Plimsoll line. 'That's not enough room for one business.'

Preston pointed to a door in the back wall. 'Through there is a lift down to a storeroom. It has the capacity to take the stock of everyone here. That's where the counter along this wall comes in.'

'How?'

'Everything will be in a catalogue.'

At first they looked at him as though all the rumours about the balance of his mind were true. Eventually it started to sound like a good idea and there was a flurry of discussion.

'It's all right,' the jeweller assured them. 'Miss Priddle insists that there are no clauses in the contract to forbid it. Of course, it means that you must produce decent photographs and specifications of your goods.'

Sonia Cupit visualised all the baby bonnets and costume jewellery. 'It would be a nightmare.'

'Not if it's done efficiently. It would work in the same way as any other catalogue shop. The counter staff will feed the number of the customer's selection into a program that will tell the storeroom what article to put in the lift.'

Mr Becker only wished he could supply books that easily. 'Sounds as though this idea has already been copyrighted.'

'There's no copyright on ideas. You know that.'

'It could take ages to retrieve the goods.'

'Not as long as being bought over the Internet. Mercy and Winston will offer complimentary cups of tea while the customer waits in the café. With an efficient call system, no one needs to wait in a queue - unlike those other catalogue counters.'

'Just how large is this storeroom then?'

'Huge.'

Monty Golden nodded thoughtfully. 'Yes, Preston Niblock, you have everything worked out, bar one thing. This needs start-up investment. Do we buy lottery tickets and invoke holy intervention?'

The jeweller pushed his hands into his pockets and leaned against the counter wall. 'I'll put up the money for all the fittings, including the café and computer equipment. I've no doubt that the Electronauts can write the software required.'

'It'll still cost thousands,' protested Vicky Wade. 'How can you be so sure we'll be able to pay it back?'

'Easily. With each of you only having to bear a fraction of the rent, you can undercut every store in Palace Parade.'

That idea had instant appeal.

But Mrs Silvestri didn't believe in fairies. 'You know they'll complain as soon as they twig what's going on.'

'Complain, yes. Do anything, no. Leave that side of things to Miss Priddle. Everything must come together quickly. In two weeks we lose the option on the unit if we aren't able to open it. Who knows, you might even be able to double your business. Everyone is a sucker for a bargain.'

As he checked through the incident book, Sergeant Whitely was aware of a small pointed face with bright grey eyes gazing up at him. Though he recognised the features, he couldn't immediately place them. Something said that they looked too well scrubbed and should have been peering out from long vanished bushes of deutzia and weigela.

'Do come away Alice,' chivvied Mabel. 'Let me talk to the constable.'

Sergeant Whitely was just about to assert his rank when he realised. 'Mabel, what are you doing here?'

'We want to know where Jenny is?' she demanded as though their missing companion had been locked in the cells for the last eighteen months.

The policeman rapidly did a mental count of the old Victoria Park residents. 'Jenny? Thought she was with you when the social workers moved you to the hostel?'

'She disappeared.'

'And we were going to have those lovely little lemon cakes for tea,' Alice added unhelpfully.

Sergeant Whitely was grateful that Mabel hadn't bought Hector as well. After his last visit it had taken an hour to tidy up the place. 'Are you telling me that she has disappeared and you don't know where she went to?'

Mabel was finding him tiresome and became imperious. 'I wouldn't be here if I knew that.'

'When did she disappear?'

'When they pulled down the pavilion,' said Alice.

For one cold, clammy moment the policeman wondered if she might have been inside it, masquerading as a heap of old clothes. No, Hector was the only one who could play dead so well the crows started to show interest.

'That was ages ago?'

'But we remember.'

To avoid a surreal conversation that would ruin his lunch, he pulled out a missing person's form. 'Right. What was Jenny's surname?'

Alice giggled. 'No idea.'

So he asked Mabel, 'What is your surname?'

'Something beginning with B - No, that was my husband's.'

He scribbled something down about the witness's selective amnesia. 'Why did you wait until now to report her missing?'

'That ghastly Christian woman told us not to come. Said we were all imagining it and were not to bother the police,' Mabel declared indignantly.

Sergeant Whitely looked at them over his glasses. 'You aren't imagining it, are you?'

Mabel leaned over the counter. 'Jenny was a big girl and we never stopped her going anywhere, but she wouldn't have been gone this long without letting us know she was all right.'

He wondered why someone capable of being as lucid as Mabel had chosen the life of a vagrant. It probably had something to do with her not wanting to remember her husband's name. He dutifully recorded the meagre information they offered, knowing it would forever languish in the missing persons' file.

Satisfied that they had done all they could for their friend, Alice and Mabel went off to the youth hostel where its young attendant was Hector-sitting until they returned.

***

After another fruitless afternoon trying to make his way through the corporate labyrinth that was Gideon Enterprizes, Conrad Makepeace sipped Earl Grey and thoughtfully stabbed his fork into a piece of lemon meringue. Over his glasses, his glance met the steady gaze of Miss Priddle. The accountant was wearing that unnerving smile which declared she knew something the rest of the world did not. He gave a deferential nod. Miss Priddle beckoned the waiter and passed him a note to take to the councillor.

What would Mrs Makepeace say if she found out that he was being asked by a woman with a reputation for amorous liaisons, business assassinations, and unnaturally high heels to join him at his table? However firm the councillor may have been when it came to campaigning for a worthy cause, he didn't know how to refuse Miss Priddle.

Carefully balancing her coffee on a bulging document wallet and swinging her briefcase in the other hand, the accountant elegantly lowered herself into the seat facing Conrad Makepeace.

'Gideon Enterprizes?' she said.

Perplexed by her perception, he swallowed a mouthful of lemon meringue before replying. 'How did you know?'

'You had that "damn Gideon Enterprizes!" look about you.'

'You're interested in them as well?'

'I have done some delving on behalf of my clients.'
'And?'
'You are looking in the wrong place.'
Makepeace regarded accountants with the same caution as he did Moltonford residents who knew the law better than he did. 'How do you mean?'
'These corporate cosmic bodies do not leave cometary tails across the firmament for everyone to gawp at.'
An analogy. He was good at crosswords. 'What dimension should I be looking in then?'
'Try a black hole, a singularity behind which information is tucked safely out of sight.'
'Some image must still remain on the event horizon?'
Miss Priddle sipped her coffee, then suggested, 'Business directories may be useful, but there is a lot of dark matter in the way. Nothing is clear until broken down into its component parts.'
Conrad Makepeace had ploughed through everything he could find about Julius Tucker the third, his ex wives, mistresses, companies, and horses. What good would another directory be to him?
Miss Priddle jotted something down in her silver notepad. 'Are you on line?'
'The Internet?'
'Try accessing these searches US investigators came up with. Don't leave your calling card.' She tore out the page and handed it to him, then swallowed her coffee, rose and strode leisurely out to the car park.
Through the restaurant's picture windows Conrad Makepeace watched the red sport's car roar into life and accelerate away.

***

Toni Zelinski's team was so thankful to be given work they fitted out the café and Catalogue Shop in the mall within the week.
The glass counter that ran the length of its back wall had the capacity to display a large range of pottery, kettles, books, records and anything up to 90 centimetres high. Racks on one side of the café were installed to hold clothes, and beside them stood an ornamental display barrow. On the other side was the café's counter and kitchen. The large floor area in between was now ready to be filled with fifteen tables and ninety chairs.

Jeff knocked in the last tack to secure the cushioned floor covering, then rolled the offcuts and swept up.

Colin buffed fingerprints from the metal surround of the display cabinet. 'Hope whoever's paying for this gets their money back.'

Jeff laughed. 'They will. Have you seen some of the rubbish in the other stores? The stuff these people sell makes it look even more tatty. We had a kettle from Ron Acton ten years ago and it's still going strong. Not like one of those plastic things.'

Colin crumpled up the cloth and tossed it into his toolbox. 'Well, good luck to them, I say. Let's hope they think of Zelinski's when they want their new workshops fitted out, otherwise I can see me spending winter in Docklands.'

'Haven't heard anything about that. They must have built up enough stock to last ages. No point in doing any more until they've unloaded that.'

'Well, they've got plenty of space to display it in that window cabinet.'

'Have you finished up in there?'

'Yeah. I've given the glass a clean, though they'll probably do that again before they arrange the window.'

'Remembered to lock the cabinet's outside door?'

'I'll collect the key when we go past, though it beats me why they wanted that installed?'

'Health and Safety. It allows access into the shop if there's a power failure and the automatic doors fail.' Jeff looked at his watch. 'We'd better get moving. They'll expect Zelinski's to pay for the security team after six thirty.'

The two men quickly tossed the tools into their boxes, picked up the bags of offcuts and darted out to the mall as the town hall clock chimed.

They made the exit just in time. The guard on the main door gave a tight smile. There would be no overtime that evening, so he returned to the control room and switched on the alarms for Palace Parade. As usual, there was nothing untoward to log, so he let himself out through the rear of the security point and left the deserted complex to Moltonford's ghosts.

In the safety lights, the new cream Catalogue Shop gleamed and in the window display cabinet's outside door sparkled a small chrome key.

CHAPTER 23

As he stepped out of the tube station, Preston Niblock tried not to reach for his breast pocket to check that the jewel box was still there. Of course it was. Being so used to handling valuable gems he was normally at ease carrying them, but no one had ever commissioned the master jeweller to reset anything quite like this before. The diamonds in the cluster were worth more than five thousand apiece, and the star ruby had probably been purloined from someone's crown jewels - he hadn't dared look in his catalogues for fear of finding out whose. With the crescent moons of diamond and pearl linked by white gold stars, the total weight of the necklace was guaranteed to leave an indentation in any heaving bosom.

As soon as he entered the hotel's plush lobby, a young man in dark glasses escorted the jeweller into a private lift. Preston had the feeling of deja vu as his frozen faced escort in the frilly shirt brought to mind the clever clockwork automata he had seen in a German collection - only his companion probably couldn't play Mozart.

The lift opened into the penthouse suite's reception room. Preston now felt inexplicably unsettled.

As he was escorted to a huge lounge with sunken couches and pond full of fat carp, a strikingly beautiful woman darted in from a semi tropical balcony. Her presence was so electric she almost crackled.

'You have it! Let me see! Let me see!'

On the verge of being enveloped by her diaphanous sleeves and expensive perfume, Preston sneezed.

A harsh voice barked, 'Hold on Hun! Give the guy some air.'

The woman handed the jeweller an embroidered handkerchief. That was also drenched in perfume. He sneezed again.

From the well of cushions rose a large, distinguished looking man. He was elderly and probably paid a hairdresser a fortune for his expertise in a rug making. Once again Preston was enveloped, this time by overwhelming bonhomie.

'Pleased to meet you Mr Niblock. Hope you didn't mind the rush. We need the necklace for this evening. We're meeting royalty!'

As that covered varying scenarios, Preston had sense enough not to ask what branch. Judging by the necklace he had just remounted, it was one that liked to see its own reflection. 'I still would have preferred it if you had not sent the item through the post.'

'Aw, what the hell - you've got the best postal service in the world.' He put his arm about Preston's shoulder and walked him over to a drinks cabinet. 'What'll you have?'

'Not for me, thank you.' Despite himself, the jeweller could hear his tone becoming prissier. 'If this was such an urgent commission, you should have really taken it to Hatton Garden.'

'You were recommended.'

'Thank you, Mr Tiller.' Preston handed him the jewel box.

A low chuckle rumbled from the old man's throat. 'Actually, Mr Niblock, that's not my real name.' He opened the box and showed Mary Bell the cluster. 'Look Hun, ain't this guy the business.'

She squealed with delight and lifted the glittering necklace to her remarkable bosom.

'Not your real name, Mr Tiller?'

'Hell no.' He tossed the jewel box to the woman. 'Right, now get lost.'

She gave a token pout and stalked into another room.

Partly because of the way he treated female perfection, but mostly at having his integrity slighted, Preston Niblock was irritated. 'Given the nature of my business, I do like to know who I'm dealing with.'

'Don't you worry about that. Whatever name I use, it's good anywhere in the world.'

The man's pattern of speech changed, although his voice was still harsh. 'Come and sit down.' He led the reluctant master jeweller to some large armchairs by the balcony where they could see London sprawl away to the horizon.

'You're an honest man, Mr Niblock.'

Preston raised an eyebrow. He had never thought that so odd it needed to be commented on. 'I hope so, though it does carry its penalties.'

'A realist. I like that.'

'What is your real name Mr Tiller? Just in case that nice inspector from the antiques recovery squad pops in to investigate the disappearance of the eye from some sacred Buddha.'

'A sense of humour-'

'I know, you like that.' Although he hadn't yet been paid, Preston felt he had the right to be annoyed. 'I also get cramp sitting in comfortable armchairs for too long.'

His client hadn't expected to find the jeweller so spiky. 'Okay. I'll cut to the business.'

Preston wasn't aware of any business other than the signing of the cheque, so let the American carry on for fear of him finding another game to play.

'My name is really Julius Tucker the third.'

Preston's memory cells immediately latched onto the reason why that should bother him. 'Oh shit!' he thought. Though foul words seldom crossed his lips, they now had the habit of jumping about his brain.

The jeweller rose from the deep cushions with as much dignity as was possible, only to find that he had lost contact with his knees. 'Gideon Enterprizes.'

'Now, now, not so hasty. Why should that bother you?'

'Because of the same reason you used a pseudonym.'

Before he could bolt, the billionaire had placed a heavy hand on Preston's shoulder and pushed him back down into the armchair. 'I heard it said that you believe your darling wife's death had something to do with the way being cleared for Palace Parade?' Before Preston could pick up the nearest heavy object and hit him with it, Tucker had launched into an extraordinary arm-waving charade that could have stampeded buffalo. 'Nothing could be further from the truth! I'm a law abiding Christian! My whole company has strict codes of conduct, and I make damned sure that everyone sticks to them!'

Far from being reassured, Preston was beginning to think that the tycoon battered Deirdre to death with his own leathery hands.

'The man sent on behalf of Gideon Enterprizes to buy your sister-in-law's flower shop was not one of my people. We engaged this realtor. When I heard how he went about it, I sacked the firm. I'm not going to have people thinking that Gideon Enterprises is in the business of intimidating people.'

Preston at last managed to cut in. 'Pity, we could have saved a great deal on the dogs and razor wire. Just why did you use this subterfuge to get me here, Mr Tucker?'

Julius Tucker calculatingly scratched his head and worked a few hairs loose. 'Well, it's like this. That young man came back with a weird story about something you said.'

For a moment the jeweller wished the cushions would swallow him. 'I said "geology".'

'Now just what did you mean by that?'

Sense told Preston to start lying then and there but he was still indignant at a total stranger making a reference to his "darling wife". 'You know damn well.'

'You're not going to spell it out for me?'

'I doubt that I need to.'

'Only, if rumour gets around that Palace Parade isn't sitting four-square on solid bedrock, that could cause a lot of bother.'

'If I thought that Palace Parade was in danger of collapsing and killing thousands of people, I would have blown the whistle when I first learnt about it. However, I believe that the civil engineer took pains to ensure the structure is sound.'

'It sure is, it sure is.'

'Unfortunately, the authorities might not take such an enlightened attitude were they to discover that it was built over empty space.'

Julius Tucker rose and went to an antique bureau. 'How much do you think your work on that necklace is worth, Mr Niblock?'

At that moment, mending several links and resetting the cluster was the last thing on the jeweller's mind. 'Whatever you think the job is worth.'

'Let's say... half a million?'

Preston had started to pull himself from the deep cushions again. He toppled back. 'What?'

'Okay then, one million - pounds of course.'

At any other time Preston would have thought up a more suitable retort but his capacity for lucidity had been swamped. 'That sounds like a bribe to me.'

'Let's say that I'm taking out some insurance.'

The affront to his precious integrity made him smart. 'I'm not in the business of blackmail.' The jeweller managed to rise and would have made for the lift, if the young man in dark glasses had not blocked his way. Preston could see enough muscle rippling underneath the frilly shirt to make the centrefold of a gay magazine.

Tucker wound his orang-utan arm about the jeweller's shoulders and escorted him back. 'I'm not saying you are Mr Niblock. I just want to be sure there are no loose ends, and that we understand each other.'

'And what happens if I refuse?'

'Refuse? This is serious money.'

'I have all the money I need.'

By the way Tucker tightened his grip, it was obvious that his ageing body had been tuned by the best physiotherapists. 'Look, I'll call you in a couple of days and you can let me know who to write the cheque out to. Or, if you don't want your bank manager getting suspicious, the money can go straight into a Swiss account - or any other account you want to open. No need for cheques. How does that grab you?'

Preston should have said, 'by the balls', but was too anxious to make the lift. 'All right, all right.'

'Good man.' Tucker gave the jeweller a hearty slap on the back that helped propel him on his way.

Hardly aware of what he had agreed to, Preston Niblock dashed from the hotel and into the reassuring normality of London's traffic fumes.

Julius Tucker poured himself a bourbon and barked into a phone. 'Okay Jamey. You get all that?'

A balding thirty-something man with a ponytail stepped into the lounge. 'Loud and clear. Even if taking bribes can't be pinned on him, he could still be caught out for withholding information detrimental to the public good.'

'Hell, I just love the way you people put things.'

Hector cautiously pushed his fish cake from one side of the plate to the other. There had to be some supernatural explanation for its continued reappearance. Perhaps if he drove his fork through the manifestation's heart, that would lay its ghost forever.

A huge schoolmarmish voice boomed about the grey emulsioned walls of the hall. 'What is the matter now?'

'Undead!' Hector blurted out.

The old man's angry exclamations unrelated to any reality Mrs Roy was familiar with were the only things that could make the formidable woman step back a little. She was totally nonplussed by the anarchic trio social services had talked her into accommodating. All her other charges lapped up their charity meals and were grateful. Mabel was dauntingly deep, and looked her overseer squarely in the eye as though she knew the length of her underwear: there was the taint of education about that one so Mrs Roy left her alone. Although Alice giggled a lot at the most unsuitable times, at least she said thank you, even when someone took away her plate before she had finished being finicky with her food.

When the evangelist's beady gaze had settled on some other unfortunate, Mabel leaned across the trestle table to ask her companions, 'Shopping Mall before tea?'

Alice giggled excitedly and Hector gave an enthusiastic grunt. Palace Parade was the only highlight of their humdrum lives and they were getting quite adept at slipping out and getting back in the nick of time.

****

Mercy looked at her usually laid back brother attacking the Formica with a cloth. 'Why are you cleaning that counter again, Winston? Rose just did it.'

'Everything's got to be just so.'

'We're opening a café, not holding a garden party at the Palace. Rose and me can cope up here. Why don't you go downstairs to the storage units and help?'

'Hell, everyone's down there. It's like a rave in a chicken run.'

'Then go behind the catalogue counter and smile as the people come in.' Winston tossed the cloth into the sink and put a comb through his beard.

'Don't you preen yourself in a kitchen!' squawked Rose. 'You want the health inspector to close us down before we open?'

A lifetime of experience told Winston never to argue with his bossy cousin. She may have only reached his gold neck chain, yet had been known to bring down stroppier men when she was a traffic warden. Now the streets were safe, yobbos had better think twice about demanding larger portions in the café.

Winston wandered off to join the newly recruited school leavers behind the catalogue counter. To them, he may have been middle-aged, but that at least meant he had some authority.

'What has got into that man?' whispered Rose.

Mercy had always though that her brother was moody because Riotous Records went out of business. Now she was beginning to wonder. 'Must be the menopause.'

When the Catalogue Shop doors opened for the first time every bit of chrome sparkled. There were fresh flowers on the tables, a glass counter under which were displayed a vast range of goods, several racks of clothes and shoes, an ornamental barrow groaning under the weight of Mrs Silvestri's health foods and a storeroom crammed with merchandise. The only thing they hadn't got round to was filling the window display cabinet - opening the main doors had been more important. The Palace Parade management would have liked nothing more than to snatch away their lease for not being able to meet their trading deadline.

Aware that there would be free coffee and doughnuts, a cluster of people had gathered outside. For a couple of hours, Vicky Wade and Monty Golden were obliged to help the Cuffe's in the café. Then the customers turned their attention to the catalogues scattered on the counter and tables. It soon dawned on the hardened shoppers that the goods here were less expensive than the special offers in the big stores and guaranteed to last longer than the usual warranty.

Most of the larger stores hadn't bothered to send anyone along to spy on the competition. It didn't cross their minds that a co-operative of local craftspeople and small shopkeepers could make a dent in their businesses, though one earnest young woman was busily writing on a clipboard.

A tall man looked over the scribbler's shoulder. 'You spell undercut with one "t".'

The young woman glared up at Conrad Makepeace, then sneered. 'And you are?'

'Just an interested customer.' The counsellor indicated the flurry of activity at the catalogue counter. 'The punters seem to like the idea of reasonably priced goods.'

The young woman tucked the clipboard under her arm. 'Depends what you mean by reasonable?'

'Reasonable means not having to pay the cost of Palace Parade's fabric and fittings whenever you make a purchase.'

'I don't know what you are talking about.' She turned on her chunky heels and strode out.

Monty Golden beamed unsuspectingly. 'Everything all right, Mr Makepeace?'

'Watch that one, Monty. She's already got this place down as a threat to commerce as we know it.'

'Great. We must be doing well.'

As the day progressed and interest had passed from doughnuts and coffee to the catalogues, there were those still tracking down free samples.

'Hello, Mabel. I haven't seen you about for some while?' As he avoided Palace Parade and had given up the church, it was unlikely Preston Niblock would have crossed her path very often.

'Mr Niblock, how are you?'

Alice darted towards him like a confused butterfly. 'Mr Noblock, Mr Noblock!'

'Alice, do behave!' Mabel turned back to Preston. 'We are all so sorry - We haven't seen you since...'

'Thank you Mabel. Where's Hector?'

Loitering near the doorway as though tempting security down to check on what he was up to, Hector peered furtively into the cream interior.

'It's all right, Hector. You can come in.' As the companions smelt surprisingly sweet, Preston escorted them to a table. 'Where did they take you after the park was cleared?'

'Bloody Bible bashers!' snarled Hector. 'Fish cakes!'

To mollify him, the jeweller brought over a tray of doughnuts and coffee. 'They're free today. Don't ruin your tea.' He knew the dreaded Mrs Roy of old. When Deirdre had been a church worker, that woman had caused her to burst into tears on more than one occasion.

Rose was casting the little gathering a circumspect look, so Preston went back for a teaspoon and whispered across the counter to her. 'They're harmless. Friends of the wife. If they're ever short of cash and want a doughnut, you can bill me.'

Rose quelled her instincts to book the illegally parked. 'If you say so Mr Niblock.'

Mabel, Alice, and Hector eked out their doughnuts and coffee until four o'clock, when the spectre of Mrs Roy loomed in their joint subconscious, and they scuttled out. As they passed the darkened window display cabinet in the mall something caught Mabel's magpie eye.

'Pretty." She pulled the small chrome key from the lock in the cabinet door and tucked it into her pocket.

CHAPTER 25

Vicky Wade gazed across the warehouse's vast concrete floor. 'Isn't it going to be nice, everyone under one roof.'

Toni Zelinski qualified her enthusiasm. 'Well, you'll have to be partitioned off because of the clay dust. How much does your kiln burn?'

Visions of huge stoneware door guardians and ornamental urns were already filling the potter's mind. 'Depends what I'm firing.'

The builder thoughtfully paced the length of the floor. 'I'll install overhead power cables. As Preston is footing the bill, I want to keep costs down.'

Mr Becker had received advance orders for the print run of his new book and was eager to have somewhere to store his next edition. 'Business is going so well we'll pay him back in no time, and with interest.'

'That wasn't Preston's idea. All he wants you to do is keep up with the surge of business in the Catalogue Shop. Nobody expected it to take off like that.'

Something occurred to Sonia Cupit. 'Where is Mr Niblock? I haven't seen him since the opening, and Lucy Tribble doesn't know where he gets to either.'

The last time she met the jeweller, Toni Zelinski had sensed that something was wrong. 'Probably taking a break, and you know he can't stand Palace Parade.'

Two of the Electronauts had already calculated the size of the dust free bubble they wanted to enclose their work area, though stopped short of asking Toni Zelinski to install an airlock. At that moment their business needed all the co-operation it could get so they decided it best not to live up to their reputation for being seriously weird. And a sterile bubble wouldn't keep out prying eyes. Any special commission that needed space lab conditions was probably best kept in their cramped cellar with the filched Star Wars software and experimental circuitry.

'Where do you want your machinists, Mr Golden?' Toni Zelinski asked.

'Can they have the back wall under the skylight?'

'They'll be under the main ventilator.'

'Keep them awake.'

'I think it might be better to have the pottery down there.'

'You're the boss.'

Yes, she was. The civil engineer at last began to feel as though she was in control again. Although fitting out a warehouse with industrial units didn't involve cranes, rippers and excavators, and it was being done on the cheap, it was real work.

Soon all the garden sheds, garages and back bedrooms were able to give up their benches, kilns, sewing machines, metal presses and welding equipment.

After everything had been installed, the health and safety inspector came to make a few suggestions, like increasing the distance between partitions and removing the metal presses and welding equipment to an adjoining building away from the books and fabric. Nothing daunted, Toni Zelinski put in a team on night shift, and the Catalogue Co-operative was back in business the next morning.

Sonia Cupit and Monty Golden refused to produce clothes similar to the production line fashions in the large stores. Unable to totally desert good taste, they gave theirs a distinctive cut and discreet monograms that quietly whispered "style". Though French seams and hand button holing were out, they made up for that with cleaner coloured, drip-dry fabrics. As a side line, they also produced large sizes that made people look slender, blouses even Miss Priddle would have worn and T shirts printed with parrots and frogs - there would have been spider webs if Monty Golden hadn't drawn the line at anything arachnid.

Mr Singh's ready to wear range of shoes were machine made by his eldest son and two nephews. Unlike Monty Golden, the shoemaker deeply resented the reduction of his bespoke trade. He believed that cheap shoes frayed the feet in the same way atheism frayed the soul. Preston Niblock had always secretly liked Mr Singh's handmade suedes with their gold piping and ormolu buckles, but would never have worn them with his tailored suits. Now he preferred sweaters, slacks and corduroy jackets, he ordered three pairs in red, gold and blue that wouldn't have looked out of place against Fran's hybrid pansies.

Next to the extension fitted out for the metal workers, Rose started a bakery to supply Mercy's café with bread, scones, doughnuts, and cakes.

Lucy Tribble packed as much as she could into the display cabinet in the Catalogue Shop, and then illuminated the shelves with ultra violet lamps. The effect was quite stunning.

CHAPTER 26

Preston Niblock sat on the bank of Bald Wendy's leat and resentfully watched the tributary dawdle past towards Coney Canal.

Once more he swore to himself that from then on he would leave curiosity to cats. At the back of his mind was the idea that, if he kept away from his phone and regular address for as long as possible, Julius Tucker would become too busy being an entrepreneur billionaire to remember that he existed. It was wishful thinking of course. Like many novices in the way of the world, Preston Niblock had admitted to the predator that he would taste pretty good served up on toast. Now he was part of the Palace Parade conspiracy, he would not be allowed to go missing. The jeweller could have always reported what he knew to the authorities of course. However, given agreement the Palace Parade Development Committee had made with Gideon, it was obvious, somewhere along the line, local government officers had their noses in the trough as well. The only person he did trust was Conrad Makepeace. Bringing down a company the size of Gideon would have crowned the crusading councillor's lifetime of fighting worthy causes. But the man had a large family. Anonymous email to the press? Tucker wouldn't have been fooled for a moment. Why didn't he just will Deirdre's insurance money to the Catalogue Shop Co-operative then jump in the Coney Canal? One glance at the murky millpond told Preston Niblock that on the tributary's journey to Bald Wendy it had accumulated a strange by-product, probably only silt, though it resembled effluent from a sewage outlet. He would have sooner cut his throat with a rusty razor. Then, that hardly had any appeal either.

The jeweller wandered up to the derelict mill, pushed open its unbolted door, and went inside. Bald Wendy's fabric was surprisingly intact. Its owner had attempted to keep it presentable for viewing by the sort of yuppies who convert old water pumping stations, oast houses, and lighthouses into second homes. The location was too isolated, and on an overcast day the aspect bleak enough to depress the bats. It was a part of England that would be forever muddy and swallowed in mist, the sort of place you went to if you wanted to disappear or find out if it was possible to be even more miserable.

Preston now realised how much he missed Deirdre. In her own humdrum way she had steered him away from getting involved, always putting an emotional cushion between him and life's irritants. The couple had been so consumed in their own small domain, they never even attempted to have a family he might now have run to - or away from. Suddenly he wanted to see grandchildren.

The jeweller ascended the rickety stairs to the lucam and looked out through the window as though at any moment a fairy would arrive, fluttering from the willows to make Gideon Enterprizes disappear with one tap of her wand. She did come, but in a red sports car speeding through the lingering mist.

****

Miss Priddle parked directly under the lucam, pulled up the straps of her four-inch high slingbacks and got out of her car.

Preston Niblock was leaning against the entrance to Bald Wendy.

'What are you doing here?' she asked.

'I fancied a ride in a taxi.'

'All the way out here? Must have cost a fortune?'

Telling the accountant that he had just somehow blundered into one would not have been a good idea at that moment. 'How did you know I'd be here?'

Miss Priddle came in and followed him up into the gearing room.

'I had a premonition.' That seemed even less likely than the accountant sitting by the fire during the long evenings and crocheting doilies. 'If a taxi brought you out here, how did you intend to get back? You refuse to carry a mobile phone and, even if the mill did have an ancient telegraph on its roof, no one would see or understand it.'

The jeweller had been so anxious to escape Moltonford he hadn't given any thought about returning. There was an irresistible finality about the thought of Bald Wendy, like a full stop on a life sentence.

'What were you thinking about?' Miss Priddle went on. Then it occurred to her. 'Is the death of your wife beginning to sink in?'

Now guilt had finished with him, there was no point in pretending. 'Partly.'

'What makes up the other percent?'

He gazed at the large crown wheel and counted its cogs to stop himself telling her. The woman may have had Achilles tendons of steel and thought in binary code, but he had no right to involve her with commercial dragons even she would be unable to slay.

'It's something to do with Gideon Enterprizes, isn't it?'

He looked up too quickly and gave the game away.

Miss Priddle placed her briefcase on a broken runner stone and took out a brandy flask. She poured a measure and persuaded the jeweller to drink it. He hated the taste of strong liquor and spluttered.

To avoid another dose, Preston wiped the water from his eyes and sat down. 'I can't tell you. It'd be too dangerous.'

She sighed peevishly and sat beside him. 'During my lawful transactions I have given more than one tycoon reason to see me dead. But I'm still here.'

'This is different.'

'Julius Tucker the third is only another tycoon.'

'How did-'

Who else was it likely to be? Neville Grablatt may be thoroughly obnoxious, but with his record he had enough sense not to exceed his powers. And who else would want to take over his sister-in-law's land?

Miss Priddle was obviously saving the velvet glove for her clients.   'So, tell me?'

Preston still evaded. 'What made you come out here?'

'Toni and Lucy Tribble were worried about you. Now, tell me what is going on?'

There was nothing for it, little short of jumping out of the window into the headrace and hoping the current would carry him from her grasp of her scarlet nails. 'Tucker tricked me into seeing him. He realised I knew about the cave under Palace Parade and offered me a bribe of one million pounds.'

'What?'

Preston was perversely pleased at her reaction. 'What could I do?'

'Demand two million.'

He looked at her steadily. 'You're not joking - are you?'

She wasn't. 'This is business. That knowledge could close down Palace Parade. Given the amount he had to sink into the place, the legal fees and loss of trade would cost him billions. Then Gideon would be obliged to demolish the shopping centre.'

Preston wasn't used to dealing with naked pragmatism. 'I don't want his filthy money!'

Miss Priddle realised that her enthusiasm wasn't helping. 'I know, I know. But the die is cast. You will have to accept the money. You really would be in danger if he thought you were going to sell the information somewhere else.'

'How can I accept a million pounds without attracting attention? I can hardly hand a cheque for that amount over the post office counter.'

The accountant dismissed his concern as though it was an annoying gnat. 'Nothing easier. What we need to do first is get you some insurance.'

The jeweller was aggrieved by her practicality. His ego would have appreciated a little more melodrama at the revelation. This may have only been a minor curtain raiser to her. To him it was Titus Andronicus. 'I can't see any company insuring me against sudden murder.'

'Not that sort of insurance. You're safe enough as long as Tucker knows that the truth will come out if you fall under a bus.'

'How safe is "safe enough"?'

'The first thing we must do is catalogue the facts. In the event of anything happening to you they will be automatically posted on the Internet and to every MP and major newspaper. It's what Tucker would expect you to do. Pity we can't lay our hands on a geological map.'

Geology was the last thing on Preston's mind. 'But what can I do with a million pounds?'

She gave him a pitying look. 'You have lived a sheltered life, haven't you?'

'Deirdre didn't encourage me to abseil down mountains or hang glide. We preferred our lives to be sheltered.'

Miss Priddle offered him another nip of brandy and, now having been anaesthetised by the first one, he took it without thinking.

'Yes, I can see your point. However, it now looks as though you have a business manager whether you want one or not. And, as your manager, I recommend that you allow me to start by opening an overseas account for your million so there will be no awkward questions from the Inland Revenue.'

Preston wasn't sure about the way she had rapidly promoted herself into his financial affairs. 'I don't want the money.'

'Think of the capital as bedrock into which you can chisel out you own little empire, dividend by dividend.'

'My imagination only runs to finding the most subtle turn in a diamante stem.'

'Don't worry, you'll find a use for the money soon enough. And by the time you do, I make sure it's doubled.'

***

In Palace Parade's committee room, the managers who had dismissed the Catalogue Shop as merely eccentric were holding an urgent meeting. Now they had a monopoly, the stores depended on selling their goods at inflated prices. Shoppers were beginning to realise that, cast afloat on a sea of plush fittings, soporific music, and luxurious displays, they had drifted into purchases they would have resisted anywhere else.

The Catalogue Shop had brought customers to their senses. Something would have to be done.

The number of customers visiting the Catalogue Shop continued to increase. There was seldom a table free and a steady stream of people carrying kitchen appliances, children's clothes, health foods, mugs, cell phones, fridge magnets, and etcetera, flowed through its entrance. The stock held over from the old factory units rapidly disappeared. Even Mr Becker's second edition on church corbels sold out. Since all the other booksellers went out of business, a book that didn't have an inane or obscene cover was now something of a novelty.

As Conrad Makepeace sat sipping his coffee in the Catalogue Shop café one morning, he noticed several customers watching an angry discussion and occasionally voicing their support. Apparently, the powers controlling Palace Parade were making their move sooner than expected. The councillor left his table and went over to the catalogue counter.

Winston Cuffe's voice stormed above the gathering. 'You can't do that! We depend on that storage space! We can't do business without it!'

The older man in the grey suit had adopted a defensive tone. 'We cannot ignore the instructions of the safety committee. The access avenue will pass through three other stockrooms as well as your own.'

'It means we will lose most of our storage space!' wailed Vicky Wade, wishing the other members of the Co-operative were there. 'You'll have to wait until we talk to Miss Priddle.'

'There is nothing she can do. The contract allows for necessary safety alterations and you will naturally be compensated.'

Winston Cuffe was now beyond words so Conrad Makepeace quickly stepped in before he erupted. 'Excuse me, but do I understand the gist of this discussion?'

Vicky Wade was in tears. 'They're taking away virtually all our storage space.'

'I'm merely delivering formal notice of safety improvements,' said the official.

Councillor Makepeace reached over and took the stapled pages. 'May I?'

The potter was right. The storage space the Catalogue Shop depended on was about to all but vanish for an access avenue.

'When is work due to start?'

'In two days.'

Winston exploded. 'Two days! Where can we find somewhere to put the stock in two days!'

'I'm sure this matter can be discussed at a higher level.' Conrad Makepeace seldom had to use his tone of authority and found it strangely gratifying to be given the excuse. 'I would strongly advise the management of Palace Parade to wait until I have put it before the next Moltonford Council meeting.'

A muted cheer rose from the customers.

The official's smile was derisive. 'This has nothing to do with Moltonford Council. This is an internal matter. We are only bound by the contract agreed with the Palace Parade Development Committee.'

Conrad Makepeace increased his tax inspector's tone. 'Anything to do with the welfare of local small businesses is our concern. Palace Parade exists only because of the concessions Moltonford Council allowed Gideon Enterprizes. This town is your landlord, and your management had better not forget it.'

'Very well, I shall inform the manager.' The official wandered out, smiling to himself.

'Is there really something you can do?' Vicky asked hopefully.

'Probably not,' Makepeace admitted. 'I might be able to buy you more time.'

Winston brought his fists down on the glass counter so heavily, the cashiers thought he would go through it. 'Man, what a set up! This means we'll have to restock at least four times a day.'

Vicky dabbed her eyes. 'The system only works because we're able to supply anything in the catalogue at a minute's notice.'

Makepeace continued to read the order. 'Of course, they are offering reparation.'

'We need storage space, not sympathy,' said Mercy.

'And that man said there isn't any more available,' Vicky added. 'What will we tell the others?'

Lucy Tribble dashed through bedding plants and under the pergola towards the garden centre café. 'Mr Niblock! Mr Niblock! Thank goodness you are all right! We were all getting very worried.' She stopped moving before her necklaces, which fell in a glittering cascade back onto her Paisley blouse.

Lucy seemed to flutter like an overweight moth when she moved, her sparkling necklaces and pendulous earrings creating fountains of crystal confetti. The bead worker's voice was pleasant and twittery, rather like the ageing canaries and finches that flew at liberty in her lounge where the furniture was draped with much laundered throw covers. Some people said that she kept a lover in the back bedroom. He must have been a sailor, because no one had ever seen him.

Out of breath, Lucy flopped down into the chair Preston Niblock offered. 'I've been locking up and putting on the alarms as you instructed.' She pulled a note from her shoulder bag. 'And here is a list of goods sold. It includes that rather nice engraved silver fob watch, and a 22 carat gold chain.' The small round woman stopped to catch her breath. 'I left early today in the hope of catching you here.'

Preston gazed across the table at his business associate. There was something distant about his expression. 'Miss Tribble, has anyone told you that your hazel eyes are larger and brighter than anything in the nocturnal cages at London Zoo?'

The poor woman looked at him in amazement.

Fran pushed a tray onto the table. 'That's enough of that Preston.' She turned to Lucy. 'I don't know where he's been. It wouldn't surprise me if he found a cannabis plantation.'

Preston giggled. 'What, and not bring you back any cuttings.'

'Where did you get to?' Lucy insisted earnestly. 'Everyone has been so worried.'

Not wanting to admit that for several days he had been slipping out of the shop before she arrived in the morning, Preston ducked the question. 'How's the Catalogue Shop doing?'

'Very well, in fact they can hardly keep up with the demand.' Her cheerful expression suddenly dropped.

Fran hesitated as she poured them each a cup of tea. 'What's the matter?'

Lucy Tribble nervously crumpled a string of red tourmaline. 'Oh dear. It's not fair. Palace Parade's safety officer insists that an access avenue must be driven through their storage unit.'

Preston let his head lean back onto the shelf of plants behind him. 'I should have known.'

'How much of the storeroom will they lose?' asked Fran.

'Most of it. Mr Cuffe is trying to work out how to run a relay of deliveries.' The beadworker then noticed that the usually immaculate jeweller was looking a little scuffed around the edges. 'Are you all right, Mr Niblock?'

'He's had an... experience, Miss Tribble.' Fran wasn't sure what had happened to her brother-in-law but didn't want to worry Lucy any more. She handed her a cup of tea. 'How are you going to get home? My Ben's back if you'd like a lift?'

'That's all right thank you. I have the bike. I thought I'd just drop by on the off chance Mr Niblock would be here.'

Preston grinned. 'I think I will fly home.'

Lucy looked at him like an accusing canary. 'Mr Niblock, have you been drinking?'

From Fran's raised eyebrow, her guess had been accurate enough. Preston's dreamy expression told the world that he was seeing it through 30% proof reality.

Lucy felt secretly smug that the master jeweller was mortal after all. She drank down her tea. 'Well, I'd better be going.'

Lucy Tribble pottered off to the car park, rearranging her beads as she went.

Fran gave Preston a long, hard look. 'What is it between you and Miss Priddle?' Preston stifled a giggle. 'She's not your type, you know.'

He waved an expansive arm at some invisible audience. 'No one is Miss Priddle's type. That summit only brave hearts dare scale.'

There was no point in pursuing the question. 'Well, at least she made the Catalogue Shop work, so she can't be all bad. Palace Parade are rotten bleeders. Fancy them taking their storage space. They could have doubled their business if it weren't for that.' Preston was still watching fairies in the clematis, so Fran decided on another tack. 'And it was you who paid Zelinski's to fit out their workshops wasn't it?' she accused as though it hadn't been an open secret.

Preston held a hot teacup to his forehead. 'I am now an entrepreneur.'

'I'm glad Deirdre isn't here to see you like this. She'd wonder what she married.' Fran got up. 'About time I did the till. Don't go away. I think you should spend the night here.'

Preston sat quietly giggling to himself until the encroaching headache had remorselessly clenched its steel talons over the top of his head.

***

A week later the relay of vans Winston Cuffe had organised were regularly cramming goods into the Catalogue Shop's severely limited storeroom space. At least the new, hastily constructed access avenue meant they were able to get in and out more easily. Realising that Palace Parade were prepared to do anything to put the Catalogue Shop out of business, the Co-operative asked Toni Zelinski to reinforce what was left of the storeroom and its lift, so the builder encased the enclosure in sheet metal. As the Moltonford Council were due to discuss the management's attitude towards Moltonford's small businesses, the safety officer thought twice about complaining.

Within weeks the Catalogue Shop had adapted to its new limitations. As convoys of merchandise flooded in from the Catalogue Co-operative's warehouse, trade once more took off. Even Mrs Silvestri expanded her range to include greeting cards, small ornaments, massage oils, and exotic fabrics.

CHAPTER 28

Now Lucy Tribble knew enough about Preston Niblock's business to order the odd watch and pair of earrings, he retreated to his workshop to make charm bracelets and hippie medallions. The beadworker became so efficient he felt obliged to give her a generous wage for being his buffer against a bizarre world.

The million pounds Miss Priddle had invested for the jeweller soon doubled. Because he refused to touch the money it continued to mount, further bending the branch his peace of mind tenuously clutched. Had Deirdre still been alive it would have given him an incentive to buy a bungalow on Capri and take several world cruises. Now Preston's instinct was to donate it all to worthy causes. His accountant pointed out how much the fund raising management of the major charities were paid, and that he might attract attention to himself. He suspected that Miss Priddle really wanted to play stock exchanges with his ill-gotten gains for as long as possible.

***

During the next nine months, the Catalogue Shop continued to make dents in the trade of other Palace Parade stores and had to increase its counter staff. As profits soared, Miss Priddle tried to relocate the Co-operative to a larger mall unit being vacated by a kitchenware store they had put out of business. Unsurprisingly, the retail cuckoo was not going to be allowed any further into the nest.

Preston Niblock's house was now full of vases, electrical appliances, shirts, shoes, Indian carpets, jazz records, and books about the more curious aspects of the English Parish church. He didn't have the heart to refuse the gifts from the grateful Catalogue Co-operative and the intricate stories woven into Mrs Silvestri's imported rugs kept him amused when his brain wanted to sleep but his conscience wouldn't let it.

The jeweller never touched alcohol again after that embarrassing day and it was months before he forgave Miss Priddle for persuading him to drink so much. At least the incident had amused Fran and Ben. Given the easygoing nature of the couple, the two ferocious guard dogs soon became pets that were taken for walks by their grandchildren. The razor wire was now under the canopy of a Russian vine, waiting for a keen gardener who preferred to pick up their bedding plants in the dead of night.

Zelinski's managed to get by with the odd contract for a school extension or private swimming pool. Moltonford Council was no longer spending on large projects because most of the population deserted the outlying amenities when Palace Parade introduced a swimming pool, gym, and health spa. Even the old lido couldn't compete and had to close down. Now only those who could afford it swam, jogged on the spot, and luxuriated in imported mud.

Over the months, Preston grew even more paranoid about the shopping mall and only ventured inside it to pay for Hector, Alice, and Mabel's doughnuts. He heard that Mrs Roy had become so exasperated with their irreligious view of the life she "invited" them to leave. They had apparently accepted with a peculiar degree of enthusiasm. Now nobody knew where they bedded down for the night, despite the continuing clean up of the streets. Anyone remaining on the pretty, paved pedestrian area for more than five minutes without moving was liable to be apprehended and given the bus fare to another town.

***

The spring evening was clear and relatively pollution free. Monty Golden said goodbye to the machinists who had been on overtime and locked up the warehouse for the night. He then strode off down Canning Road to his small shop. As it was his own property he couldn't see the point in selling it at a loss, so he and his wife continued to live in the flat above it.

***

At 3.0 o'clock a.m. Jimmy McBain rolled over in his sleep and wrinkled his nose. He sneezed. Feeling another asthma attack coming on, the ten-year-old got up and went to the window. He sneezed again. That wasn't pollen or traffic fumes.

He threw back the curtains and opened the window. Acrid smoke was billowing from fingers of livid flame consuming the Catalogue Co-operative's warehouse.

Gasping for breath, Jimmy dashed downstairs and phoned for the fire service.

By the time four pumps arrived the warehouse was a furnace. As cylinders exploded in the adjoining metal workshops it was impossible for the fire fighters to get close.

115

Water was poured down from a hydraulic platform while three-inch jets on the ground tried to penetrate the wall of flame.

Eventually, all that remained was a pall of smoke and lake of water in which the carbonised pages of Mr Becker's latest tome and charred children's clothes floated. The sewing machines, kiln, and metal presses were now blackened stumps, fused in the fierce heat. The plastic of the Electronauts' computer terminals had melted, creating bizarre structures resembling mouldering alien heads.

****

Having an erratic sleep pattern, Preston Niblock was in his workroom engraving zodiacal signs onto a brass tap fitting for an astrologer.

He suddenly decided that Deirdre's plants that were eking out an existence in the back bedroom needed watering. He dutifully filled a plastic jug and took it in to the row of schlumbergera, which had been provoked into flower because of the deprivations they had undergone.

When he had topped up the saucers of each one, he happened to glance out of the window. There, like an immolating phoenix on the dark side of town, was a bright bloom of flame. At first he thought there had been a crash on the motorway.

Then he pinpointed its location. The terrible implication momentarily numbed him.

By the time the jeweller's taxi arrived at the warehouse it was totally gutted.

The sight of the smouldering ruin made unpleasant memories flood back. This is what had happened to Frank Merryweather and Deirdre; consumed in a blaze so fierce that any evidence of what had caused it was incinerated.

This time he was angry.

Preston Niblock turned to a senior police officer. 'Was it arson?'

The man buttoned his tunic to conceal a pyjama top. 'It will naturally be investigated Sir. Do you have any special reason to suspect arson?'

Then the jeweller remembered that he no longer had any right to be virtuous. He qualified his statement. 'I didn't think that the sewer rats lit up until seven in the morning.'

A familiar voice suddenly bludgeoned the night air. 'Arson, dear fellow? Why on earth would anyone want to burn down such an admirable enterprise?'

Preston turned to face Neville Grablatt. The man was as overbearing as ever and exuded false sympathy from every pore.

'And why are you so sure it wasn't arson, Mr Grablatt?'

The councillor planted a large hand on the jeweller's shoulder and guided him away from the policeman. 'Excuse us. Mr Niblock has not so long ago had a similar tragedy overtake him.' As soon as they were out of earshot the avuncular persona melted away. 'Look, Niblock, don't make waves.'

Preston stepped back, momentarily nonplussed by the man's sudden aggression. 'What are you talking about?'

'Do I have to spell it out for you?'

The jeweller refused to be intimidated. 'I never realised you had a dictionary, Mr Grablatt.'

'All right then. You've been paid off. If you want to keep your integrity, molecularly as well as locally, I would advise you to keep your suspicions to yourself.'

Preston didn't know which surprised him more, the fact that the bully was privy to his deal with Julius Tucker, or that he was able to put so many words together in one sentence and still make sense.

'And if I do feel the need to express myself, Mr Grablatt?'

'Don't push it.'

'Councillor Grablatt, if anything happens to me Mr Tucker will not thank you for the consequences.'

The alligator eyes reflected the glare of a spotlight and the jeweller could see that the man was unsure.

He decided to make the most of his hesitation. 'Good night Councillor Grablatt.'

Preston quickly strode back to his taxi before the creature decided to pursue him. Once home, he bolted the doors and sat on the stairs. There was no point in waking the Co-operative just yet to tell them that their livelihoods had burnt down during the night.

CHAPTER 29

Conrad Makepeace birdied the ninth and told himself, 'The woman may be related to Morgana Le Fay, but she won't top that.'

Miss Priddle couldn't care less about golf and only played it to humour important clients. Stiletto heels were not welcome on the putting greens and her ego needed to feed on greater challenges.

She conceded the final round so the councillor could demand the information she had every intention of giving him anyway. 'We believe the warehouse fire was arson. I doubt if anything will be proved. It's Frank Merryweather's all over again.'

Conrad Makepeace thoughtfully replaced the sleeve on his putter. 'At least they'll get the insurance.'

'That's hardly any good if they aren't able to obtain new premises.'

He led her down the cockleshell path to the clubhouse. 'If health and safety refuse them permission for another industrial Co-operative warehouse they can appeal, though I wouldn't hold out much hope.'

'We know damn well the fire wasn't started by welding equipment. What arc welder would leave his equipment on?'

'I know. However, the economy of Moltonford is now so dependent on Palace Parade the council daren't put their fists up to Gideon. If I can just prove that just one store is tied to Julius Tucker, I'm sure the rest of the sordid business will spill out. Then we'll have them.'

Miss Priddle stopped to scrape some mud from her pink golf shoes. 'Given the time an appeal will take, that won't do the Catalogue Shop any good.'

'I'm sorry, but they must have made a fortune during the last year.'

'Not the point. Local businesses are being decimated by a company who would take out a patent on the gene for motherhood.'

'I didn't think you bothered with the subtleties of ethics?'

'No one who attacks a client of mine gets away with it.'

He gave her a wary glance. 'So I've heard.'

Miss Priddle stopped to make sure no one was watching. She reached into the side pouch of her golf bag and pulled out a document wallet. 'You won't find this by surfing the Internet.

There's enough in here to get an enquiry under way. Don't involve me.'

After his extensive investigations, this seemed too easy. 'How did you come by it?'

'Never mind. Just remember, a clever lawyer could run enough rings round these documents to give Gideon Enterprizes time to cover its tracks. In fact, they've probably been juggling the companies since I got the information.'

The councillor set his jaw. No tax-evading pike had escaped him when he had been an Inland Revenue inspector, and he was damned if this barracuda was going to get off the hook either.

***

Nothing could be salvaged from the wreckage of the warehouse. The small depot from where the Catalogue Shop's vans made collections had stocks that would last barely two weeks.

At first, few of the Co-operative could see the point in fighting on. Then, like Preston Niblock, they became angry.

The management of Palace Parade was confident that the Catalogue Shop would have to give up the lease by the end of the month. Only Mrs Silvestri, who brought her stock in from wholesalers, hadn't been affected by the fire and the Cuffes could carry on running the café for as long as there were enough customers.

Monty Golden and Sonia Cupit took over the workroom in his old shop and continued to make a limited range. Mr Singh and his son did the same. As Vicky Wade had a second wheel she was able to buy firings at another pottery until a new kiln could be installed in her shed. The Kitchen Collection had lost all its machinery so Ron Acton could never hope to meet the demand and, though they were capable of breaking into the most sophisticated security systems of any national defence grid, the facilities in the Electronaut's cellar were hardly geared to turn out electronic goods in bulk.

The only way the Co-operative could restart production was in another town where they would be allowed planning permission. But deliveries would be a logistical nightmare. Everything depended on their appeal against the chief health and safety officer's decision.

***

Mabel pulled her blanket up to her chin and tried to stretch out. 'Hector, will you stop snoring.' She nudged him, then realised where the unseemly din was coming from. 'For pity's sake, Alice, someone might hear us.'

'Nah,' yawned Hector. 'Bleeders gorn home.'

'All the same... 'Mabel yawned and turned over.

The accommodation may have been cramped, but the space under the shelves of the Catalogue Shop's window display cabinet was more private than Mrs Roy's hostel. As long as the camera scanning the mall didn't catch them going in and out, they would never need to go back into accommodation with tin lamp shades, cold charity, and accusation pointing from every biblical print.

The soporific fragrance of incense from Mrs Silvestri's scented candles pervading the cabinet could have wafted away any odours liable to arise from bodies in such close proximity. Now not even that mattered. The companions had developed the habit of staying clean and regularly visited the washrooms managed by the sympathetic attendant at the youth hostel. In its own way life was bliss. Oblivious to the tribulations of the unsuspecting proprietors, they slept on.

CHAPTER 30

'Bald Wendy?' echoed Toni Zelinski. 'Why is the place called Bald Wendy for pity's sake?'

Preston gazed at the deserted carcass of a building. The mill must have been at the very bottom of the English Heritage's conservation list.

'Meant to be Auld Windy.'

'But it's a water mill, not a windmill?'

The last thing the jeweller felt inclined to do at that moment was argue over regional irony. 'Shall we go?'

Toni took a hard hat from her general foreman and strapped it on. 'Are you sure you want to come with us?'

'Of course I don't want to come, but you've not been down there and I have. Will the outbound motor on that inflatable be powerful enough against the current?'

'That thing could sail up a waterfall.' Toni's boots bit into the steep bank as she half strode, half skidded down with her foreman.

'What about sharp rocks?'

'Toughened and double shelled.'

Preston secured his helmet, and then toppled into the dinghy after them.

They carefully nudged through the thicket of weeping willow concealing the ancient gate across the tributary's tunnel.

The civil engineer trained a torch on one of the rusty hinges. 'Right Owen. Loosen that for us.'

The foreman stepped onto the bank. Though the metal was corroded, the brackets holding the hinges had been driven deep into the rock. Owen took an acetylene torch from his backpack, lit it, and cut the metal. When one side was free they were able to ease the gate wide enough for the inflatable to squeeze past.

They were swallowed by pitch darkness only a matter of metres inside the tunnel. Owen switched on two powerful lamps at the prow.

There was something sinister about the way the oncoming water lapped at the smooth walls, making a ponderous sucking sound as though trying to swallow the dinghy into its depths. It made the jeweller even more apprehensive than when he had lowered himself down the limestone chimney after Arnold Mold. His companions were no doubt used to standing in cofferdams with nothing but a few piles between them and millions of tons of water. The nearest Preston had been to such an experience was in a wrap around aquarium. If the water did suddenly rise in this tunnel, there were no air pockets to head for.

After they had motored on for three kilometres the River Nox tributary took a curved course under a vault of rock and Toni Zelinski carefully guided them through the increasing swell.

Preston felt the Universe closing in. 'If this ceiling gets any lower I'm turning back, even if you aren't.' He pressed against the side of the dinghy, clutching the safety rope as though some tentacle was about to reach up and pluck him into the slurping, murky water.

'It's only because the rock here is harder. It'll even out. The water is much lower than when it came up to Bald Wendy's wheel,' Owen tried to reassure him. Life jacket or not, he had no intention of plunging in to save a terrified jeweller.

The limestone walls opened out into another cave.

'Hold on!' warned Toni Zelinski. 'The river's branching off so there might be some turbulence.'

At the junction of the tunnels, she appeared to be steering them into a bottleneck.

'This limestone must be pretty ancient,' Owen observed.

Without warning, they found themselves in a large cave.

'This is it,' she announced.

Preston was beyond worrying whether he made sense. 'Thought the river was Cretaceous?'

Owen scrutinised the ceiling. 'That fissure looks deep.'

'Further up, you can touch the roof.' Toni sounded as though she was enjoying herself. 'A fold in the rock must have pushed it down when the valley was formed.'

'Is it stable?'

'It's had eighty or so million years to collapse if it wanted.'

'Hold on tight!' called Owen.

Toni Zelinski held the rudder fast to stop the inflatable being pulled through the arch of an adjoining cave.

'Arnold says that if you get sucked in there you don't come out!' Preston called, more in terror than desire to inform.

The powerful outboard motor negotiated them past the churning water.

Preston pointed to a wide sloping floor. 'Just here. Palace Parade is now directly above us.'

They disembarked and he took the builders up the ancient beach to the access cover that used to lead to Victoria Park.

Toni shined a torch into the short chimney partly filled with hardcore. 'This rock can't be any more than two metres thick.'

Owen whistled. 'And it's taking the weight of that shopping mall?'

'The main load-bearing columns have been sunk either side of the cave and into the bedrock. The beams that span the ground floor are propped midway on columns sunk only a metre deep. The basement ground was levelled for raft foundations.'

'But that span's huge?'

'It's stable enough so as long as there aren't any rock movements that dislodge the central beams.'

Preston couldn't take his gaze off the limestone ceiling where the curtain of stalactites distantly glittered in their torchlight. 'What would happen then?'

'As the load-bearing foundations aren't cantilevered, the floor would crack down the middle.' The civil engineer made a "V" with the sides of her hands. 'The outside columns support the galleries as well as the whole weight of the building. With the central pillars gone, Palace Parade would split lengthways, collapse and bring down this cave roof.'

The jeweller was horribly fascinated. 'Then?'

'Everything would disappear into the bowels of the earth.' She added as an afterthought, 'Except the outer columns of course. They've been sunk too deep.' Toni Zelinski rotated to take her bearings. 'The other end of the mall must be in that direction.' She carefully paced out her steps and led the other two over the boulder-strewn floor for half a kilometre. She stopped and pointed at the cave ceiling. 'The Catalogue Shop must be somewhere about here.'

Preston started to wonder if he was doing the right thing. 'You are sure it's possible?'

The builder laughed. 'Of course, drill that out that in no time.'

'But you have to find the exact spot.'

'We can pulse sound waves through the floor above. That will give us the location and rock density.' She shone her torch on the jeweller's worried expression. 'Trust us, we're builders.'

Owen hoped the master jeweller wouldn't have second thoughts. The work would keep them going for a few weeks.

'You aren't going to change your mind over a few drips in the roof are you? My father spent his working life a mile underground, sometimes knee deep in water, and lived to be ninety five.'

Preston wasn't sure what coal mines had to do with drilling holes into a shopping centre. All the same, he couldn't back out now. 'Sure you can do it without anyone guessing what's going on?'

'We'll have to bring in the plant and generators after dusk and work through the night.' Toni stopped analysing the ceiling. 'Don't worry, no one will blab. I'll only use teetotallers.'

'Don't joke Toni. You've no idea of the consequences if this gets out.'

'It won't, Preston. I promise. You've brought us too much business.'

'When can you start?'

'As soon as that barge is delivered and you have the lease on Bald Wendy.'

'No problem.'

Owen detected some ambivalence in the jeweller's reply. 'Can you trust the others in the Catalogue Shop?'

Preston wanted to believe he could. Now the Co-operative had lost their appeal against the health and safety officer's decision they would either have to approve his idea, move twenty miles away to the nearest town, or go out of business. Best of all, if no one knew where they were, they could never be burnt out again.

Toni thought over the logistics. There was enough current in the river to drive a turbine. They would have to buttress the area round the shaft and working area and put in dampers to suppress any vibration. As long as they kept the workshops well away from the mall area, the sound wouldn't be picked up.

'It will have to be a platform lift-' she announced out loud, but Preston interrupted before she could finish.

'A what?'

'The lift must fit flush with the floor in the storeroom.'

'But we don't want stock suddenly shooting through it like the demon king.'

'I think it's time we got you back, Preston. It must be way past your bedtime.'

'Don't patronise the person who writes the cheques.'

Toni mischievously edged up to him. 'I thought that was Priddy?'

Sooner than face more innuendoes about his relationship with the accountant, the jeweller decided to go quietly. Then something occurred to him. 'Do you think anyone came down here to check things out before Palace Parade was built?'

Owen shrugged. 'Well Bald Wendy's gate hasn't been tampered with. Not unless there's some other way in?'

Of course. They would have used the Victoria Park entrance. When that was sealed they probably thought the Bald Wendy end was secure enough.

'Oh we'll make it more secure than a bank vault, don't you worry,' said Toni.

CHAPTER 31

Mercy Cuffe weighed a cauliflower in her hand. 'This is good stuff. Can I have a look at those carrots?'

'I can see flies,' squeaked Rose.

Mrs Silvestri also had misgivings about how much space the organic grower would want. 'Isn't it too hot in here for vegetables?'

The thirty-something man with the woollen hat and fair beard didn't register the scepticism in her tone. 'I've got a cold cabinet. Fit in that space against the wall, easy.'

'And how long did you want it for?'

'Until I can find another outlet. The council estate was okay after they got over the novelty of fresh fruit and vegetables, but it was a short lease. The old High Street was the best location.'

Mercy liked the idea of having fresh tomatoes and lettuce ready to hand. Rose would no longer need to go to the food hall to buy expensive ingredients that went off within a day, and his modest stall would help them justify retaining the unit. 'Well, he is one of us, Marie. How can we turn away someone who refuses to wash organic vegetables for the supermarkets?'

'Does he know what has been happening to our business lately?'

The market gardener reached down into his crate and pulled out a root of ginger. 'I grow this in pots.'

Mrs Silvestri cautiously examined it. 'All right then. Can you supply peppers?'

'The greenhouse ones won't be ready for a couple of months.'

She was prepared to forgive him that. 'Okay then. But if business begins to pick up we'll need the space back.'

'Understood.'

***

Miss Priddle gazed past her computer monitor at the jeweller's innocent expression. 'You are doing what?'

Preston didn't bother to repeat himself. The accountant never missed anything the first time and she was only asking to give herself a moment to think.

He sat back in his chair that was under the foliage of a variegated fig decorated with silk winged bees. 'I would like you to pull out some money for Toni Zelinski.'

'How much?'

'Just enough to buy a carbide blade capable of cutting through 100 million-year-old Cretaceous limestone.'

She continued to stare at him as though he were a dinosaur. 'Julius Tucker is not a man to play beggar-my-neighbour with. If he finds out what you're doing - you are dead, whether or not that means incriminating material being pushed through the media's letter box.'

The full impact of what he was involved in began to strike home. 'What else can we do?'

Miss Priddle saved the program she had been working on, pulled up her sling backs, and collected her briefcase. 'If you want to compensate everyone connected with the Catalogue Shop, you have enough to do that without this performance.'

'But they have the right to those businesses. Some of them took a lifetime to establish.'

The accountant went to the door. 'Forget that I asked to marry you.'

'Not even to inherit that two million after Tucker has had me dismembered?'

'Lose that gerbil expression and come with me.'

Preston was bustled down the stairs and into her red sports car. He had now been in it so often the passenger seat should have had the impression of his narrow backside.

He passively watched the scenery flash past, not bothering to ask where they were going. As long as she didn't force brandy down his throat or ask him to design them an engagement ring each, he was prepared to wait and find out.

The jeweller hadn't expected to arrive at Bald Wendy.

Miss Priddle got out of the car and slammed the door after her. Preston meekly followed into the gearing room.

'Why all this drama? You know Toni Zelinski can be trusted.'

The accountant looked at her client as though she was scrutinising an interesting blob of ectoplasm. 'Not so long ago I had a dream about this place.'

'A dream?'

'Shut up. I don't often have portentous dreams and this was the real thing.'

Preston wasn't sure what to make of his computer-minded financial manager having premonitions. 'What was it about?'

Miss Priddle suddenly turned to face him and jabbed a finger towards a pile of debris. 'Just there.'

'What?'

'You, with blood pouring from your face.'

Preston stepped back and nearly fell down the steps. 'You didn't really believe it, did you?'

'Not until this morning.'

The jeweller walked across the floor and perched on the cracked millstone to avoid the area. Whether she was psychic or not, he decided to keep clear of that particular spot from then on.

Miss Priddle relaxed. The dream was probably a once in a lifetime aberration and would never happen again.

'The thought of having a few extra facets added to my face is pretty disconcerting.'

'It would only take one misplaced word.'

'I know that.'

'Of course I trust Toni, and her work force. And everyone who goes along with your little scheme will probably guard it like their grandmother's will. But there is no such thing as a total secret, Mr Niblock.'

'Why won't you call me Preston?'

'Because I'm annoyed with you.'

The jeweller wilted. This was the only woman with a sting his wife wouldn't have been able to dissolve over tea and crumpets.

Then he remembered that Gideon was responsible for Deirdre's death. 'I still intend to go ahead, whatever happens. And I don't like bullies.'

'Bullies? I would have put Julius Tucker into a more dangerous category.'

'I meant Neville Grablatt. The night of the warehouse fire he threatened me.'

'Why?'

'He's one of Tucker's creatures. He knows about the bribe.'

She had already guessed that much and wasn't surprised that the councillor had tried to intimidate the jeweller. 'Why didn't you tell me?'

'You were annoyed with me over something else at the time.'

The accountant went to a small window and looked out at the bleak landscape. 'Well, in that case there's nothing else for it. I'll have to fiddle your books so you can explain sales against deliveries, amongst other things.'

He became defensive. 'There wasn't any intention to cheat on VAT.'

She was surprised, given what the jeweller had already been up to, that he considered the prospect so reprehensible. 'You don't have any choice.'

Even though she was in cahoots with an ex Inland Revenue inspector, Preston had no doubt that her ingenuity could stretch to it.

Relieved that his financial manager hadn't insisted on tagging him like an expensive dog, he was whisked back to his shop.

Miss Priddle returned to her office and started work with the exotic software the Electronauts had designed for her. It had so many hidden subroutines she could see where she had been before she got there.

CHAPTER 32

After the last customer had left, Sonia Cupit bolted the doors of the Catalogue Shop then turned to the others, wondering if it was safe to talk.

Winston Cuffe had ceased to trust the Palace Parade management on any level a long time ago and suggested they find somewhere else.

Vicky Wade's living room was safe enough, and her husband was out for the evening so she could fit everyone in.

'This needn't affect you,' Mercy reminded the potter. 'You'll probably be better off working at home.'

'I know, but Mrs Silvestri and me still need to use the storeroom. And I rather like the idea of a pottery in a Cretaceous cave,' Vicky whispered.

Monty Golden hadn't a clue why it would appeal to anyone, but the potter's ceramics had always been a mystery to him anyway. 'Right then, let's do it. Everyone got a lift to Vicky's place?'

The small convoy wended its way out of town to her sprawling cottage. It was set in the middle of an orchard so isolated the resident wildlife could be heard munching in the leaf litter. The party filed across the flagstone courtyard and negotiated the potter's wheel in the small kitchen to enter a low beamed living room. Had Ron Acton's team and all the Electronauts been there as well, they would have had to stand outside and lean in through the windows.

The meeting was subdued.

The Co-operative had been offered a survival package that they wanted to accept, though the consequences of the scheme being exposed didn't bear thinking about. All of them were habituated to working within the rules, even if they did perpetually let them down. And how far could they trust all the other people who needed to be involved?

The Catalogue Co-operative sipped dandelion coffee from rustic mugs and watched Vicky's chinchilla dart about the furniture like a horizontal yo-yo.

Having found a lucrative niche in the book market, Mr Becker wasn't going to give up now. 'Well for pity's sake, do it. If you don't, you'll end up with state pensions and nothing to leave the kids. We can only be hanged once if we are found out.'

'So you're going to join us?' asked Winston.

'Probably too damp down there to store books, though it would be a marvellous address for a publisher of ancient landmarks. The Cave Under The Parade. I could call my imprint Troglodyte Press.'

Sonia Cupit wasn't in the mood for levity. 'Your virtuous volumes would be safe enough. We'll each have our own damp proof units to store finished goods before they go up in the lift, but God had better be on your side if you try to send out letterheads with our location on them.'

Rose still had misgivings. 'If we can only go in and out under cover of darkness, that means some of us may never see daylight.'

'That only applies to the barge. The builders are going to dig a tunnel in the bank that comes up through the floor of Bald Wendy. Those of us using the dinghies will have our own landing bay. We'll be able to come and go as we want as long as we wear life jackets and have someone reasonably sane at the helm. Those who aren't up to doing that can always use the storeroom lift. As long as the number of people coming and going from the Catalogue Shop is staggered, anyone watching will have no way of telling that they aren't working in the storeroom.'

'Why not just install the workshops in this old mill?'

'And get firebombed again?' said Sonia. 'Even Bald Wendy isn't too damp to burn.'

Rose brightened. 'Okay then. Can't we change that name though?'

Sonia at last laughed. 'What? Bald Wendy? Afraid not, it's been stuck for too long.'

'I just hope I don't meet any woman called Wendy, that's all. I wouldn't be able to stop myself looking for their joins.'

Mr Singh finished his dandelion coffee. 'Well, it seems we all agree. When do we have to be ready for the Jolly Roger?'

'It'll take a couple of weeks to install everything, then Mrs Zelinski can ferry us in to see it,' explained Sonia. 'She'll contact everyone to let them know how things are going.'

Monty Golden polished his glasses. 'And where is the money for all this coming from?'

'We'll pay it back soon enough once we're in business again,' said Winston.

'Loans usually involve interest. One without string attached sounds very much like manna from Preston Niblock?'

'If the man wants to help us, why not let him?'

Monty Golden had a better idea than the others of just how much money was involved. He said nothing. If his friend had put a gun to the head of his bank manager, that was his business.

***

Whenever Preston Niblock sat in the office of Miss Priddle that bad habit, guilt, always returned to overwhelm him.

The accountant handed him a substantial document. 'Well that's settled. We are now Wentworth Developments.'

'Wentworth Developments?"

'Shall I give you a rundown of its portfolio?'

Lights had already started to flash behind his eyes. 'No thanks.'

'I've written a piggyback program to handle the accounts of the Catalogue Shop. It will only declare half of what goes over the counter.'

Despite taking a million-pound bribe, Preston still hadn't reached an accommodation with his honest streak. 'Is that really necessary?'

'Without it, questions will be asked about where all the goods are coming from. However much time Winston Cuffe and his friends spend driving about the country to put spies off the scent, some deliveries must be seen to be made. There is a limit to the life of this scam, but it would be pointless winding it up too soon.'

'How long?'

'Let's see how the acquisition programme goes. There is no guarantee people will desert the mall for a new shopping precinct, even if there is a bargain on the other side of the road.'

'It must work.'

'Because it is generally assumed that nothing can survive outside Palace Parade, and the location can't be used for car parking because listed buildings are involved, planning permission should be easy. The problem will be setting up small industrial units. Conrad Makepeace believes Moltonford Council will want assurances that they don't work as a co-operative and are kept well away from each other this time.'

Preston fidgeted in his chair. 'I wish you hadn't involved him. He's got a reputation to think about. Being in league with criminals like us could blot his copybook at the clubhouse.'

'He only knows what I tell him. If anyone needs a decoy, it's us.' She suddenly remembered something. 'Did you ask your sister-in-law for one of the dogs?'

'I'm not so sure about that.'

'One of them is bound to like you.'

'The only way they would like me is medium rare.'

'A dog would be your bodyguard and smoke detector rolled into one.'

Preston knew that Lucy Tribble would only feed it Smarties and make it daft as lights. Fran's grandchildren, Jim and Josey, already dressed them up. They would push them about in prams if they could lift them off the ground.

Miss Priddle gave her tedious client a critical look. 'You've lost weight?'

'Probably all that potholing.'

'I want you to see a doctor.'

Preston rose. 'Now look, I've earned the right to be bald and skinny!'

'If anything happens to you, everyone else will dropped in the shit the moment your will is read. Not even I can make all your assets disappear overnight. Bear that in mind.'

'Can I go now? I want to make a daisy chain.' Miss Priddle cast him a hard look. 'In silver and topaz to fit the throat of a duchess.'

She nearly asked what had happened to that pearl choker she had ordered just before his wife died. That might have triggered recollections she wasn't qualified to council anyone about.

'You may go.'

CHAPTER 33

The nanny goat fixed Ben with an annoyed gaze and lowered her horns.

'Fran! What did that farmer say about them butting you!'

His wife dashed from the tool shop where she was stocktaking. 'For pity's sake Ben, get off that fence! The animal hardly reaches your knee!'

'It's not my bleeding knee it was aiming for!'

Fran wished she hadn't talked her husband into retiring. Life had been easier when he was laid up with lorry driver's backache and not able to get under her feet.

'Look, Ben, just pick the damn thing up and put it back in its pen. This is meant to be a children's farm, not a circus.'

Gingerly the large ex lorry driver got down from the creaking fence, successfully cornered the escapee and wound his arms about its legs. It bleated and tried to bite his ear as he managed to drop it back in its enclosure before it started to breathe fire.

Fran stood watching with hands on her hips. 'Are you sure you really want to do this? Jackie and Rita like working with animals.'

'It's my idea. I'll see it through.'

'You're not disarming landmines, Ben.'

'All we need now is half a dozen peacocks and a wallaby.'

Fran's expression clouded. 'You are not having any peacocks!'

'Only a pair. I'll keep them away from the plants.'

'If you bring so much as one into the garden centre it'll be served up with side salad.'

She left her husband to sulk and play with the Vietnamese pot bellied pigs. Soon a group of toddlers arrived to pat the rabbits, and he was back in his element.

***

The young woman with club-cut hair and maroon lipstick examined Bald Wendy's damaged door. 'How long has the property been like this?'

The round man in the tweed suit shrugged. 'Couple of years. Wind most probably. It's too remote out here for vandals. One of the reasons I bought it.'

'I was given to understand that you only intended to lease? Are you sure about selling?'

'To be honest, I want the thing off my hands before it becomes old enough to be listed.'

The agent followed him up to the large milling room. 'Requires a great deal of renovation.'

'Original millstones those, and all the gearing is in place.'

'Given the low level of the river, that is somewhat academic.'

'What is your client going to use it for?'

'Initially as storage. Perhaps later on it could be adapted for living space.'

The owner of Bald Wendy said nothing. He knew from bitter experience that no one with the sort of money to convert the water mill would choose to live in that bleak spot.

The agent bounced on the oak floor. A somewhat risky operation. The large room over the gears driving the great spur wheel was taking the weight of three sets of millstones in situ, not counting the odd runner and bedstone still waiting for some ancient craftsman to dress them. Over the grinding stones, the teeth of the crown wheel were locked into gears for driving the hoist, plus various long forgotten devices invented by the miller, and the floor was littered with ankle ricking equipment neither of them could identify.

'Must have gone into liquidation rather suddenly?' the agent noted.

'I understand it wasn't worth converting to industrial use when the large roller mills started producing white flour.'

The agent toyed with the possibilities created by the recent fad for health foods, but she knew of no other client who would invest in a mill on the way to nowhere, and raising the height of the leat to reach the wheel would have been an engineering nightmare.

The young woman ascended the creaking ladder to peer about the bin floor still dotted with age hardened ears of wheat, barley, peas, and beans. There was a hatch leading into a small loft space. As a good agent, she should have examined that as well. She knew she could make a decent bargain whether it was riddled with woodworm or not and her immaculately styled hair told her it was bound to be filled with bats.

After another brief inspection of the large rotten wheel hanging from its post as though some frustrated monster rodent had gnawed its way out of it, the agent referred to a letter on her clipboard. 'If you are prepared to come down four thousand I will be able to make you an offer for its freehold.'

The round man huffed and puffed and tried to pretend that it was a bitter pill to swallow, secretly glad to get the white elephant off his hands.

***

As soon as night fell, Toni Zelinski and her team drove out to Bald Wendy and automated the old rusty gate concealed by the willows.

Owen and his crew hewed out platforms inside the tunnel on either side of the River Nox. They removed the corroded brackets and fitted hinges that swung the gate up like a garage door. After widening one of the platforms into a small landing bay, the team tunnelled through the clay of the bank towards Bald Wendy.

On the other side of Bald Wendy, Toni Zelinski and her foreman waited on the bank of the Coney Canal. Eventually the phut-phut of an engine could be heard. The shape looming through the early morning mist seemed much larger than when she had first checked it over.

At a signal from her torch the canal barge drifted to a halt. Once safely moored, a scruffy looking man in overalls, bandanna, and earring jumped ashore.

'You Mr and Mrs Giblin then?'

'That's right.' Owen took the delivery note offered him and signed for the craft.

'You've got some beast there. Used to ferry coal - that thing. Sure you know how to handle a vessel that size?'

Owen beamed a wide, Welsh smile. 'I've had some experience.'

The man gave a rough chuckle. 'Only hope the little wife don't mind. That thing needs a good clean up before it's fit to live in.'

Toni assumed a fixed grin and just managed to stop herself tipping the scruffy creature into the canal. 'We did an inspection before buying it.'

Owen sensed the bad vibrations coming from his boss. 'Thanks a lot. We need to get moving right away. Could this boat do ten miles before midday?'

'Possible. Bear in mind the local locks are only open during the day.' The deliveryman slid a small dinghy from the barge's roof, launched it, and climbed in. As he opened its throttle he called back, 'You do know the length of this thing, don't you?'

'Oh yes,' said Toni Zelinski. 'I laid my needlework tape out on the deck and measured it.'

Unsure about the strange edge to her voice, the deliveryman turned his dinghy back up the Coney Canal and sped off.

Owen scratched his chin. It looked as though they would have to knock the corner off the bank to turn it into the tributary. Toni insisted that, as it had a low draught, they could use the hoist and drag it across. Owen wasn't so sure; he could see them bringing enough bank down to block the tributary. That would raise the water high enough to turn the ancient mill wheel.

Toni had her way as usual. The canal barge was hoisted from the water and then man and machine-handled across the bank until it was parallel with the River Nox tributary.

Out of sight, under Bald Wendy's sluice arch, Owen and a couple of men gave the boat a thorough going over for leaks. Its caulking was sound enough, though the roof needed to be camouflaged and the floor reinforced to take the drilling equipment.

***

The longhaired Alsatian looked steadily at Preston as though trying to work out whether he was there to take it for a walk or as a light snack.

'Why on earth did you call the creature Tiny?'

Fran looked up from her ironing. 'Because he's smaller than Tinker.'

'Are you sure you don't mind parting with him?' the jeweller asked.

'Of course not. He eats too much and I can't keep up with the hairs.'

'Thought about having him clipped?'

There was a low growl.

'Don't mention baths either. Apart from that he's quite a sweetie.' She obviously thought that Preston needed the Alsatian as a companion.

'He is a decent guard dog, though?'

'Sure.' She gave him an enquiring look. 'What do you need a guard dog for? I thought your place was secure enough to repel Attila the Hun.'

'I don't like the idea of Lucy being there on her own.'

Fran tossed the last blouse onto a hanger - Ben now had to iron his own shirts. 'She's not had any bother has she?'

There was no point in mentioning the obnoxious Neville Grablatt. The idea of Tiny choking on a chunk of that man might have made Fran change her mind. 'No, but I wouldn't be much use if someone did come in waving a baseball bat.'

'You need to work out.'

'That's what the doctor said.'

'Why did you need to go to the doctor?'

He ignored the question. Ever since Deirdre died, the man kept telling him to get out more. He spent over thirty years sitting in the same room, going nowhere and doing nothing. Suddenly he was almost pensionable and needed exercise.

Fran sat at the table with Preston. Tiny growled. 'Shut up, dog.'

The Alsatian languorously sprawled on the floor without taking its piercing gaze from the jeweller.

'Tell me, Preston, why didn't you and Deirdre go out once in a while?'

For a moment he wasn't sure. 'I didn't think she wanted to. We seemed happy enough with our own company.' Despite himself, Preston suddenly wanted to burst into tears.

Fran grasped his shoulder. 'I'm sorry. I didn't mean to upset you.'

'It's all right. It's just the thought that she's not coming back.'

'Would things be different if she did?'

'It's too late to wonder about that now, isn't it?'

'I meant... there's nothing between you and Miss Priddle, is there?'

Preston shuddered at the thought. He meant as much to her as a moth did to a praying mantis.

Under the tight skirts and Harvey Nichols blouses, it did cross Fran's mind that the accountant could have been a transvestite, and the image had some difficulty escaping her imagination. 'Preston?'

'What?'

'You've never had any fancy for... your bread to be buttered on the other side?'

Given his vaguely effete aura and genius for designing women's jewellery, it was probably surprising it hadn't crossed anyone's mind before. 'Not all men harpoon the first passing female as soon as they lose their wife. I do know how to boil an egg, and -'

'And?'

'Deirdre may not have been macho man's ideal mate, but I only ever wanted her. If that makes me an ageing queen, then pass the eye shadow.'

'All right. I'm sorry I asked.'

Preston was relieved that Fran hadn't guessed the real nature of his relationship with the accountant. She would have had a nervous breakdown trying not to gossip about it.

CHAPTER 34

Conrad Makepeace glanced through his newspaper, then left it open on the table to take a sip of coffee. Although the Catalogue Shop café was not so busy as it used to be, its business was still brisk. He wondered how they managed to pay the Palace Parade rent and bring in a profit, yet didn't underestimate their financial manager. In fact, he was glad that he had never encountered Miss Priddle when he had been a tax inspector.

Then something in the newspaper centrefold caught the councillor's eye. Julius Tucker the third was in London to attend yet another charity function. Facing the article was a colour photograph of the billionaire accompanied by his latest girlfriend. She was wearing a necklace with a diamond cluster the size of his alimony.

Conrad Makepeace had seen that distinctive piece of jewellery somewhere else. Not knowing why, he suddenly felt uneasy.

He finished his coffee, then left the mindless bustle of the shopping mall to try and mentally retrace his movements to the first time he had encountered that diamond cluster. Though common sense was telling him that it could hardly be important, intuition insisted that it was. Over the years his eyesight may have weakened, his hair thinned and prostate persuaded him to play no more than nine holes of golf, but his instincts were still pretty sound.

The councillor strolled the length of the old High Street, passing the run down side roads that had once been filled with shoppers. As he wandered towards the garden centre he mentally ticked off each junction. After Canning Road, he looked up at the residential houses on the top of the hill.

Makepeace stopped dead in his tracks.

Of course - it was so obvious he could have kicked himself. When he had taken his wife's cameo to Preston Niblock to have the collet replaced that same diamond cluster had been sitting on the jeweller's workbench. There could be no mistaking a galaxy of stones like that.

The implication didn't bear thinking about. The jeweller involved with Julius Tucker? Neville Grablatt definitely was. That bladder of unctuous malice's tongue wouldn't have missed the chance to get acquainted with the billionaire's anal region.

But Preston Niblock? The man who had lost his wife because someone was in such a hurry to build Palace Parade?

The councillor rested on a bench facing the shopping mall and tried to convince himself he had been mistaken. Unfortunately necessity had taught him how to identify expensive jewellery, and his imagination just didn't play tricks like that.

***

After a small reception booth had been built by the entrance and its floors cleared of debris, Bald Wendy was secure enough to take deliveries. As soon as the excavating equipment and prefabricated workshop sections arrived, they were ferried to the cave. The tunnel from the landing bay, which led through the clay bank, was buttressed and pre cast steps laid up to Bald Wendy's gearing room.

***

Toni Zelinski came up into the Catalogue Shop from the storeroom. 'The equipment's installed and running.'

Mercy Cuffe finished putting the table flowers in the fridge and wiped down the counter. 'Fine.' She hesitated. 'What does it do again?'

'Pulses a signal down to the cave so they can drill up to the exact spot.'

'Sure you don't want me to stay overnight?'

'It's not necessary. I should think you need your sleep after a day in here.'

'Business has picked up again, but we're only half full, and I'll be glad when Rose has her bakery to go to and stops trying to slap parking tickets on prams.'

'Thought she loved children?'

'Don't you believe it. She had five. Life as a traffic warden was light relief from bringing up that lot.' Mercy put out the lights and picked up her bags. 'Ready?'

Toni pushed her helmet into a canvas knapsack, buttoned a full-length coat over her work shirt and jeans, tidied her hair, and then changed her boots for trainers. 'Ready.'

Mercy locked up and they went out through Palace Parade's main entrance.

Half an hour later the shopping centre was totally deserted, the lights switched off and the mall spangled by security LEDs.

Palace Parade's maintenance engineer, who had a small residence adjoining the far end of the shopping mall, was at last able to go out for his regular pub dinner and pint.

***

Inside the Catalogue Shop's window display cabinet, three interlopers attempted to settle down for the night.

'It's too early to go to sleep,' moaned Alice.

'You always managed it during the winter,' Mabel snapped.

'But it's still light outside.'

'Why should that bother you inside here? It doesn't bother him.'

Hector's snores were rattling Mrs Silvestri's scent bottles.

'That's because he doesn't know any different.'

'What do you want to do then? After the mess you made in the ladies last time, we agreed that we only go into the mall if our bladders can't hold out any longer.'

Hector woke with a start and kicked a panel in the cabinet. 'Crocodiles!' A chink of light from the Catalogue Shop appeared through the resulting crack.

'Look what you've done!' scolded Mabel. 'Now we'll have to fix it.'

The fascia had only been tacked to the back of the display cabinet to give the effect of panelling. Mabel bundled the other two away and carefully removed it before they could do any more damage.

She cautiously peered into the interior of the Catalogue Shop. It was bathed in the glow of the safety light over the café counter.

'We'll have to find a way of fastening it from the inside.'

'Latches,' twittered Alice. 'The big hardware place has twirly latches with sticky backs.'

Mabel knew what she meant. 'All right. We'll have to pull it back onto the nails for tonight then fetch some tomorrow.'

Hector had other things on his mind. 'Doughnuts. Find doughnuts.'

Mabel crawled out into the shop. 'There won't be any until tomorrow. I'll see if there's some soup.' Mabel seldom unlocked the other cabinet door into the café for fear of one of them following her. She guarded that key like a year's ration of milk stout.

Alice gathered together her voluminous skirt and followed her through the small gap. 'I'm coming out! I'm coming out!'

Mabel went to the fridge. 'All right, but don't touch anything.'

Alice pirouetted about the café, almost knocking the chairs from the tables. 'I'm a fairy.'

'I know dear.' Mabel found an opened loaf of wholemeal bread and some margarine. 'We can risk a slice of toast each. Do you want some jam?'

'Yes, yes.'

'Bleeding brown bread!' Hector had also escaped and was crawling across the floor on all fours.

'You can get up now Hector. You're out.' Mabel looked in the fridge again. 'They don't have any white.'

Hector went to the greengrocer's cold cabinet. 'Turnip!'

'No! Don't touch the vegetables! They'll notice.'

Hector grunted and sat on the floor beside the counter.

Mabel decided against trying to operate the huge toasting machine and gave them a slice of bread each instead. Alice joined Hector. The two sat munching their small snack in silence for a while.

Then Hector started to fidget. 'My bum tingles.'

Mabel couldn't face having to escort him out to the gents again. Compared to the mess Alice made, every hurricane should have been called "Hector". 'I told you to go before we came in.'

'My bum tingles as well,' giggled Alice.

Even though they had spent the last ten years locked together in vagrancy, they couldn't both be having the same anal delusion - could they?

Mabel joined them on the floor. Her backside tingled as well.

'Ooh...' Alice stopped munching. 'The ground's gone wobbly.'

Mabel had enough sense to be more worried than they were. 'Probably a generator,' she lied. 'Stay here.' She went to the door behind the counter that led to the lift. It was locked.

'Down there,' she said to herself. 'They're coming up from down there.'

The men shut down the compressor powering the carbide tipped drill and Owen scrutinised the hole in the cave ceiling. 'Good night's work that, boys. We'll be through in no time. Find any dinosaurs?'

'Were they wandering about when this stuff was laid down then?' asked Cliff.

'Shouldn't think so. They had sixty million years to get out of the way.'

Another team was installing a turbine by the river. Further along the cave, baseplates were being bolted onto the limestone for the frames that would support the prefabricated workshops. Ventilators were also brought down, even though the River Nox moved enough air through the cave to give any bat that lost its way a nasty chill.

Cutting steel columns to buttress the ceiling had caused the biggest headache. The noise had skirled about the cave system like a demented banshee and not even liquid filled ear defenders had been able to shut it out.

Water for the toilets and the tanks of the metal workers could be pumped from the river. Making a saddle connection to the pipe that ran through the storeroom and supplied the Catalogue Shop café would siphon off clean drinking and washing water. A bed was levelled for a track to take the trolley that would shuttle goods to the storeroom lift and lights were garlanded along its length.

In case any cavers did eventually find a way down, care was taken not to permanently damage the limestone or leave too many suspicious traces. As much as Toni Zelinski would have liked to create a mystery for conspiracy theorists, she didn't want to oblige any of her descendants to make reparation for her desecration of the cave's curtain of stalactites or rare rock formations.

Eventually the barge, sinisterly plying the three kilometres of tunnel, brought in the first deliveries of new equipment and machinery to replace what had been lost in the warehouse fire. Because Bald Wendy made a plausible collection depot for canal traffic, the Co-operative's suppliers asked few questions about its address, apart from how the odd pantechnicon was expected to find it from the nearest main road.

***

Lucy Tribble, glasses perched on the end of her nose, deftly continued to thread a quartz necklace, unaware of the customer until a large shadow blocked her light.

The beadworker glanced over her glasses, squinted, and then recognised the visitor. 'Why Mr Grablatt. Forgive me, I was far away.' She carefully laid her work in her tray. 'What can I do for you?'

Neville Grablatt gave an oily smile. 'May I see Mr Niblock, please?'

He believed it to be a straightforward question, but Miss Tribble was suddenly thrown into a tizzy. 'Oh goodness! Now I'm not sure. Did he say he was in or out? I mean, he did say he was going out, but I'm not sure when. Let me buzz.' She pressed the link to his workroom. There was no reply. 'I wonder if he's in the garden. No, not this time of year. All that pollen.'

Councillor Grablatt's manner hardened. 'Do you know whether he's in or not?'

'I know this sounds bizarre, but I really wouldn't like to commit myself.'

Grablatt's voice took on a menacing edge that quite escaped Lucy Tribble. 'Do you know where you are?'

There was a deep growl from under the counter.

'Now, now, there's no need for that, Tiny.' Whatever was making the noise was far from tiny.

Miss Tribble tried to pick up the thread of the conversation. 'Really, I do know this must be vexing. Perhaps you would like to leave a message?'

As Grablatt was only putting in an appearance to intimidate the jeweller, he could hardly jot that down on a piece of paper, and the growl beneath the counter was getting louder. 'I'll return at some other time.'

'I will tell Mr Niblock you called,' Lucy wittered as the large man left. Sure he wasn't coming back, she turned to the corner cupboard. 'It's all right Mr Niblock. He's gone.'

Preston opened its door from inside and jewel boxes tumbled down on top of him.

Lucy Tribble was unable to stop herself laughing.

'It's not funny. That man is a cross between Al Capone and the Creature from the Black Lagoon.'

Lucy Tribble dabbed her eyes with a tissue. 'He certainly is imposing.'

'Did you know that twenty years ago he was jailed for grievous bodily harm - to an all-in-wrestler?'

'No?'

'He worked as a bouncer at a London night club.'

'Well, after that, what was left but local government.' Miss Tribble returned to her beads. 'Will you being going out today?'

'Not with Godzilla prowling the neighbourhood.'

Though unsure why her business associate's antipathy to the man verged on paranoia, Lucy had the discretion not to ask. Why should she? Her beadwork was selling and she had a wage into the bargain. The jeweller could spend all day hiding in cupboards, or standing on his head in the kitchen sink for all she cared.

Conrad Makepeace flattened his lean frame even closer to the neighbouring privet hedge as Neville Grablatt stepped from the shop. He wished he hadn't been driven to spy on Preston Niblock. A lifetime of being suspicious was difficult to put aside, and it was unlikely Grablatt possessed any trinkets delicate enough to require the attention of a master jeweller.

Discouraged, Makepeace slowly strolled back down to the town centre. Should he say something to Miss Priddle? Conrad Makepeace had always liked the jeweller and given the man's recent bereavement didn't want to do anything that would cause him even more grief. Perhaps the dossier he had accumulated on Gideon Enterprizes with the accountant's help would be enough.

CHAPTER 36

Bald Wendy now had an imposing notice over its new door, OLD MILL DEPOT, even though only delivery lorries and the odd barge plying the nearby Coney Canal would see it.

Not having any hair for them to get tangled in, Preston Niblock insisted that the loft be left to the bats. Toni Zelinski and most of her crew did have hair, so the job of patching up the roof went to a couple of apprentices she had failed to talk into short back and sides.

After two more nights, Owens' team was ready to break through into the Catalogue Shop's storeroom. Mercy, Winston, and Mrs Silvestri had cleared out as much stock as they could and stacked it behind the catalogue counter upstairs, hoping health and safety wouldn't decide to pay a midnight visit.

When the drill broke through, the noise skirled about the steel shuttered storeroom and reverberated the length of the access avenue. In case it triggered the shopping complex's sensors, the team cut the drill and went to work with masonry chisels.

By morning, the hole had a lid that fitted flush with the floor. Beneath that, a hydraulic platform lift was installed and the inside of the tunnel fitted with cladding to absorb any noise it made.

Despite her confidence in the precautions taken by Palace Parade's civil engineer, Toni Zelinski was familiar with the fickle behaviour of all things natural and attached a sensor to monitor rock movement to the ceiling of the cave.

She arrived back at Bald Wendy in time to see the headlights of a red sports car and leapt from the barge onto the bank before it reached the sluice arch.

Toni Zelinski believed that even Miss Priddle would have known better than to wear a tight skirt and high heels for her tour of geology's underworld. She probably had nothing functional in her wardrobe apart from a pair of pink golfing shoes.

'Priddy, you can't come in here dressed like that.'

'Why not?' In the light of her friend's torch, the accountant clambered down the steep bank to meet her and only saved herself from being pitched into the water by digging in her stiletto heels.

The civil engineer promptly propelled Miss Priddle back up to Bald Wendy and found her some overalls, boots, and helmet.

The accountant felt as though she was being kitted out for a space walk. 'Is all this really necessary?'

'You're the one who demanded to see what Preston is spending his money on, and I don't want a stiletto heel puncturing a dinghy. I fail to see why he should have to pay for that as well.'

The accountant tucked the remains of her crushed coiffure under the helmet and looked at the slabs of concrete laying about the gearing room floor. 'I didn't realise that you were rebuilding the pyramids in an enclosed space.'

'Not yet. I suspect that may be the next little scheme you talk Preston into.'

'Me? Talk him-!' Miss Piddle stopped. She knew it would be pointless trying to explain to Toni that the man was much deeper than she could ever guess.

The two women went down the tunnel in the mill's floor to the small landing bay.

Now there was no more damage that could be done to her appearance, the accountant sprawled back in the dinghy.

As they entered the tunnel, she watched the river's ceiling, which would have been in danger of flattening her coiffure if the helmet hadn't already done that, in the prow light. 'Did you install the precautions I specified?'

'Yes.' The civil engineer proceeded to reel off the list. 'I can understand why this has to be kept secret, but what is the worst that could happen if it did leak out? Gideon would be in more trouble.'

'Someone would lose their life.'

Toni knew her friend too well to believe she was joking. 'I don't understand?'

'You don't need to.' Miss Priddle's smile looked positively satanic in the light reflected from the rock walls. 'Don't worry. You and your team will be safe enough as long as they keep their mouths shut.'

Toni knew they would. Even if one of them did blab, no one else would back them up.

When they reached the main cave the accountant's business acumen started to calculate whether it would have been more lucrative as a tourist attraction. It was unlikely Gideon Enterprizes would have welcomed the promotion, STEP DOWN THROUGH THE BASEMENT AND SEE THE WONDERFUL STALAGMITES SUPPORTING PALACE PARADE.

Now all the workbenches, metal presses, sewing machines, Electronauts' sterile workshop, ovens, and other machinery had been installed in the work units they looked almost comfortable.

Suddenly Miss Priddle recalled the time she had been trapped in a lift with a steam engine enthusiast. 'What happens if there's a power cut?'

'If the river turbine fails there are enough backup generators.'

'And?'

'We've taken a spur from one of Palace Parade's power cables.'

'What!'

'Just to help regulate the input. Given the energy that place soaks up, no one will notice.'

'How did you manage to shut down their power without setting off the alarms?'

Toni smiled enigmatically. She had no intention of admitting she had got access to Palace Parade's transformer and security panel.

The accountant didn't really want to know. She had her secrets as well. Toni was entitled to hers.

'When can the Co-operative come down?'

'Everything will be up and running by the end of the week.' The civil engineer hesitated. 'Don't tell me they're going to have problems with the lease of the Catalogue Shop?'

'The management did try to make things awkward by sending in people with clipboards to poke around. Now Conrad Makepeace sits in there for an hour each morning and the inspectors tend to keep away. They've got an organic greengrocer, you know?'

The last thing on Toni Zelinski's mind for the last two weeks had been carrots and cauliflowers. 'Really?'

'He's going to move into the garden centre when this place gets underway.'

Now it was the builder's turn to worry about security. 'He doesn't know what's going on down here, does he Priddy?'

'Goodness no, and Preston's sister-in-law thinks that the Co-operative has moved into industrial units out of town.' Miss Priddle analysed her friend's expression. Even in the half-light it radiated misgivings. 'What's the matter?'

'Nothing. I just have this bad feeling.'

The accountant also remembered the dream she had about Preston Niblock. 'What bad feeling?'

'About Bald Wendy.'

'What about it?'

She shrugged. 'I don't know.'

'Not haunted is it?'

Toni laughed. 'No, not that place. I've renovated real haunted houses in my time. This doesn't even have the ghost of the miller's cat.' She paused. 'In fact, it doesn't even have rats.'

'You don't have premonitions do you?'

'God no. Though I had a great grandmother in Eastern Europe who knew Rasputin.'

'Didn't know you were Russian?'

'We're not; the Zelinski's were just passing through before Lenin shook things up.'

'Still think the name Featherstone would have been better for business.'

'Bob wouldn't wear it. He couldn't cope with being mistaken for a civil engineer. The nearest he gets to heavy construction is lining the fishpond with plastic.' Toni looked at her watch. 'Time we got back. Nights are still short.'

'I suppose I had better arrange your cheque.'

'Yes please. Payday tomorrow '

Mabel persuaded Alice not to riffle through the goods stacked behind the counter and lured her and Hector to the café kitchen with some bourbons found in a biscuit tin.

Alice was intimidated by Mercy's scrubbed surfaces and polished taps. 'Wash hands, wash hands.'

Mabel had misgivings about her sudden burst of hygiene. 'Be careful not to splash all over the place. It took ages to clean up the last time.'

Mabel placed some chairs at a table and was eventually able to make them settle down.

'Turnip,' Hector mumbled through his beard.

'No!' snapped Mabel. 'Do you want to end up back with Mrs Roy?'

Hector muttered obscenities, then sulked.

After a biscuit, slice of bread and glass of water each the companions sat contentedly watching the winking safety lights in the mall.

Alice had nearly dozed off. Then a raw, skirling noise suddenly vibrated the floor. She leapt up and darted about the café like a frightened rabbit.

Even Hector stopped sulking. 'Robbers! Save the bottles!'

The skirling stopped. It was replaced by the sound of something chipping at the floor below.

'They've found us! They've found us!' wailed Alice.

Mabel raised her hand. 'Quiet!' She listened. 'It's from down there. It's all right. They won't come up.'

It didn't matter. Hector and Alice had returned to the sanctuary of the display cabinet, leaving Mabel to clear away crumbs, wipe up splashed water, and replace the chairs on the table.

***

Ben rubbed his back. It was inevitable he would do something to make the pangs return. After one of his mates from the haulage business had seen him feeding the rabbits, he needed to restore his aura of machismo. Unfortunately, carrying timber for the new greengrocer's stall was not the way to do it.

The fair-bearded market gardener retrieved the wood Ben clutched precariously in one hand before it fell and crushed his feet.

'Let me do that mate.' Used to hefting bags of potatoes up onto trucks, he easily balanced the planks on his shoulder and marched off to the main entrance where they were being assembled.

'Never mind, Ben. You can always wrestle the goats again after they've finished digesting that pullover you left on the fence.'

The ex-lorry driver turned painfully to see a mustard-coloured jacket and green trousers that clashed horribly with the ornamental grasses. 'Don't you have any bleeding work to do Preston?'

The jeweller had no intention of admitting that he was trying to avoid some local government thug. 'Thought I'd take a walk.'

'Why not try the shopping mall?'

'Did that last year. Still got the headache.'

'Well spring in this place is just the thing for hay fever.'

Preston picked up Ben's tool case and helped him stagger over to the café where he brought them some tea. 'Who's looking after the animals?'

'Jackie. She takes it in turns with Rita.'

'Hear you need some stables? Though I wouldn't want to get under the hooves of the pony that could take your weight.'

'Fran won't allow it until we get the freehold of Machan's old yard.'

'Shouldn't be difficult, it's been empty for ages.'

'He wouldn't sell to Gideon.'

'Don't worry about it. All he needs is the right price and a guarantee it won't be turned into a car park.'

Ben sat back and looked at his wife's brother-in-law. It occurred to him that the jeweller only needed to grow his remaining hair and tie it back into a ponytail to look like a demented social worker.

'What are you up to, Preston Niblock?'

'I've no idea what you are talking about.'

'You always know what people are talking about, just never used to let on. Since you lost Deirdre you've turned into a different person.'

'I hope he's better looking?'

'And you don't wear a hat any more.'

'That's hardly constitutes a transformation of my molecular structure.'

'You know what I mean.'

Preston said nothing. The change had scared him a little as well. With Deirdre, his routine had been so regular the dawn chorus could have taken their cue from him. Now his body clock had enslaved him to any whim that dare peep over the parapet of life. The idea of taking million pound bribes, setting up a scam to undermine a major company, and having to hide from Moltonford's principal thug, would hardly have crossed his mind had Deirdre been there.

He picked up the teapot. 'Milk?'

***

With some trepidation, Monty Golden, Sonia Cupit, Mr Singh, Rose, Ron Acton, and two Electronauts caught the early morning dinghies to their new premises. This was one experience they would be unwise to tell their grandchildren about.

The Electronauts treated the ride as though it were a trip in a virtual reality program designed by some ecological demon. They had no idea real life could be so weird. Rose kept glancing about as though looking for illegally parked stalagmites and Ron Acton frequently reached out to touch the wall of the tunnel, fascinated by its rilled texture.

Having convinced herself that they were only punting on the River Nox, Sonia Cupit poured some tea from her flask and sipped it. Monty Golden felt the weight of Nature closing in and experienced an overpowering urge to jump over the side and swim back.

Mr Singh ignored it all. In the light of a pocket torch he sat tut-tutting at the sketches for a new range of shoes designed by his son. They were stylish, comfortable, and inexpensive, and the bespoke shoemaker hated every machined stitch. The endless gloom didn't lighten the thought that he would be cutting the templates. But then, as Monty Golden was frequently saying, business is business.

Feeling as though they had just spent an eternity in the intestine of a flatulent serpent, the Co-operative reached the main cave.

Toni Zelinski led them on a brief tour. Having seen all the boulders, adjoining caves and stalactites of interest, they followed her up to their workshops. By this time Monty Golden was clutching Mr Singh's arm as though they were entering the jaws of Hell.

153

Once inside the insulated units, it was impossible to tell that they were underground. While the rest checked that their machinery and other equipment was in place, Mr Singh produced a flask of coffee and made Monty Golden sit down.

When everyone was satisfied, Owen went to the only spot by the river that would allow a mobile signal and phoned back to Bald Wendy to instruct the waiting team to load up the barge with tools, raw materials, flour, sheet metal, and components.

Within a couple of days a small, trustworthy work force dribbled in and out of the Catalogue Shop to start up production.

***

At last Toni Zelinski had the opportunity to look more like a woman than a troglodyte in a helmet.

Miss Priddle finished her fruit salad, dabbed her lipstick with a serviette, and then reached into her briefcase. She handed the builder her cheque.

Toni looked at it for some while. 'Are you sure Preston is able to cover an amount this large?'

'Trust me, I'm an accountant. If everything goes smoothly, I estimate they will be able to pay him back within three months.'

'Will it go smoothly, Priddy?'

'Oh yes. I promised not to blaspheme for at least six months.'

'I can't shake off that uneasy feeling.'

'Hide that cheque. Here comes company.'

Toni slipped it into her shoulder bag.

Miss Priddle pretended to be surprised. 'Fancy seeing you, Mr Makepeace. Would you like to join us?'

'You look flustered?' Toni observed.

Conrad Makepeace sat down. 'I have been pursuing chimeras.'

'I hope they didn't see you coming?'

The last thing he needed at that moment was sparkling repartee. 'I wish I were younger.'

Miss Priddle was unable to forget that round of golf she had almost played with him. 'You are still remarkably fit.'

'I wish I were Preston Niblock. He does seem to be getting younger. He's not the man I used to know.'

Miss Priddle sensed he was angling. 'How do you mean?'

'He's leading a different life. Never there half the time.'

She wondered why the councillor was stalking the jeweller when his life's ambition was to expose the corruption between Gideon Enterprizes and local government. 'Would you like to join us in a coffee?'

Winston filled his van's tank with petrol, made a mid morning delivery of Vicky Wade's mugs and health food supplies for Mrs Silvestri to the Catalogue Shop's storeroom then, when he was sure he was being followed, hit the road. While he and some friends continued to lay false trails across the region, goods from the cave workshops came up on the platform lift through the storeroom floor.

The original intention had been to refill the limited space every night, but turnover in the Catalogue Shop rapidly picked up when customers realised that it was back in business. To be able to cope with the extra demand, Toni Zelinski rigged the stockroom lift to the Catalogue Shop to work in sync with the platform lift in the cave so it wouldn't be noticed operating during the daytime.

***

As soon as the management of Palace Parade realised that the threat to Gideon's cartel was back, smart suits circled the Co-operative's outlet like sharks waiting to pick off fish from a shoal. Mercy smiled sweetly at them and, whenever they purchased something bulky to take back to their inspectors to dismantle, offering them a free coffee while they waited. The inspectors never found anything wrong with the goods, of course. The Co-operative was well aware of the consequences of giving the management any excuse to pounce.

***

After wandering the mall, Hector, Alice, and Mabel found that their regular table had been taken when they arrived for their doughnut and tea. They were relegated to a cramped corner under a plastic palm.

Conrad Makepeace still came in every morning to watch for signs of trouble. The shopping centre management assiduously avoided him, though he was surprised to see Neville Grablatt. However deep in cahoots with Gideon Enterprizes, the man seldom showed his face in the Catalogue Shop.

Grablatt had one of the managers with him. Makepeace raised his newspaper and pretended to read while the two men took a cursory look around then left.

Nearby, Mrs Silvestri had been watching from her stall.

'You saw that?' she asked Conrad Makepeace.

'Yes. I think business has picked up too rapidly for the management's liking.' The councillor gave a disarming smile. 'How did you manage it?'

'The work is stored in new premises,' she smiled back. 'A long way out of course, but they have regular deliveries.'

It seemed plausible enough. 'Let's hope nothing goes wrong.'

'Oh no, nothing can go wrong this time.'

***

As the mist lifted, Preston and Tiny sat on the steps of Bald Wendy watching the livid sun go down. Given the increasing congestion on the roads, he'd never seen the point of going in for another car. That was before he had bought a property half way to nowhere and pair of driving glasses.

Tiny was still unsure whether to treat his owner as pack leader or provider of the evening meal and tolerated his company with uneasy grace. Unable to bring clippers near the Alsatian, the jeweller had been obliged to order a high performance vacuum cleaner from Ron Acton. Not wanting to go into the Catalogue Shop to collect the machine, he had arranged to have it delivered on the evening barge.

'I hope you appreciate the aggravation you cause, dog?'

Tiny looked at Preston with that "are you talking to me?" expression.

'I dread to think what Deirdre would have made of a permanently moulting baggage of flatulence. If I'd wanted the lingering smell of compost I would have scattered a bag of the manure from Ben's animal corner up and down the hall. And I could have bought a fur fabric rug from any second-hand shop. You ruined that tapestry one with the mosque and flowers Mrs Silvestri gave me. You're meant to pray on it, not chew off the fringe then lug it into a corner to make your bed - Are you listening to me?'

But the Alsatian had picked up the sound of something else.

Preston was suddenly nervous. The area wasn't noted for its abundant wildlife. Here, nesting birds didn't even show interest in the fur he had combed from Tiny.

'What is it?'

The dog suddenly lost interest, and then farted.

'Must you do that, you flatulent mutt!' Preston got up and went inside Bald Wendy.

The evening delivery of raw materials was stacked ready for the barge and Mr Singh was just coming up through the gearing room trap door from the tunnel. The jeweller quickly closed the outside door.

The shoemaker helped his eldest son carry up a box of offcuts. 'You look nervous, Mr Niblock?'

'This place makes me imagine things.'

'You say that - Mr Golden will not come near it after dark. Leaves overseeing the late shift to Miss Cupit.'

Preston tried to shake off his unease. 'How are you finding the workshop?'

'I still prefer to hand-make.'

His son gave a secret smile. Off the rack, ready to wear shoes were his forte. He wished his father would return to his shop and fuss around with ormolu buckles, gold piping, and Cuban heels.

'I'm glad I was never faced with that decision,' empathised the jeweller.

'I don't understand why you still work at all?'

'After you've all paid me back I may retire,' Preston lied. Nothing would have driven him out of his mind faster than having to spend the rest of his life in an armchair or on a golf course.

'No, you are a changed man, Mr Niblock.'

If the jeweller heard that once again he would have probably turned green and rampaged through Moltonford. When the Buddhists say that all things change, they probably don't mean as dramatically as he had. From neatly ironed shirts and conservative ties, he now wore outsize sweaters or sleeveless jackets imported by Mrs Silvestri. His trousers were no longer pressed and shoes mostly suede because he couldn't be bothered to polish his leather ones. After seeing the silver anchor the greengrocer wore in his ear, he had the urge to pierce a lobe as well, but didn't keep the equipment. The logistics of piercing the navel of a twelve-year-old, even with her parent's permission, would have been too much for him. After Lucy Tribble demonstrated how she could do it with one of her needles, an ice cube, gas ring and cork, he changed his mind.

At least Preston still did some housework. With a dog that made the place like a wool carding factory, he had to.

CHAPTER 39

As Miss Priddle gazed out of her office window, she half listened on the phone. 'So they wouldn't wear it? Why not?'

Conrad Makepeace was beginning to wonder why he had ever become interested in the public good. 'Some of the companies apparently don't exist.'

'Ah yes.' She tapped the receiver with her gold pen. 'Of course they exist; they've just assumed different personas. By the time you've tracked them down, they will have changed again. Sorry I wasn't more help.'

'You did warn me.' Conrad Makepeace hesitated. 'There is something else we need to discuss, though.'

'Of course. What is it?'

'Preston Niblock.'

***

Having won a battle, but not the war, Neville Grablatt sat silently smouldering with rage in the deserted council chamber. Though unable to work out how, he was convinced that the jeweller was responsible for supplying Conrad Makepeace with the revelations about Gideon Enterprizes. Even worse, Grablatt was afraid that Julius Tucker suspected him. Preston Niblock had every reason to bring down the company. He believed it was responsible for the death of his wife and had been bullied into accepting a bribe he promptly used to fund a co-operative that undercut the goods in Palace Parade

What to do about him, though? Breaking his back would have made Grablatt feel better but, with his record of grievous bodily harm, it wouldn't have been a good move. He would have told Tucker of his suspicions if the billionaire hadn't taken a perverse liking to the small, inoffensive jeweller. Somewhere, deep down inside, Tucker was after all a family man, albeit several times over, and didn't care for the thought of persecuting a widower, especially one who had been widowed on his behalf.

Neville Grablatt eventually got up and strolled across to the shopping mall where he could glare at the Catalogue Shop. Perhaps a sudden infestation of something obnoxious could close them down for a while. He was determined to put them out of business, even if he had to engineer the seven plagues of Egypt.

***

'What makes you think that Preston Niblock is connected with Julius Tucker?' If Miss Priddle nibbled another bread stick she would have to loosen her skirt.

Conrad Makepeace furtively glanced about the deserted restaurant. 'He recently worked on the diamond cluster his mistress was wearing to a charity function.'

Miss Priddle stopped nibbling. 'Are you sure? Couldn't it have been something similar?'

'I've a good eye for these things.'

'It might have been an innocent commission?'

'Given what he believes Gideon Enterprizes did to his wife?'

Something deep down in the accountant's soul said, 'Oh dear!' If problems had to arise, the last person she thought would cause them was Conrad Makepeace. She bore the man no malice, and the best way she could prove it was by keeping him innocent of what was going on. 'How much do you trust me?'

He was puzzled. 'Why shouldn't I trust you?'

'There is something I cannot tell you.'

'So how much do you trust me?'

'It's not up to me. You must take my word for it that Preston Niblock is the best ally you have if you are still interested in toppling Gideon Enterprizes.'

'Of course I am.'

'In that case, stop wasting your time watching him and pay more attention to Neville Grablatt. He's in deeper than a brick trying to float on quicksand.'

Makepeace tried to sound resolute. 'If I'm to do anything, I need to know the whole truth.'

She shook her head. 'Oh no. Take my word for it, you don't.'

'Why not?'

'Because this way you stay alive.'

***

Mercy scrutinised the contents of the biscuit tin. Although she now checked it every morning she wasn't yet quite paranoid enough to count how many were left in the opened packets. And she wouldn't have wanted to encounter the mouse that could prize off a lid that had broken more than one of her fingernails. There had always been more pressing problems when she opened the shop.

Mrs Silvestri came up from the storeroom. 'Can you call your brother, Mercy? I'm out of pumpkin seeds and lecithin, and will need another box of jasmine candles.'

'Sure. Has Rose started sending up the bread yet? We have to open in twenty minutes.'

'She says it's coming up right away.'

Agitated, Mercy once again wiped the café counter. 'Why does she do this to me?'

Mrs Silvestri came over and took the cloth from her. 'Relax; you mustn't let things get to you. I'll help you with the sandwiches until your girls arrive.'

'They're still watching us, you know. I'm sure that great thug with the silk scarf is up to something.'

'He hasn't caught us out yet.'

'And what did they need to send pest control down into the storeroom for? We've never had trouble with pests, other than those wearing that hideous crown on their epaulettes.'

'They do it to all the storerooms.'

Mercy poured them both a coffee, and then relaxed. 'I'm sorry, it's just that I've always wanted a café so much. I would have started one long ago if Winston hadn't opened his record shop instead.'

'Before the year is out you'll be able to buy your own premises.'

'Outside Palace Parade? Probably only get weirdoes and down and outs.'

Mrs Silvestri smiled reassuringly. 'No. Things will change. Has Preston ever let us down?'

***

Despite all the tricks to damage the Catalogue Shop, from infesting it with cockroaches to superglueing the lock, the other stores were forced into a discount war they wouldn't win. As customers continued to make the Co-operative's outlet their first port of call, the counter staff and deliveries had to be doubled. Having hit business in Palace Parade so badly, the accountants had no option but to bring it to the attention of Julius Tucker the third. By the end of the year, all he had to show for his great shopping mall venture was another ulcer and embarrassing deficit.

***

Neville Grablatt regularly made a point of standing outside the Catalogue Shop to glower at the customers. It took more than the frown of an inflated councillor to put off hardened bargain hunters, and Preston Niblock seldom, if ever, passed by to be intimidated.

Grablatt was now expected to get some eccentric motion carried at Moltonford's next council meeting. After all, Tucker was paying him enough. But the wealthy autocrat totally misunderstood how local government in the UK worked. Since Conrad Makepeace's failure to prove that Gideon had a cartel, suspicions lingered, and no councillor wanting re-election was going to help damage something as popular as the Catalogue Shop.

CHAPTER 40

'Office relocation?' Mr Rupel of Merchant & Merchant Estate Agents Limited turned the words round in his mouth as though he could taste them.

The young woman with the club-cut hair and maroon lipstick watched him make a meal of the proposal. The agent was unable to understand his hesitation. After all, she was buying property on behalf of a client, not asking to join the local hunt.

Mr Rupel had been approached before for a similar project and that deal had fallen through. This time he had no option but to sell the derelict supermarket for his client and cut their losses. He assumed that Wentworth Developments wanted to clear the site and fill it with a bland high rise. As nothing that close to the town centre was allowed to overlook Palace Parade, he knew that planning permission wouldn't be granted. Their agent appeared to be a big girl and capable of eventually working that out for herself, hopefully after he had closed the deal.

'Two hundred thousand is the asking price.'

'I'll offer one ninety.'

Mr Rupel looked down his nose at the strange henna haircut. 'This is a prime town centre site.'

'Not since Palace Parade. The properties on this side of Moltonford will now only be taken by offices. That means rebuilding. One ninety is a good offer for the land. The bricks aren't worth anything.'

There was nothing else for it; the building had been on the books of Merchant & Merchant for two years, the supermarket's owner needed a sale, and Merchant & Merchant needed their percentage.

Mr Rupel left to draw up the contract and the young agent for Wentworth Developments remained in the aisle that had once contained household goods.

She pulled out her phone. 'One ninety. Three down, ten to go. I hope our client knows what they are doing? If these properties aren't cleaned up soon, the drug dealers will move in.'

She returned the phone to her briefcase, saw the pile of droppings on the floor, then looked up at the smashed skylight. Several pigeons peered down at her.

'And you'll be first to go.'

∗∗∗

Dear Gideon Enterprizes,

We retail high-class fashions for the ladies' market, including hats, handbags and other accessories, and have for some time now been trying to lease a modest unit in Palace Parade. However, despite repeated approaches, the management has ignored our letters.

Understanding that the councillor, Mr Neville Grablatt, was the driving force in persuading Moltonford council to approve the building of your shopping mall, we also approached him in writing. We were disappointed to receive a reply from this gentleman that inferred that Gideon Enterprizes have a somewhat "incestuous" policy when leasing units in Palace Parade. Not fully comprehending the meaning of his letter, we would like some clarification of your policy, as we feel sure there has been some misunderstanding about our application.

We look forward to hearing from you,

Yours faithfully,

As she read the letter out, Miss Priddle doodled an invisible abstract on the screen with the cursor. 'That should slow down the overbearing Neanderthal for a while.' She backdated the letter, tapped in the name of a recently bankrupted shop, and then printed it.

Toni Zelinski wasn't so enthusiastic about the tactic. 'They're bound to check back to see if they received any correspondence.'

'One of the secretaries in the main office told a spy that, after they've sent out the form reply, they file any letters like this in the waste bin.'

'Grablatt will deny writing it of course.'

'Not before Tucker's given him some grief.'

'This is a dangerous game, Priddy.'

The accountant cast the civil engineer a sly glance over the top of her glasses. 'At least I don't buy military devices constructed from blueprints the Electronauts hack out of top secret files.'

Toni was taken off guard. 'Why would I want to buy a military device?'

'I've heard that this one can detonate a megaton blast with only a grain of explosive and not leave any trace.'

'That's ridiculous!'

'Or was it a detonator that can be triggered by a signal that normally wouldn't register in transmission blind spots?'

Actually, it had been a transmitter capable of sending a readable electromagnetic signal through a mountain range. The civil engineer already knew everything she needed to about detonators.

The short woman seemed to rise indignantly without leaving her chair. 'What on earth would I need a device like that for?'

'I've no idea. The games I play are far less risky.'

'Sending letters like that? I doubt it.'

The accountant signed the correspondence and pushed it into an envelope. 'If it helps make Grablatt think twice about harassing Preston, then it's worth it.'

'What harm is that wart hog liable to do him?'

'Believe me, Grablatt is dangerous. You'd be surprised at the sort of people who are allowed to stand for election as councillors.' Miss Priddle tossed the letter into the OUT tray. 'Now. We're exchanging contracts for Benn's supermarket, the terrace at the bottom of Melon Street, the old sorting office, and Machan's Builders yard. We're about to make an offer for the café bar next to that, and Henderson's are willing to let Wentworth buy their factory if the price is right.'

'Sounds good.'

'Can you draw up plans?'

'Start right away. Most of those properties can be renovated. Henderson's will have to come down because it's a rabbit warren.'

'Be the ideal spot for a garden and shopping precinct.'

Toni Zelinski heaved a sigh. 'I hope you've got this right, Priddy. Preston's taking a hell of a gamble in raising this sort of money. If everything goes pear-shaped he could well end up with Mabel and her friends.'

'Odd that.'

'What?'

'No one has any idea where they've been sleeping since God's handmaiden threw them out. Not so much as the sighting of a carrier bag in old Bindal's doorway.'

'I'm more worried about Preston at the moment. I owe it to Deirdre to make sure he doesn't lose everything.'

'Don't worry, I wouldn't let him lose quite everything, believe me.' The accountant left her chair to go to the window and gaze at Palace Parade. 'Just look at that place.'

The builder joined her. 'It's still there.'

'Trade will never be as brisk on this side of town as it used to. If people know they can find bargains and the rents are pegged low enough, it could work.'

'And what if someone tries to burn them out again?'

Miss Priddle turned to look at her. 'Well, you'll be installing the sprinklers.'

***

Fran stood on the seat of the trackless bulldozer and bounced up and down.

A small voice squeaked from below, 'Be careful, Gran!'

'Look Jim,' she swept out her arms. 'Imagine all this filled with chickens, sheep, wallabies, rabbits, and donkeys.'

'You said that granddad could only have a donkey if he forgot about the wallaby.'

Fran sometimes forgot that the young had the recall of a fly on the wall equipped with a camcorder. She climbed down and helped Jim pick his way through the dangerous rubble left several years ago by a builder not noted for his sense of the vertical. After two of his houses fell down, it wasn't surprising he followed by going into sudden liquidation.

'Where can I have my flowerbed?' asked Jim.

Fran looked at the shattered concrete, collapsed corrugated iron sheds, and piles of rusty metal. She wished she had the imagination of an infant. 'I rather think Auntie Toni will have to bring her big diggers in here first.'

'Can I drive one?'

What did she have to mention big diggers for? 'Why not come and help granddad feed the rabbits.'

CHAPTER 41

Alice stopped twirling about the café to listen.

Mabel pulled her felt hat over her ears. 'Oh no, not again.'

The thought that some subterranean monster was chewing its way through the floor to cart them off to a hell for wayward vagrants was making Hector and Alice more jumpy than the fleas that had at one time been their constant companions.

'Crocodiles!' Hector blurted out.

Mabel left her chair. After spending so many restless nights listening to the whirring and muffled voices, there was nothing else for it. She would have to find out where they came from.

'Now don't make any noise,' she warned Hector and Alice as though they were likely to invite the monster up into their cosy little parlour.

From the cover of Mrs Silvestri's barrow, they watched Mabel open the catalogue counter's gate, go to the door of the lift lobby, place her ear against it, and listen. She could hear people talking. It was usually locked but, as Mabel put her weight against the door, it swung open. Tentatively she stepped into the small space stacked with boxes.

Reverberating inside the lift shaft, the words were now audible. Mabel's old heart fluttered. Nobody should have been inside Palace Parade at that time of night.

Having come so far, she had to find out what was going on. What if these intruders were to suddenly burst into the café? The thought of having to return to Mrs Roy and her hymns restored the old woman's strength.

She pushed the lift button. There was a horrible whirring noise that frightened her back into the café.

The voices must have heard. Peering over the counter, Mabel saw the lift door slide open. There was no one inside it.

With a sudden burst of courage, she darted back into the lobby and leapt inside it. Before she could change her mind, the doors closed and the lift went down. Terror stricken, Hector and Alice watched as their friend disappeared from sight.

Fearful of what would greet her, Mabel flattened herself against the side of the lift.

The door opened to silence. Warily she glanced about the storeroom. In a corner was a wide hole surrounded by containers and filled with a hellish light. Something was ascending from the depths of the earth. Against what vestiges of common sense she had left, Mabel recalled Mrs Roy's dire warnings about the Devil rising up to claim his own. Transfixed, she watched as a stack of large crates rose through the floor. Then, lit by a dazzling beam of light, the head and shoulders of a sinister creature from the Underworld came into view.

Mabel suddenly found the presence of mind to push the lift button. The doors closed and it whirred back up.

'Did you hit the lift control, Ron?' the man yelled down before he was level with the floor.

'Sorry, probably caught it with my-' The voice was cut off as the platform arrived.

Mabel tumbled out of the lift and hid behind the café's counter. Seeing that the monster hadn't devoured her, Hector and Alice stopped panicking and were now concerned about the change in their usually imperturbable friend.

'Crocodiles!'

When Mabel realised that nothing mammalian or reptilian was pursuing her, she peeped from behind the cake display cabinet. 'The Devil!'

Alice screwed up the corner of her long skirt. 'Down there?' she whispered.

'Coming up through the floor.'

Alice squealed.

Mabel cautiously came out of her hiding place. 'Quiet or he'll hear us!'

'Do we have to move now? I like it here.'

'We have to keep quiet. He lives in a large metal box just below us. He won't hear if we keep quiet.'

'Aardvarks!' declared Hector.

***

Julius Tucker the third did not like being disturbed during a manicure. 'This had better be important, Bart?'

The thin young man in the collarless suit held a letter. 'I think it is.'

'Well, spit it out.'

'This arrived at head office yesterday. They faxed it straight to us when they saw his name.'

'Whose name for pity's sake?'

'Neville Grablatt's.'

Tucker waved the manicurist aside. 'What's he been up to?'

'He apparently suggested to some dress retailer that, when Gideon Enterprizes selects tenants, its policy is somewhat,' the

168

young man was reluctant to allow the word out. The last time Tucker heard something like this he exploded and hi PA had trouble matching the broken glass fittings. 'Incestuous.' He stepped back and waited for the fallout.

The billionaire lunged from his chair and snatched the fax. 'Give me that!' He pushed on some glasses and scoured the letter. 'What the hell is this! Grablatt couldn't be this stupid!' He turned on his aide. 'Where is the letter from this firm?'

'Palace Parade management was instructed to disregard any such approaches and send a standard refusal. Only larger companies got the regular spiel about availability and being contacted when something came up, but the small firms...' He continued to back away. 'They apparently never kept it.'

'I want to see Grablatt!'

'Could it have been a misunderstanding? The English have got a different way of using our language.'

'Incestuous means the same thing if you're living on the moon. That son-of-a-bitch is becoming a liability.'

'We wouldn't have got Palace Parade up without him, Mr Tucker.'

'He was paid enough and still hasn't done anything about that damned shop.'

'Given the stuff that other councillor dug up, he's probably finding things tricky.'

'Yeah, I wonder who told Makepeace where to dig?'

A harsh breeze cut through the disused café bar. Mercy Cuffe didn't feel the chill. This was her dream. Not even dry rot could spoil it.

'You like the idea then?' asked Preston.

Of course she liked the idea. Why did the man have to keep asking?

'The brewery baled out when the off licence in the mall opened.'

Mercy continued to shine her torch into every nook and cranny. 'I'll make it a place for the kids to come, and won't even bother with a drinks licence.'

'A café bar without booze?'

'There isn't a restaurant in this town which caters for families unless they want to eat and drink out of polystyrene and cardboard. And I could turn that function room into a daytime cinema where people can leave their kids while they go shopping.'

Preston wouldn't have thought about that. But then, what did he know about children?

Mercy must have been reading his mind. 'You didn't have a family, did you, Mr Niblock?'

'Only my sister-in-law's. When you have been the solitary offspring of parents who believed that children were a punishment for mortal sin, they somehow seem optional.'

'Didn't you want children?'

Preston shrugged. 'It just never happened. Not everyone has the reproductive capabilities of a feral pigeon.'

'Would you have done, though?'

'Perhaps.' Deirdre might have, but she never made an issue of it. Deirdre never made an issue of anything. Sometimes he wished she had thrown her weight about more.

Mercy righted a stool that had been lying on its side for the last two years, and brushed it off. 'That's the trouble with life, you can never go back.'

'Pity, I think I must have missed the point somewhere along the line.'

Mercy smiled. 'No, not you Mr Niblock.' She pulled out her mobile. 'I've just remembered I have to get an order for pesto and black pepper to Winston before Mrs Silvestri sends a search party down to the storeroom.'

Mercy left and Preston wandered through the boarded-up premises lit only from the open door and a skylight. Was he doing the right thing, encouraging people to believe that they could restore their businesses as though Palace Parade never existed? Between them they had the money to try virtually anything. But to rebuild an alternative town centre? Would those who had become used to the mindless comforts of Palace Parade cross the road for a decent cappuccino or custom made shoes?

The jeweller delved into the pocket of his new trench coat for a tissue to wipe the dust of the furniture from his hands and pulled out the key ring Deirdre had bought him as a joke. At the time, the fluorescent orange frog seemed absurd, now he was beginning to like it.

Preston heard a movement near the door and turned. The huge figure of Neville Grablatt was blocking the light.

There was nothing else for it. Never show a bully you are intimidated. 'What do you want?'

The cat had cornered its mouse at last and the councillor remained in the entrance, cutting off Preston's escape. 'Now I was just about to ask you the same thing?'

The man was bound to find out sooner or later. 'I'm considering buying the place.'

The councillor came in and lounged against the far end of the bar. 'Really?' There was no surprise in Grablatt's voice. 'Of course, you have enough money to indulge such whims, haven't you.'

'Why should you be so interested?'

'Let's say that I am here to help you keep on the straight and narrow. If a certain gentleman thought that you were stepping outside your agreement or becoming too visible, he might decide to rewrite the contract.'

Preston could feel the man's crocodile eyes louring at him in the dim light. 'And what I am supposed to have done?'

'You know Conrad Makepeace quite well, don't you?'

'I have mended several pieces for him.'

'You're a very clever man, aren't you?'

'I could even chase you a gold nose ring, but the temptation in bringing callipers near those porcine nostrils to measure their thickness would be too great.' The jeweller felt his bravado slipping away. He might have coped in a brief encounter, but the man's continued presence was too intimidating. He had to get outside. 'I'm locking the place up now.' He strode to the door.

Grablatt caught his arm, his huge hand encircling it as though it was a child's wrist.

Preston tried not to think of the bruise it would leave. 'Let go of me.'

'Or what?'

'This is not some night-club and you are no longer a bouncer.'

At the reference to a past he thought confidential, Grablatt increased his grip. 'You know a lot of things, don't you Mr Jeweller?'

Preston's common sense told him to shut up. However, his innate perverseness never bothered about the odd bruise or broken bone. 'That knowledge is not so secret as you would like to believe.'

'Perhaps you've been mentioning one or two other things to Mr Makepeace as well?'

Preston mentally apologised to Tiny for all the names he had called him and wished he had brought the Alsatian along for a walk. The dog could lay moulting on his bed every night from now on if he would just appear in that doorway. Unfortunately, at that moment, Tiny was too busy catching the Smarties tossed from Lucy Tribble's plump little hand.

Grablatt sensed the man's terror and gave a small chortle of delight. 'Of course, I can't prove it was you who pointed Makepeace in the right direction. I'll find out soon enough though. And then we'll have another little talk.'

Preston was near to panic. 'I don't know what you're on about. Let go of my arm!'

Grablatt released him, only to seize the jeweller's coat collar with cat like maliciousness before he could make the door. 'Not so fast.'

Preston's heart started to thud again. 'Now what?'

'I don't know how you're making the Catalogue Shop work, but I'm pretty sure it would be a good enough reason for Tucker to have you served up on a waffle.'

Preston compelled himself to calm down. He turned back to face the man. 'And just what are you going to do? Put a light to your backside and go into orbit?'

'As you said, I've got a record. That was because there were witnesses. I never made that mistake again.'

Preston wanted to run out before his knees turned to jelly. For all he cared, the pigeons and Neville Grablatt could have the run of the derelict saloon, but the man still held him by the coat. Had he been wearing one of his casual jackets he would have been able to slip out of it and leave it in the thug's hand. Perhaps it was poetic justice for wanting to display his formerly immaculate persona to a woman twenty years younger than himself. Damn fitted sleeves!

Before Preston could wonder who else Grablatt might have done to death, another figure appeared in the doorway. It had the presence of a peccary about to gore flesh. 'Not interrupting something, am I?' said a deceptively light voice.

Grablatt quickly released Preston. 'Mrs Zelinski!'

She stepped inside. 'Not interested in buying the place are you, Mr Grablatt? I would have thought that nightclubs were more your style.'

Now she had confirmed that more than one person knew about his days as a bouncer, the councillor was unnerved. 'No, Mrs Zelinski, I was just having a quiet chat with Mr Niblock.' The large man pulled himself to his full height and strode out.

Preston slumped onto an inglenook seat. 'Thank you,' he gasped. 'I just needed someone with a knowledge of bulldozers to turn up at that instant.'

'Sounded bad?'

'That man thinks I told Conrad Makepeace about Gideon Enterprize's company scam.'

'I'd pour you a drink, but it doesn't look as though the bar's open.' Toni helped him to the door. 'Are you all right?'

'Just a mild case of terror. The bruise will probably disappear in a couple of weeks.'

'You should keep away from that gorilla.'

'Don't you think I've tried.'

'Let's go for a coffee. What did Mercy say?'

'She'll take it.'

After the vigorous rustling of iridescent quills and a call penetrating enough to stampede the donkey, the peacock fanned out its tail and rotated precariously on the potting shed, much to the delight of the watching customers.

Fran's voice suddenly reverberated through the garden centre. 'Ben, if you don't get that bloody thing back in its pen I'll skin it!'

'I didn't know it had flown out,' he called back, afraid she would appear at any moment clutching a lethal garden implement. 'I'll get it down.'

Why, when Ben had two adult sons, were they never around when he had to climb ladders and arrest large birds pumped full of testosterone? Fortunately the greengrocer was always tuned into his landlord's predicaments and put down the crate of parsnips he was carrying. By the competence with which he shinned up the ladder and folded the displaying peacock like an ungainly fan, it looked as though he should have been raising wild boar as well as growing organic vegetables.

'Here you go.' He handed the bird over to Ben. It immediately pecked him.

Satisfied that the little drama would be continued next week at the same time, the onlookers wandered off to buy their hellebore and summer bulbs.

'They told me the creature wouldn't show any interest until spring and the bloody thing's already got a full tail?' complained Ben.

The greengrocer retrieved his parsnips. 'Oh they don't waste any time, those birds.'

'But Toni Zelinski's foreman says that the large pens won't be ready until they've laid the turf.'

'Thought about clipping its wings?'

'If it makes a habit of getting up there too often it'll end up in the gift shop as table decoration.'

'As long as they can't get into the greenhouses - and they might leave the shrubs outside alone.'

Knowing his luck, Ben doubted it. He looked longingly over to the muddy acre that had once been Machan's yard. The ground had been levelled, a large pond with fountain installed, and the foundations for animal accommodation laid. All it needed now was the turf, sheds, spring, and the small flock of laying chickens Fran had insisted on him keeping to help with the running costs.

Once the children's farm was open, Rita and Jackie would have to work full time making sure a goat didn't devour the occasional toddler's fingers.

Ben tossed the peacock back into its cage, then took a bucket and went to the store for the sheep's pellets. About to enter, he heard Fran inside talking on her mobile phone. It sounded confidential, so he listened at the door.

'Of course he's going to be upset. I keep telling you it won't be that easy. He's changed. He'll never be the same again.'

Ben wondered if there was some family matter he should have remembered being told about.

'What you did was wicked... No, of course I won't tell anyone, but I don't see the point in hurting him any more.'

As Fran finished the conversation she called, 'It's all right Ben, you can come in.'

'Sorry, didn't mean to interrupt.'

Fran looked at her husband as though he was about to arrest her. 'How much of that did you hear?'

Ben knew there was a bombshell coming and wasn't sure whether it had his name on it. 'Not enough to make sense. Is it something I need to know?'

'Yes, but you won't like it.'

***

The VAT inspector gave Miss Priddle a glance of defeat. As with her make-up, there wasn't a flaw in the accounts for the Catalogue Shop. 'Given the volume they're handling, they've made an extraordinary job of keeping track of everything that goes over the counter?'

'I wrote them a standard program that prices and itemises each sale.' The accountant offered him a floppy disc. 'Every transaction is on here if you would like to go through them.'

Knowing he wouldn't find any flaw in that either, he declined. His business was tallying receipts and turnover; he wasn't interested in how they were generated. He only knew that the VAT due meant that the Catalogue Shop's profits were higher than any of the other major stores in the mall and the Co-operative's expense receipts would keep his office busy for a week if he allowed it. If this woman was a crook, she was able to fiddle the books as though they were a Stradivarius.

'Tell me, Miss Priddle, I understand that you are also the business manager for Wentworth Developments?'

She paused. 'I am, but would prefer it not to be common knowledge. As some of my clients have had rather unfortunate experiences with incendiary woodworm, we prefer to keep a low profile.'

The inspector nodded and gathered up the mountain of paperwork. Miss Priddle handed him a couple of carrier bags for what he couldn't crush into his briefcase. Then he left, hoping someone else would have the delightful experience of checking the books of Miss Priddle's clients next year.

After twelve months, the Catalogue Shop had done so well it was surprising that no one had thrown a petrol bomb through its window.

If anyone on the Coney Canal had seen the barge under the sluice arch of Bald Wendy being loaded during the night with raw materials, they hadn't thought anything of it. Once the vessel's sinister shadow had disappeared through those willows, who was likely to follow?

The spies tailing Winston Cuffe's fleet of vans had long since given up trying to keep track of the warehouses they visited, so now he had the opportunity to fit out a small recording studio.

Yes, everything was going so well, Miss Priddle knew the worst must have been about to happen. She wasn't sure what.

CHAPTER 44

Mary Bell giggled, then added another coat to her lipstick. Neville Grablatt watched, resentful he would never be able to afford a woman like her, not that she would cast one to look in his direction if he could. Women in Mary Bell's class drew the line at malevolent hippos, however well manicured.

Teasingly, she turned to check her seams in one of the hotel room's full-length mirrors. Her erotically contorted figure was reflected from several glass panels and Grablatt fought back an erection.

Julius Tucker strode in and tossed her a roll of bank notes. 'Don't use the plastic till I say so. Got it?'

'Sure Juli.' His aide helped Mary Bell on with her coat and then she wiggled her way to the lift that took her down to a waiting taxi.

'Bet she's not going to Palace Parade,' Grablatt thought to himself.

The manner in which Tucker poured himself a drink without asking whether the councillor wanted to join him spelt trouble.

'So the Catalogue Shop's still trading, Grablatt.' It wasn't a question.

'We tried everything. Cockroach infestation, triggering the café's extinguishers and spiking a delivery of fruit juice. They just got more sympathy.'

'And sympathetic people spend more money.' The billionaire took a swig of whisky. 'Dammit man! Why couldn't you find some other way to close them down?'

Grablatt felt a surge of anger but knew the guard at the door had a gun in his jacket and there would be a bullet through his brain if he took one step too near his boss. With Tucker's money, a body his even size could disappear without trace.

'I know something's going on, but I can't get at it.'

Tucker tossed the dregs of his drink onto the roots of an ornamental cycad. 'I'll tell you what's going on! Palace Parade's not going to cover its start up cost, let alone make a profit! I am paying you to look out for us!' He calmed down a little. 'Now, what do you know?'

'I think Preston Niblock has something to do with it.'

'What? The jeweller?'

'His wife was killed in the Merryweather fire and his friends driven out of business. I know he was the one to refit that warehouse for them.'

Tucker gave a contemptuous snort. 'That man wouldn't have the balls to cheat on Gideon. He's just got a guilty conscience and trying to make things right by the others.'

'And I'm convinced he's the driving force behind the Catalogue Shop.'

'Proof?'

Grablatt hesitated. 'I haven't found any yet, but I will.'

'You'd better.' Tucker slumped onto a settee. 'But then, Grablatt, perhaps you don't want us to find out who's really been cheating.'

'Cheating?'

'The dossier that Makepeace fella put together - Who the hell tipped him off?' He looked the councillor straight between the eyes as though taking aim.

Grablatt shrugged. 'I don't know.' Then he was compelled to confront the chilly truth. 'You don't suspect me?'

'Show him, Bart.'

The aide pulled a fax from his jacket. The billionaire snatched it. He thrust the paper at Grablatt and watched his expression like a tiger stalking a water buffalo.

Grablatt read the letter Miss Priddle had forged. It was ostensibly from a dress retailer. 'I never wrote this! It's a bad joke!'

'No Mr Grablatt, this is a dangerous joke.'

'Why the hell would I put something like that in writing, and to a firm I've never heard of before?'

'A small business, recently ceased trading according to Bart.'

'I found the entry in an Internet listing of UK companies,' his aide added. 'All we need now is a law suit accusing us of putting them out of business.'

The thought that even this hippo wouldn't have been so thickheaded as to send the letter had crossed Tucker's mind, yet suspicion lingered. With somebody like the corrupt councillor, it was difficult to avoid.

'I tell you what, Grablatt. You prove that the jeweller is cheating and you're off the hook.'

'How the hell can I do that?'

'I don't care. Shake it out of him if you have to. You've done that to much harder cases before now, haven't you? Why do you think Gideon approached you in the first place? Your glittering wit and business acumen? You're a bum, Grablatt, and a thug. We needed a heavy hand at the seat of the action, that's why. I don't care how you do it. Find out who's trying to stitch us up or I might continue having a few suspicions of my own.'

Neville Grablatt backed to the door. Tucker hadn't finished, though.

'And why haven't you found out how this shop is shipping in its goods?'

'There were several vans and umpteen different warehouses. They never took the same routes.'

'Are they buying in cheap and selling cheap?'

'All the machinery was destroyed in the warehouse fire. They must have bought new equipment. We can't be so sure about the electronic stuff, but the kitchenware, pottery, clothes, and shoes are definitely made by the same people.' In desperation, Grablatt clutched at a straw. 'Why don't you just raise their rent?'

'You numbhead. They've got an airtight contract. Goodwill to the local shopkeepers, wasn't it? Your idea! Your idea has dropped us straight in the crap!'

'Look, Moltonford Council insisted on that clause. I can't do any more. Makepeace has already made them suspicious enough.'

'Then you had better find out who's at the bottom of it, hadn't you. I don't want to see your fat face again until you have!'

Smarting from the onslaught, Grablatt spent the rest of the day prowling Soho. The place had been cleaned up, yet he still felt at home there. One or two people recognised him and ducked out of sight, although he was too occupied with ideas about how to save his own skin. If he had to commit another murder it wouldn't be difficult. Getting away with it was the problem.

CHAPTER 45

Jack O'Brian glanced again at the main mall monitor. He didn't believe his eyes that time either. Suddenly the figures disappeared. He couldn't put it down to his liquid lunch in the pub this time.

He called down to the security office on the first level. 'Intruders in the mall, outside - well they were outside - the Catalogue Shop.'

'Were outside?'

'Looked as though they vanished into that display cabinet.'

'You been on the bottle again, O'Brian?'

'I'm not seeing things. You'd better check it out.'

This was all security needed minutes before locking up, a search of the main mall for phantoms that disappear into walls.

Chief Security Officer Regan called in two men doing their final rounds and they surrounded the Catalogue Shop.

'Couldn't have been a rat, or something, could it Guv?' asked Clive, his second in command.

'What, filching the sunflower seeds?'

Regan pulled out a bunch of master keys and riffled through them.

Clive hammered the emergency door with his fist.

'What do you think you're doing?'

'If it was a rat it might dash out.'

'Can you see any holes for a rat to get-' Regan cut his words short. On the other side of the automatic glass doors an old woman in a voluminous skirt was pirouetting across the floor of the café. 'Bloody hell!'

'That's Alice,' beamed Clive. His smile faded. 'And Mabel... and Hector.'

Regan quickly unlocked the main doors of the shop.

Alice continued to pirouette about the men trying to grab her; Mabel immediately put her hands up and surrendered. Hector stood in a corner, stamping his feet and shouting, 'Aardvarks! Aardvarks!' the worst imprecation he knew.

Eventually the companions were rounded up and escorted back to the security office.

'Say nothing, we're prisoners of war,' Mabel declared, and would only give her Christian name and social security number.

Hector might have said something if he hadn't forgotten how to make the words come out in order. Mabel, Alice, and Jenny may have rescued him from the meths years ago, though only after his brain had been scrambled.

Alice just giggled, so she and Mabel were put into the room reserved for truant schoolchildren while Regan sat Hector down in front of a cup of tea spiked with brandy.

The 'Crocodiles!' and 'Aardvarks!' gradually gave way to an erratic volley of bemused reasoning, albeit mainly in monosyllables.

'What were you doing in there Hector?'

'Biscs.'

'Apart from the biscuits?'

'Hide.'

'Hiding from what?'

'Monster.'

'What monster?'

'Down.' Hector stabbed a thumb in the direction of the floor.

Regan sighed. This was getting nowhere. He wanted to go home to his dinner. He knew the management wouldn't be happy that three men had clocked up a couple of hours overtime interrogating two down and outs who refused to say anything, and one only too willing to talk but not make sense.

Clive poked his head round the door. 'Social services will have someone down in twenty minutes Guv. Want to know if we're going to prosecute?'

'Prosecute? What for, being batty and destitute?' Regan swigged back his tea. 'Hector here thinks there's a monster's living in the storerooms.'

'Sounds too rational for him.'

'At least they haven't done any damage. Phone Mercy Cuffe and tell her that someone's been dipping into the biscuits. Don't make a big production of it. All we need now is to give the Catalogue Shop an excuse to sue the management.'

'They'd love that.' His deputy laughed and left to make out a report.

'What are we going to do with you Hector?' Regan looked at the roll of bedding materials the old man had insisted lugging in with him. 'I suppose Mabel has the key? You wouldn't know what one was for, would you?'

'Monsters! Downstairs!'

Conrad Makepeace pulled his Wellington boot from the mud and tried to keep up with Toni Zelinski. She seemed to skim over it like a chunky lily-trotter to where she intended to create a square of shops.

The civil engineer stood on the steps of Henderson's factory and spread her arms as though she could encompass the place. 'Once we've demolished this monstrosity, we'll have an area four times the size of Victoria Square. Through that way,' she made a slicing motion towards a single storey outbuilding sandwiched between several unused offices and derelict shops. 'We will lay a pedestrian precinct straight down to the High Street. What do you think?'

Makepeace liked the idea. 'That will face the main entrance of Palace Parade.'

'How soon can the proposal be drawn up?'

'Our architect is working on it now. When do you need it?'

'Before the year's expenditure is decided.'

'We're not asking for a grant. Only planning permission.'

'Oh no. After what local government sank into Palace Parade, you must ask for a grant. When they refuse and you decide to go ahead nevertheless, they will find it very difficult to deny planning permission.'

Toni Zelinski hadn't got round to thinking of that. 'Won't they start asking questions about Wentworth Developments, though?'

'Grablatt probably will, but anything he says now is going to be taken with a pinch of salt.' Makepeace joined her on the steps. He could never shake off the feeling that the councillor from Hell was always listening. 'I take it you are going to include factory units?'

'That's up to Wentworth.'

'Come on, if you want my co-operation in promoting this scheme you have to be straight with me.'

'Any workshops will be well away from each other, and probably fronted by their own shops.'

'As long as I have something to say when the question comes up.'

Toni sat on the steps. 'I don't know. They're so touchy about any factory space, anyone would think that the Catalogue Co-operative actually set fire to their own premises.'

'It's policy to blame the victim when the truth is inconvenient.'

'The Co-operative should do more shouting.'

'Bringing business in Palace Parade to its knees isn't exactly the work of shrinking violets.' Makepeace paused. 'Just how are they managing to do it?'

'You'll have to ask their accountant.'

'Miss Priddle? The web that woman spins ...'

'I know. With luck, Priddy one day might drop anchor in the humdrum ocean everyone else has to stop themselves drowning in.'

'I wouldn't have put it quite like that.' Despite the risk to his bespoke overcoat, Makepeace sat beside her. 'Those goods in the Catalogue Shop are too reasonably priced. To make a profit, they can't be outlaying for much more than materials and labour?'

'I understand the workers are on a percentage system and the ground rents are very, very reasonable.'

'And all underwritten by Preston Niblock no doubt.'

Toni Zelinski just smiled.

CHAPTER 46

In Palace Parade's executive canteen, Mr Meeks, the manager of the food hall, probed his steak like a cautious bird. 'You can never be sure about meat these days, can you?'

Neville Grablatt was swallowing his in huge chunks. 'Came from your own store, should be all right.'

'Of course. Thank God there is still something the Catalogue Shop can't undercut.'

'They only sell bird food.' Grablatt wiped away the gravy from his chin and took a swig of beer. 'Heard the food hall was going to be enlarged?'

'Now business in the clothing section is so bad, we might as well fill it with groceries. That's the only thing Palace Parade can make a profit on.'

'What about the outside chains who've been queuing up to rent space? Aren't they going to kick up?'

'Oh, that's covered. The food hall is controlled by the same company. It's a legitimate expansion.' Mr Meek took a sip of his wine. 'At least our three vagrants didn't manage to infiltrate that. We would have had to condemn half the stock.'

'Vagrants?'

'Yes. Didn't you hear? Three down and outs had been sleeping in the Catalogue Shop's display cabinet.'

Grablatt was suddenly listening intently. 'Go on?'

'We don't know how long for, but they didn't do any damage.'

'I've got an idea who you mean.'

'They're quite harmless. In fact, one of them is so addled he kept going on about some monster living in the storeroom.'

Grablatt laughed. 'Given the sort of stuff he used to put away it's a wonder that's all he sees.'

'Oh, he claimed to hear them as well. Says they try to burrow their way up every night.' Mr Meek placed his knife and fork over the half-finished meal. 'Have to get back. You know what it's like upstairs. Just as well I know too much to get the sack.'

Grablatt let the manager go. He was busy wondering what sort of monsters Hector could be hearing apart from crocodiles and aardvarks.

***

Two counties away, high on the range of hills that created the River Nox's drainage basin, the snow was at its deepest for decades. The enthusiasts who had been making the most of it were greeted one morning by cordons and signs declaring BEWARE, DANGER OF AVALANCHE. This gave them a strange thrill. Avalanches? That sort of thing only happened on the Alps. However, being England, they dutifully shouldered their sledges and snow boards, and went home.

Two days later the temperature rose to 12°C and the snow melted before it could do anything more dramatic. The meltwater percolated rapidly down the fissures in the limestone basin and soon the River Nox was churning turbulently through the network of tunnels beneath.

Rose was just loading a second tray of scones onto the delivery trolley when she felt the change in air pressure. It had been chilly outside the prefabricated units with the winter river flowing through the cave, but this cold atmosphere had nothing to do with spring arriving. She put down her tray and ran back along the track to the other workshops.

Within minutes a worried Co-operative was lining the riverside.

Winston had taken a day off from his recording studio to help load the lift. He remembered the stories his grandmother had told him about tidal waves. He hurtled over the boulder-strewn ground, shouting at the others. 'Get back up here!'

He had hardly herded the workers to the summit of the ancient beach when the River Nox surged.

In some places the water struck the ceiling, and then crashed up the sloping floor of the cave. The angry maelstrom stopped short of the lift and workshops, leaving the only escape route through the storeroom of the Catalogue Shop. Even Mr Regan's hungover security team wouldn't fail to notice over thirty people in overalls walking out all at once into the mall.

The river carried on surging with meltwater for some time. After a couple of hours it found its level, though it could still be heard roaring in the sump of the adjoining cave. The river turbine had been overwhelmed. The emergency generators kicked in and the lights along the trolley track illuminated the sediment and other debris that had been churned up in the gloomy foam.

'My God!' shouted one of Sonia's machinists, 'There's the prow of a boat.' She pointed.

The others caught sight of an old upended longboat pirouetting in the swirling water.

Rose gave a strangled cry. A skull had come bobbing from the adjoining cave. The human remains and debris from the racing teams that had been lost in the caves over one and a half centuries ago appeared.

Eventually the adjoining cave's sump sucked back its ghoulish flotsam.

For safety's sake, Winston ferried the workers back up in the Catalogue Shop lift at twenty-minute intervals, sending Monty Golden first. The tailor already had the horrors about the cave. The thought that he was a whisker away from being washed back to Bald Wendy by the monstrous flood was going to make his hand shake for the next week.

Toni Zelinski took a team down as soon as the river was low enough and checked over the river turbine. There was no trace of the skeletons churned to the surface.

'Think that surge undermined anything?' asked Owen.

The monitor on the cave ceiling wasn't indicating dangerous movement in the rock.

'Too soon to tell. I want the whole team on alert and ready to move if we have to. The lift must be prepared to take passengers at any time and nobody is to work down here during the night.'

Owen went down to the receding river, the only place where his mobile would work, and phoned on the instructions.

CHAPTER 47

Hector, Alice, and Mabel clustered in a corner well away from the television where the regular residents sat transfixed. That colour set was worth its weight in tranquillisers to the management, then they had never had to deal with characters like the new arrivals.

Mabel couldn't get used to the smell of urine and disinfectant and had been told, that here, they would be bathed. Mabel was quite capable of bathing herself. Why should anyone need to do it for her? Hector always needed a little help because he thought the showerhead was a rattlesnake - but let anyone bath her? Chance would be a fine thing. It was just as well Jenny wasn't around to see what they had come to.

Alice decided that the large man entering the seedy lounge wasn't a policeman. Over the years she had learnt to recognise the difference. And he was too smartly dressed to be one of those young, exasperated people who said nice things yet were totally ineffectual. Whatever this man did, he would certainly be effective.

Neville Grablatt strode over to their isolated corner.

'Don't you dare say anything to him,' Mabel hissed.

'Biscuits,' said Hector.

'Especially about the biscuits.'

An attendant, who was usually dashing about with laundry, bedpans, and medicine, brought Grablatt a chair so he didn't need to look down at their grizzled hair and the pink crocheted hat Alice refused to take off. 'We will have to keep the dears here now. They're far too old to be wandering the streets,' she patronised.

'Fuck off,' said Mabel.

Alice giggled and the woman left, scowling under her politic smile.

Grablatt assessed the opposition. The women obviously weren't going to say anything to anyone in authority and it was unlikely Hector had any idea where he was.

'Well, well, fancy managing to live in the mall all that time without anyone finding out.'

This visitor's aftershave smelt too official for Mabel's liking. She decided to improvise her response. 'Piss off.'

Grablatt put on his best canvassing manner. 'Now, now, I'm here to help you. Wouldn't you like the council to build a nice warm home where older people like you could have a room to themselves?'

Mabel had got used to sleeping in company, though wanted to hear more before she told him to piss off again. 'When?'

'The plans are being drawn up now.' He neglected to add that was as far as they would go.

Grablatt drew closer and Alice tried to match his smell with the aromas in the display cabinet.

'Parma violets,' she announced.

Grablatt swallowed his indignation at the slur on his £40 a bottle aftershave. 'How did you manage to hide for so long?'

Alice and Mabel eyed him suspiciously. Hector growled, mainly because he couldn't remember.

'Hector, you said that there were monsters below the café? What did you mean, monsters?'

'Be quiet!' snapped Mabel. She had no intention of sharing the monsters that had been lurking beneath their night-time lodging.

Grablatt smiled menacingly. 'Do any of you know a jeweller called Niblock?'

If there was one thing Hector could remember from the wreckage of his memory, it was the scones and cakes Deirdre Niblock used to bring them when they were in Victoria Park's pavilion.

'Cakes, Niblock, yes!'

'Shut-up!' snapped Mabel so angrily that it confirmed Grablatt's suspicions.

The councillor never waited to find out the real reason why Mabel wanted to protect the jeweller. He wouldn't have been interested to learn that Preston Niblock had been paying for their coffee and doughnuts for longer than Hector could remember.

He dipped them a derisive bow and left.

Mabel was beside herself. 'Oh dear, this must mean Mr Niblock's in trouble.'

'Why?' It was the most rational question Alice had asked for years.

'I don't know, but that man is evil.'

'Aardvarks! Yes!'

'Keep out of this, you stupid old fool!' Mabel turned to back Alice. 'I have to warn Mr Niblock.'

Alice still looked baffled. 'What about?'

'That big ogre asking about him.'

'All right then.'

'You have to stay here with Hector.'

Mabel waited until the lone attendant was up the other end of the corridor, and then slipped out.

The old woman was unsure where she was, but could see the flag of Palace Parade fluttering in the distance. Mabel scurried towards it and eventually found herself in the town centre. From there it was easy to find Preston Niblock's street.

Lucy Tribble was gluing stones to earrings when the harassed woman slipped in without tripping the new buzzer that had been installed against the eventuality of Neville Grablatt, not some ancient waif.

'Well hello Mabel. What are you doing here? I heard they found you living in the mall? That was very naughty.'

The old nails protruding through fingerless gloves clutched the edge of the counter. 'I have to see Mr Niblock.'

'All right, but I don't think even he can help you now.' Lucy rang up to the workshop.

Preston was bemused by Mabel's disjointed story. It was worrying when someone who has a full time job looking after their own welfare is so bothered about someone else's.

Preston thanked Mabel, took several packets of biscuits and some tubes of Tiny's Smarties from the pantry, and put her in his car.

As they drove away, Neville Grablatt stepped from the shadow of the neighbouring hedge.

CHAPTER 48

Although the jeweller had lost weight, his neatly pressed trousers puckered uncomfortably under his knees and the conservative waistcoat now felt too tight. Unfortunately, this exclusive restaurant was not the place to give in to a slobbish whim and release a few buttons.

Mary Bell cooed and gently giggled as she caressed the bracelet in which small galaxies of diamonds were partly eclipsed by cabochon moons of milky opal.

The young woman's expression glowed as though Julius Tucker had just returned her credit cards. 'How did you manage it with only that silly little photograph to go by, Preston?'

'I had all the stones in stock.'

'My mother will love it.' Mary Bell leaned across the table and her exotic fragrance took the jeweller's breath away. 'Did I tell you she was dying?'

He was too tense to sneeze and tried to ignore the novelty of a hot flush. He discreetly withdrew the hand that was a little too close to her orchid corsage. 'I wish I had known sooner. It's just as well I like to keep track of my work and phoned when I did.'

Mary Bell held the bracelet up to the light and Preston took the opportunity to dampen down his internal combustion with a mouthful of spring water.

'Oh that necklace was just great. I wear it to all the charity galas, though Juli thinks I ought to try something different now.'

The craftsman would have offered to create another necklace for free just to see it lying against that warm brown bosom. While Mary Bell continued to coo over her mother's bracelet, he dabbed the perspiration from his neck and told himself to calm down.

'Thank you so much, Preston. I'll get Juli to send you a cheque as soon as I get back.'

That did dampen the jeweller's fire. 'I'd rather you didn't. He might misunderstand.'

'Misunderstand? Oh no, really?'

'We have this agreement which does not include me doing his nearest and dearest a favour.'

'What a funny way of putting it. There's no need to worry though. Juli trusts me totally. He knows I wouldn't see another man.'

The thought of being mistaken for the lover of the billionaire's mistress was hair raising, even for a bald man. 'So he never has you followed?'

The shimmering lips pouted. 'Of course not. I wouldn't like that. My last boyfriend had me followed, and I couldn't stand it.'

Preston hoped Mary Bell was as dim as she sounded. He fastened the bracelet round her wrist. 'It has a double safety-catch so you have to secure this before closing the clip.' He demonstrated.

'Hey, that's cute.'

'My invention.' It had never been in the jeweller's nature to brag, but that safety-catch had confounded anyone else's attempt to duplicate it.

'How do you make something this wonderful?' Mary Bell shared the vague misapprehension with so many others that all works of art somehow spring into being from an ethereal production line.

Preston Niblock was used to the incredulity of clients. 'The opals are mounted in rub-over collets and the diamonds grain set in pierced platinum...' Mary Bell's expression was becoming glazed. He stopped. 'It's easy after you've done it several times.'

Mary Bell lightly rubbed the milky stones with a fingertip. Her lovers had given her far more expensive clothes and jewellery, yet this was the nearest she would ever get to that irreplaceable heirloom before her mother died. 'You must let me do something for you in return, Preston.'

He desperately tried not to sound coy. 'That wasn't my intention, Mary Bell,' he lied. It was a risky tactic. She might believe it.

'I like you. Why shouldn't I do something for you?'

As her lips formed a kiss, Preston felt as though he was going to melt all over the expensive tablecloth. He had never been so close to temptation in his life. One off encounters with Julius Tucker and his lover had pushed him into universes he didn't know existed. Would a night of bliss with a billionaire's mistress be worth tossing out his carefully calculated ploy for and ending up as an interesting conversation piece for the fish?

'No, I don't want anything from you. I'm not like Neville Grablatt.'

Mary Bell wrinkled her nose in disgust. 'That man. Ugh! He gives me goose bumps.' Her tone changed. 'He isn't your friend then?'

'Goodness no. He's been trying to convince Mr Tucker that I'm at the bottom of a plot to destroy Gideon.'

He either spun a convincing yarn, or she was more trusting than he dared hope.

'Now don't you worry about that.'

He feigned alarm. 'You won't repeat what I said to Mr Tucker, will you?'

'Of course not, but that nasty Grablatt is not going to hurt you.'

Her choice of words sent a shudder down the jeweller's spine. 'Only, it might create a misunderstanding if Mr Tucker knew I had seen you, however innocently. He might think I was trying to use you to influence him.'

'Don't you worry about Juli, Preston. I know exactly when to massage his... erogenous zones.' She slid her elegant hand across the table and linked fingers with his.

Preston wondered if anyone else in the restaurant had noticed this very expensive woman wafting temptation in his direction.

He hoped so.

***

The turf was now laid and several rabbits were trying to take a meal from its thin grass. Leaving Jim and Josey to round them up, Ben tried to herd the goats and sheep from the other side of the garden centre into their new quarters. Several nibbled primrose trays later, he eventually managed to drive them into the pen.

Fran watched from a safe distance. She preferred her stock to not jump around and anything mobile living on it easily flattened by a boot.

The phone rang. Having waited over an hour for the call, she sprinted into the house and snatched up the receiver.

'Hello!' She caught her breath. 'It's okay, you did say you hadn't any idea when you could get away. How are things? ... Okay, if you're sure that's what you want, we'll see you in a couple of days... No, I'd rather Ben collected you. I don't want anyone knowing before we're ready. How much time can you take off? ... I know you don't intend to stay. The place has really changed since you saw it last. We've just got the children's farm fitted out. It won't be up and running until the weather's warmer, then the animals will start breeding I suppose. It at least means fresh eggs for the café and some for the greengrocer to sell on his stall... And you won't recognise the town centre... All right then. I'll give you a ring tomorrow. Your switchboard will put you through if you're not in your office, won't they? ... Fine. Bye.'

Ben stooped by the kitchen step to pull off his grandchildren's muddy boots. 'She phoned back then?'

'Yes. She's decided to do it.'

'Well, guilty conscience, isn't it.' Ben then yanked off his Wellingtons and followed the children inside. 'The kids want to go to the pictures.'

'It's too late. John will be picking them up in an hour.'

While Jim and Josey watched television, Ben and Fran cooked spaghetti.

'Did you see Preston this morning?' he asked.

'No, where was he off to this time?'

'Don't know, but he was wearing a sharp suit and a hat.'

Fran stopped stirring the boiling pasta. 'Dear God, perhaps he's found a fancy woman.'

'What? Him? Shouldn't think so. He doesn't have the first idea of how to chat up for a woman.'

Miss Priddle picked her way up the steps of Bald Wendy as though inspecting a ship about to be named in her honour.

Toni Zelinski called down from the newly painted lucam overhanging the lower floor. 'Be careful when you come in Priddy, the trap door's open!'

'What are you doing up there?'

'A bit of glazing. Just come in will you, and close the door.'

Miss Priddle went into the gearing room, carefully teetering round the entrance to the tunnel. A perspiring face looked up at her.

'What's happening?' she asked.

The workman wiped his nose on the back of a muddy sleeve. 'Replacing a couple of rods in the roof buttress. That surge of water swept through it and loosened them.' He tossed a heavy length of steel from the tunnel and it clattered to the floor in front of her.

'You are busy little bees, aren't you. Pity I couldn't get Bald Wendy any insurance. Unfortunately it would have begged some very awkward questions.' Then she saw Preston Niblock lounging on some wooden crates. 'You're early?'

'Thought I'd bring Tiny for a walk. He likes it out here. His ancestors probably evolved in the sort of mist that shrouds this place on a bad day.'

Sprawled on the floor like a large outcrop of beige candyfloss, Tiny looked up.

'Enjoying his exercise I see.' Miss Priddle noticed that there was something self satisfied about the jeweller. Lounging nonchalantly had never been in his repertoire. He always used to sit as though he had a ramrod shoved up his rectum. 'What have you been up to that I ought to know about?'

'Me? Nothing? You have a suspicious mind.'

'It should be paranoid, but I don't have the energy.' She placed her briefcase on the crates next to Preston. 'Now let's get down to business.'

'Is it the triplicate signature in blood this time, or have you just blundered me into another ten million and want to buy out Gideon Enterprizes?'

'In your dreams. Ten million wouldn't pay for their executive toilets. I need to know how long you intend to carry on with Bald Wendy?'

'The others want to stick at it for as long as they can, but Toni isn't happy about that river surge. Reckons some of the water could have seeped into fissures and built up pressure in the bedrock.'

Miss Priddle pulled out the accounts the VAT inspector would never see. 'Well, the Catalogue Shop has covered the cost of installation and plant, raised enough for the redevelopment of the new shopping precinct and there is a generous float to relocate and support the businesses while they establish themselves. Need promotion by Saatchi & Saatchi of course. You can afford that as well.'

'What you're really saying is, you want everyone out of there?'

'Ever since they picked up Mabel, Alice, and Hector, I've been uneasy. They must have heard the lift being operated during the night.'

Preston slid off the crates. 'Mabel came round gabbling something about Grablatt trying to intimidate them into incriminating me.'

Miss Priddle sensed he was being guarded. 'And what did you do about it?'

'Do about it? What could I do about it? Pick up the thug by the collar and tell him not to do it again?'

'You've got Tiny.'

'Lucy Tribble has got Tiny, I have a mobile mattress of hair which a flock of weaver birds would set up looms for.'

Toni came down, wiping putty from her hands. 'That was a job for an apprentice.'

Miss Priddle had no sympathy. 'We need all of them in town working on Wentworth's new shopping precinct. I'm sure a little grouting never hurt anyone.'

Toni sneered at the manifestation in lemon silk. 'You wouldn't go near a piece of sandpaper in case it grazed those painted nails. If we are going to move the operation out of the cave I'll have to recall a crew from town. There will be quite a few holes to make good.'

Preston thought things were getting too far ahead. 'Hold on, why don't we take a vote on it?'

'All right. I am not happy about the stability of that cave roof and recommend a tactical withdrawal.'

The mere mention of sandpaper had made Miss Priddle involuntarily examine her nails. 'Shall I go down and see what they think?'

'Not in those shoes you won't, Priddy. I'll do it.'

'All right,' agreed Preston. 'What happens to Bald Wendy afterwards?'

Miss Priddle was looking in a security mirror and tweaking a few hairs back into place. 'Change its name. Never sell the damn place with it.'

Night was drawing in so Preston and Miss Priddle didn't wait to hear the outcome of the vote. Only after the accountant's sports car roared away did the jeweller pull out onto the narrow road in his small hatchback.

Watching the mill forecourt from a thicket of weeping willow and making a note of the people coming and going from Bald Wendy was the nearest thing the region had to a large aquatic life form. Neville Grablatt had found it worthwhile squelching about in the heavy clay mud, shining a torch through the bars of the cave entrance gate, and seeing the dinghies floating by the small landing bay.

It was all too good to be true and he could barely keep everything to himself until he found out exactly what was going on. These people were sharp. Exposing their presence in the cave would have rebounded on Gideon for constructing Palace Parade directly over it.

He had to neutralise the ringleader.

***

On the way to his private jet, Julius Tucker and his entourage swept through the airport reception lounge like oil royalty. Mary Bell wiggled after them, posing and pouting for the press. Tucker didn't mind. Letting the world know he had a woman like that made him feel good. This mistress was even civil to his ex wives and never drank or threw tantrums. She did like spending money, though always stopped short of apartment blocks.

Once in the air, Mary Bell brought Tucker his bourbon and snuggled up beside him to watch the rugged cliffs below wind away to the horizon.

'I do like Scotland, Juli, they have so much heather.'

'And the Loch Ness Monster.' Unable to separate a statement from a joke, the billionaire chuckled.

'I know someone I would like to feed to it.'

'Who's that Hun?'

Mary Bell giggled. 'No one, Juli. I don't hardly know him.'

'Who?'

She pouted. 'That big brute with the smarmy smile who comes to see you sometimes.'

The description fitted quite a few of his acquaintances. 'Which one?'

'I think he's a politician in some pokey little town somewhere. I'm not sure. You know I never listen when I shouldn't, don't you Juli.'

Tucker paused. 'You mean you overheard something?'

'Oh, I didn't mean to! He was in the lobby talking to some small man in a bowler hat and pin striped suit.'

Tucker had already identified Grablatt, so the other had to be from Palace Parade. 'Yeah, that sounds like one of the managers at the shopping mall. What were they saying?'

'I didn't understand. Something about a set-up.'

'Set-up?'

'Yes. That big gorilla wanted to avoid being suspected of something, so he was setting up someone else.'

An angry flush infused Tucker's neck. 'Who?'

'Oh, I never heard that much. I think they recognised me and moved away. It was when I was waiting for the car to go to that classy concert, remember. I had to send the porter back up because I'd forgotten my ticket.'

Yes, Julius Tucker remembered the day Neville Grablatt called with one of Palace Parade's managers. The billionaire had nearly blown a blood vessel when he learnt how much the shopping mall was losing to the Catalogue Shop. His analyst had spent a couple of hours trying to calm him down.

Mary Bell couldn't have known what was going on and was too dim to lie about something like that.

So it was Neville Grablatt after all. Gideon would have to review his contract.

CHAPTER 50

In the deepest basement of the town hall, the borough surveyor unlocked the bar securing the map drawers.

'Who else knows they're here?' demanded Neville Grablatt.

'No one. There is only one key to the cabinet and I went down and did the bedrock survey myself.'

'What about the workmen with you?'

'They thought I was only investigating a cavity that was going to be filled in with hardcore.'

'So how could anyone else have found out about the cave?'

'Search me. A Gideon agent tracked down all the other maps and we got rid of them.' The surveyor removed the bar and pulled open a drawer. 'This is the latest geological map I know of. It's Victorian.' He laid the map out on a desk. 'What are you looking for?'

Grablatt never answered. Under the dim light he followed the course of the River Nox with his thick finger and squinted to find landmarks. And there it was, Auld Windy, the mill sitting on the River Nox tributary that flowed from the network of caves under Moltonford.

The surveyor was growing concerned. 'What's the matter? No one's rumbled us have they?'

'It's nothing I can't sort out.' The councillor's tone suggested he was contemplating murder.

'Only if there is something going on I need to know about it. You have to book tickets to Tonga well in advance.'

'Burn this,' Grablatt ordered, and then left, having convinced the man he would be wise to transfer his bribe money to a foreign bank.

***

Lucy Tribble tossed Tiny his last Smartie then replaced her needles, glue, wire and beads back in her work box. 'Now you be good. I have to go, it's getting late.'

As she was putting on her coat, Lucy noticed a letter on the doormat. She thought there was something odd about the way it had surreptitiously appeared. The envelope was addressed to Preston, so she phoned up to his workshop.

The jeweller came down and took it from her.

Inside the envelope was a typed note from Toni Zelinski.

'Unable to reach you on the phone. Need to see you at Auld Windy right away.'

Lucy picked up the outside line. 'It's dead.' She rattled the connection. 'As the link with the workshop was working, it didn't occur to me there was anything wrong.' She unbuttoned her coat and returned to her chair behind the counter.

'What's the matter?'

'Something's not right, Preston.'

He laughed and put on a jacket. He took his car keys from their hook and went to the shop door. 'There's no need to wait around. Tiny hasn't ripped anything up for weeks now.'

'I don't think you should go.'

'Why on earth not? There's nothing surprising about Toni wanting me out there.'

'Then why didn't she come in instead of pushing a note through the door? I've been sitting here all the while.'

Preston didn't like to suggest that it was because Lucy would have kept her talking. 'You go home and get your tea. There's no need to wait around.'

'At least take Tiny with you.'

'God no, he'll only want to go for another walk.' Not waiting to argue he left and drove off in his hatchback.

Lucy was beside herself. She could sense when something was wrong. It was like threading beads: the shapes and colours had their own innate arrangement - life's undercurrent was like that. Preston Niblock may have crafted expensive jewellery; he had never spent a lifetime threading beads that had personalities of their own.

'What am I going to do, Tiny?'

Tiny looked at the door, then back at her. Now she wished she carried a mobile phone. Lucy remembered the public telephones opposite Palace Parade. It was only fifteen minutes there and back.

The beadworker pulled her coat on. 'You be good, Tiny.' She trotted off clutching some change from the petty cash.

***

As Toni Zelinski closed her mobile phone and walked back into the restaurant she looked puzzled.

'What's the matter?' asked Conrad Makepeace.

The civil engineer slowly sat down. 'That was Lucy Tribble. She says that Preston received a note from me telling him to go to Auld Windy.'

Miss Priddle took a sip of fruit juice then turned her attention to the hors d'oeuvre. 'What on earth for? I'm sure the woman's sweet, but she does tend to get confused about things.'

Toni paused. 'No she doesn't.'

Makepeace chuckled. 'Why would anyone want to send him a note from you?'

'Lucy also says that their phone is dead.'

Miss Priddle studied the prawn on her fork, wondering what reincarnation it had gone on to. 'I tried to nag that man into carrying a mobile. Said he didn't want the embarrassment of beeping in public.' Then it struck her. 'What did you say the mill was called in that letter?'

'Auld Windy?'

'Something is wrong.'

Though unsure why they were so concerned, Conrad Makepeace waved the waiter away as he came over to take the order for their main meal. 'Are you sure?'

If anybody else knew about Bald Wendy they could have easily seen the three of them together, very publicly eating a four course meal. It would be the ideal opportunity to lure him out there.

'Just what is going on at this mill?' Makepeace insisted.

Miss Priddle slowly lowered the prawn as a ghastly dream came back to her. 'Oh my God, just pray I'm not psychic.'

'We've been rumbled,' hissed the civil engineer.

'Will you tell me what is going on?' Conrad Makepeace demanded too loudly for comfort.

A friend of his wife's was two tables away and already wondering about the councillor's rendezvous with the civil engineer and middle-aged femme fatale.

Miss Priddle beckoned for the bill. 'Did you bring the Land Rover with you?' she asked Toni.

'Yes, I let the boys have the car tonight.'

'I'll probably get there before you.' The accountant snatched some money from her bag and thrust it at the waiter as she dashed out.

'What is going on for pity's sake?' repeated Conrad Makepeace as he chased the two women out to the car park.

When they were out of everyone else's earshot Toni Zelinski told him, 'I think that Neville Grablatt is going to kill Preston Niblock.'

The last of the day shift had gone by the time Preston pulled up. All the lights had been switched off and Bald Wendy loomed bleakly like a tired leviathan against the grey dusk.

There was no sign of Toni's Land Rover and night was closing in fast so he waited by his car. He then realised why everything about the place gave Monty Golden the horrors. It didn't need a ghost to be menacing.

As the air was chilly, Preston went into the gearing room, leaving the door unbolted for the civil engineer. Although she was unlikely to be tinkering about in the dark with sash cords or putty, he threw on the master light switch and darted up to the milling room, checking for signs of repairs in progress. There wasn't so much as a screwdriver or bottle of linseed oil.

From the lucam he looked out into the chill dusk, but could see no headlights in the distance. This wasn't like Toni Zelinski. She was as reliable as the governor on a traction engine.

The jeweller went back downstairs to the phone in the small delivery booth adjoining the gearing room. It was dead.

This would be the last time he refused to listen to Lucy Tribble's forebodings. He now had one of his own that was virtually tangible.

Preston tried to think clearly. If someone had lured him out here, where were they? Then he remembered that he had left the door unlocked. He dashed over and secured all the bolts.

Now what? The only other way out was down the tunnel and into the cave system. He didn't fancy wending his way along the tributary in a dinghy by himself and up to the lift of the Catalogue Shop which would be closed anyway. Perhaps he could hide in the loft with the bats. It would be better to wait up there all night and risk coming down in the morning to discover he had been making a fool of himself. The most sensible course of action would be to make a dash for his car and drive off.

Before Preston could reach the door, the lights went out. A large shape bore down on him like a bloated Nemesis.

***

Jealously guarding the corner they had claimed as their own, Mabel, Alice and Hector sat with their malt drinks, reminiscing. The harassed attendant realised they were harmless enough and capable of looking after themselves so no longer bothered them. All the companions needed were food, warm water, and a little respect.

'Isn't it strange, I'm just beginning to realise how much I miss Jenny,' mused Mabel.

'Jenny!' Hector echoed the sentiment as though hammering it back into his memory.

Alice toyed with the hem of her skirt. 'Why did she go off like that? We had those lovely cakes with lemon icing from Mrs Niblock.' Alice's recollections tended to be selective and mainly revolved around cakes she had nibbled.

'Cakes!' said Hector.

'You've had your cake,' the attendant said automatically as she passed.

'I really liked those small ones in the little cases with cherries on,' Alice wittered on, unable to stop the flow. 'And those nutty, crunchy, honeyiee... '

Mabel put her out of her misery. 'Flapjacks.'

'Crocodiles!'

'Not here, Hector. They went away a long while ago.'

And so the conversation stumbled on while the colour television on the other side of the room blared out game shows, soaps, and national lottery numbers.

***

Miss Priddle's car screeched to a halt by Preston Niblock's hatchback. She hurtled up the steps, only to find the door bolted.

Conrad Makepeace and Toni Zelinski arrived in the Land Rover and she teetered back down to meet them.

'He's here, but the door's locked.'

Makepeace looked up at the large dark building. 'There aren't any lights on. Could he have gone somewhere else?'

'There is nowhere else to go,' Toni told him. 'But there is another way in.'

'Oh no,' groaned the accountant. 'Not in this skirt.'

The civil engineer pulled the electronic key from her shoulder bag. 'You two stay here. I'll have to climb round and push a dinghy out so you can reach the tunnel entrance.' Toni handed Miss Priddle the powerful torch she always took with her, even on dinner dates. 'You hold this. And keep an eye on the door in case someone comes out.'

Makepeace was unable to fathom what was going on. 'I'll watch the door. You two do whatever you have to and get us inside.'

Like a chunky gibbon, Toni swung from the half-raised gate, over the water. She dropped down onto the small landing bay in the tunnel and brought out one of the dinghies.

The builder took Miss Priddle and Conrad Makepeace back inside and led hem through the passage up to Bald Wendy.

'What the hell is this place?' demanded the councillor.

'Quiet,' the civil engineer warned. 'This tunnel has an echo.'

'Whoever's in there must know we've arrived,' hissed the accountant.

As Toni Zelinski reached the trap door into the mill, she pulled back the bolts. 'Are you ready?'

If Neville Grablatt was really in there committing murder, Conrad Makepeace was determined to be the one to execute a citizen's arrest. 'I'll go first.'

Carefully he lifted the trap door and, by the light of Toni's torch, walked up into the dark gearing room. She quickly followed and threw the master light control.

As Miss Priddle climbed up, illumination flooded the building. There was no one else about. Working on the assumption that her premonition had been genuine, she went straight over to that corner of the room. Crumpled on the floor in an untidy heap was Preston Niblock. Blood gushed from a head wound.

Toni dashed over and tried to find a pulse.

'Is he dead?'

'No, but he needs a doctor. It looks as though he's gone several rounds with a psychopathic kangaroo.'

Makepeace was outraged. 'And Grablatt did this!'

Miss Priddle was quite matter of fact about it. 'Probably. He's been trying to find an excuse for ages.'

'But why? I know the man's a thug, but this-?'

'Long story.'

A familiar voice reverberated about the room. 'Then why not tell it to him?' Grablatt stepped from the cover of the mill's gears and into the light.

Makepeace would have rushed at the man if the two women hadn't held him back. 'You don't seriously think you're going to get away with this Grablatt?'

'Of course I am Conrad, or haven't the two ladies told you what's been going on.' The thug took a handkerchief from his breast pocket and wiped the blood from his fist. 'Oh yes, after what Mr Niblock has been up to he's very lucky to still be alive. You see, he double-crossed a gentleman far more dangerous than me.'

'He must be talking about Julius Tucker,' whispered Toni. 'But I don't know what else he's on about.'

Miss Priddle did, so she kept quiet.

Makepeace pulled a mobile phone from his pocket. 'I'm calling the police and an ambulance.'

Grablatt stretched out a large, warning hand. 'I wouldn't do that if I were you, Makepeace.'

'Stop me.'

Grablatt gave a terrible leer. 'Because if you do,' he pointed to the unconscious Preston. 'He will most certainly die. In fact, I'm beginning to wonder why I didn't finish him off before you arrived.'

Without any apparent regard for the size or dangerous disposition of the thug, Miss Priddle teetered back over to Preston. 'This is all getting very silly.'

'Keep away from him!'

'My goodness, don't you bulge when roused.'

'Priddy!' Toni warned through gritted teeth.

Grablatt closed in on the accountant. 'I said get away!' The monster could have easily beaten everyone there to pulp without pausing for breath.

Miss Priddle seemed oblivious of the fact and hitched her tight skirt up to her thighs so she could kneel next to the jeweller.

Grablatt seized her arm.

Like a suddenly released spring, Miss Priddle shot up and crunched her shapely knee into his genitals. Grablatt's eyes glazed for a moment. As he crouched and staggered back, Toni kicked him in the back of the knees and he folded up like a huge anglepoise lamp.

Without thinking, Conrad Makepeace seized the heavy metal rod that had been used as a roof buttress and placed himself between the women and Grablatt. 'Quick, get Preston outside!'

Toni unbolted the door then went back to help Miss Priddle.

Grablatt quickly recovered. Rearing like an enraged killer whale, he lashed out at Makepeace and landed a blow that sent him spinning. He turned on the women. Tossing them aside like rag dolls, he seized Preston Niblock.

Beyond reason, Grablatt would have broken the jeweller's neck if he hadn't been suddenly stopped in his tracks.

Makepeace struck another blow with the metal bar, and caved in the man's head.

Neville Grablatt toppled forward like a vat of lard, dead.

'Dear God!' Makepeace was unable to take in what he had done. Then cold reality drove home its lance. 'Where's the toilet?'

Before Miss Priddle could ring the bell, a young man in a dressing gown opened the door.

'You'll have to give me a hand; I can't manage him by myself.'

The doctor padded out to the Land Rover in his slippers. Between them they carried Preston Niblock round to the surgery.

'I hope no one is watching this. The neighbours already suspect me of running a very peculiar practice since someone saw that lame alligator being brought into the waiting room.'

'Just think of the money my accounting will save your practise if you can put him back together.'

'You're serious about waiving your fee, Priddy?'

'Naturally.'

'What's been going on then?'

'He had a bad fall.'

They put the patient on the couch and the doctor examined the jeweller's injuries. 'Fall - be damned! He's been worked over. Fee or no fee, if he's got internal damage he's going to hospital.'

'Just examine him will you.'

When Preston regained consciousness, diagnosis was easier with his co-operation. The doctor sewed the cut in his face made by Grablatt's ring and gave a couple of broken ribs some support with a bandage.

'He's going to have a patchwork complexion for a couple of weeks and if he gets too many headaches he'll need an X-ray. He's not badly concussed and there's nothing broken. The steamroller seemed to concentrate more on his body.' The young doctor scratched his beard. 'So why don't you want the police to know about it?'

'Because the thug who did this would come back and make a more permanent job of it,' Miss Priddle lied.

'All right. Give me the patient's address and I'll keep an eye on him for a couple of days. Not unless he can go to his own doctor?'

'You're kidding? Old Marchment alerts social services if he glimpses so much as a graze on a mother's knuckles. He'd probably call out the Territorial Army if he saw Preston.'

'Is there anyone you could take him to?'

Miss Priddle consulted her watch. It was half past two. 'I'll look after him for tonight.'

They helped Preston back into the Land Rover and the doctor returned to bed to dream about what he could do with the funds that lucrative little transaction would save his practice.

***

Toni Zelinski wrapped the metal bar that had crushed Neville Grablatt's skull in a sack then helped Conrad Makepeace drag the huge body across the storage area and to the loading bay in the sluice gate arch. The civil engineer went down the tunnel to collect a second dinghy. She moored it under the sluice's trapdoor and spread out a pickup truck tarpaulin inside it.

Every fibre of Makepeace's integrity insisted he should not be doing this, and that the court would understand how he had acted to save another man's life, but experience told him that juries were fickle. Fewer things can be more irrational and easily influenced than twelve average people good and true who would rather be somewhere else. Then there was that other small factor to be taken into account; the one Conrad Makepeace was just about to travel along the tributary of the River Nox to witness.

'You'll have to help me with that.' Toni Zelinski pointed to a concrete block originally intended as one of the steps down into the tunnel. It was virtually the same weight as Grablatt.

They dragged it to the trap, winched it down onto the tarpaulin in the dinghy, then lowered the metal bar and body of Neville Grablatt on top of it. The double-shelled inflatable sat low in the water but somehow never folded up and sank. Toni Zelinski laced a nylon rope through the rings of the tarpaulin and made a tight package of the bulky objects.

She and Makepeace then got into the other dingy from which Toni attached a line to take the gruesome cargo in tow.

In the light of the prow lamps, Conrad Makepeace saw the subterranean tunnel gouged out by the River Nox, the world that had been long forgotten by cavers until Preston Niblock met a palaeontologist on the beach.

The councillor was silent until they reached the large cave with the Catalogue Co-operative's workshops. 'Are you seriously telling me that this place is directly under Palace Parade?'

'The limestone here is less than a couple of metres thick in parts. I suspect that the recent increase in water pressure penetrated some fissures and weakened it.' Toni Zelinski carefully guided the inflatables through the swell being churned up in the adjoining cave.

'Dear God! Gideon built Palace Parade knowing that this was underneath it? I've often wondered why the Victorians filled the centre of Moltonford with a park and constructed no buildings heavier than two storeys.'

'Now do you understand what would happen to everyone concerned if you so nobly elected to go for trial? We could never keep this quiet, and Preston's life wouldn't be worth a light.'

Now the councillor understood how deeply the jeweller was implicated, he didn't have any option. At his age, life imprisonment for humane pest control had no appeal. 'Now what?'

'During the last river surge, some boats and bodies of rowers lost down here one and a half centuries ago were brought to the surface. As soon as the water returned to its normal level, they were sucked back down into this adjoining cave again. It acts like a sump. Not even Neville Grablatt's rampaging ghost would be able to escape from it.'

Makepeace had no time to question the moral certainties that had ruled his life. If his old Methodist congregation could see what he was doing now they would have excommunicated him.

The water flowing through the arches of the other cave gurgled and surged, making the dinghies roll unnervingly.

'Are you sure this is safe?' asked Makepeace.

'Of course not. Your life jacket wouldn't save you from being sucked down there - so don't lean out!'

The civil engineer reached across to the other dinghy, disabled the emergency cylinder, and released its pressure. Makepeace seized her jacket, trying to keep his balance in the turbulence. With a soft, slow glug the craft containing the body capsized, committing its revolting cargo to the deep.

When the load fell from the deflated dinghy the outboard motor of their own vessel cut out.

Toni tried to restart it as the swell buffeted them towards the wall of an arch jagged with stalactites. In the sharp shadows fretted out by the prow lamp, it was like being swallowed by the jaws of the monster in your worst nightmare.

'For pity's sake release the other dinghy!' called Makepeace.

'No, it could be washed out and traced.'

Suddenly the motor spluttered into life.

Sodden and shaking, they towed the deflated craft back to the main cave's shore.

In the lights perpetually powered by the river turbine, Conrad Makepeace saw the Catalogue Co-operative's workshops. He marvelled at how they had managed to pull off a scam on that scale without being discovered. The councillor's stunned respect for the law weakly waved its truncheon at his complicity, though his conscience told him that the Co-operative had every justification. Most of them had been put out of business and two people had lost their lives for the sake of a multi billionaire's profits.

'What now?' he whispered for fear of hearing his voice come accusingly back at him.

'You go home and pretend nothing happened. Will your family want to know where you've been?'

'For a midnight swim, fully clothed?'

'Oh God.'

'It's all right, I keep a fresh change at the club. I'll tell Anne I slept there. If she doesn't believe that her friend, the one who saw me dash out with you and Miss Priddle, will no doubt embroider something else suitably lurid. What are you going to do?'

'You needn't worry about that.'

By her tone, he knew full well that he should.

CHAPTER 53

Preston Niblock woke the next morning under a canopy of pink drapes and breathing air thick with expensive perfume.

He nearly called out, 'Mary Bell!' but sneezed instead. He thought his bottom jaw was going to drop off so didn't do it again.

Suddenly a familiar face was looking down at him. He couldn't immediately place it. It wasn't the billionaire's mistress. The sophisticated apparition placed a cold compress on his face, then the invisible elephant sitting on the jeweller shifted position and he passed out.

The next thing Preston knew, he was lying on a tartan sofa and enveloped by the smell of frying onions. He shrank back at the large figure looming over him before realising that it was only Ben.

'Fell down some stairs?' The ex-lorry driver had seen the aftermath of too many fights to believe it. 'That concrete must have been travelling at a hell of a lick.'

Preston shrank to the end of the sofa. 'I can't remember.'

'And what were you doing, wandering about building sites in the middle of the night?'

'Ben!' Fran called from the kitchen. 'Leave him alone!'

Ben mumbled something about the jeweller's sanity, before leaving to feed the livestock.

Fran brought two mugs of coffee in.

After Preston had sipped a couple of mouthfuls, the revolting jigsaw started to slot into place. Then, as if that wasn't enough, he noticed the set of simulated crocodile skin suitcases behind an armchair. They were too elegant to be Fran's and whenever Ben travelled, he lived out of an old army knapsack.

'I'm sorry Fran. I would have never let anyone bring me here if I'd known you had company.'

'You had no choice. You weren't conscious. Anyway, Miss Priddle's potpourri gave you an asthma attack. Doctor had to come in and replace the stitches. You must have been well out of it if you can't remember that. We could have hardly dumped your bleeding carcass in the shop for Lucy Tribble to find.'

'What about Tiny?'

'She took him for his walk.' Fran swallowed a mouthful of coffee. 'So why were you wandering about a building site in the middle of the night?'

The image of Neville Grablatt laying into him like a threshing machine was difficult to dismiss. 'The shops have to be ready sooner than we thought. I was helping check them out.'

Fran could tell he was lying. 'Toni Zelinski's foreman should be doing that. Come on, what have you really been up to?'

Preston tried to hide behind his coffee mug but Tinker pushed his wet nose under his free hand. 'Nothing,' he said weakly. He was surprised to discover that he was still wearing his watch. 'I'd better be getting home now.'

'Not in that state you won't.'

'Tiny will need feeding.'

'Lucy can do that.'

'That's what I'm afraid of. She feeds him Smarties and ginger nuts.'

'You are staying here.'

He may have married a meek little woman who had always let him have his own way, but her sister didn't just lay down the law, she nailed it to the floor. Even her fifteen-stone husband daren't cross the line.

'Who have you got staying then?'

'Just a relation.'

That was plausible; Ben's side of the family had mentions in all the local parish registers.

Fran gave him a hard look. 'Dear God, you look a mess.'

***

'Evacuate?' The short ex-traffic warden squared up to the six foot two Owen as he blocked the way to Bald Wendy's tunnel. 'I can't evacuate, I've got twenty loaves to bake before half past eight!' Rose's high-pitched complaints were shrill enough to wake the bats.

'Sorry darling. No one is to go back down there. It's not safe. The lift to the shop has been sealed, so no one will be able to come down and help you with your kneading anyway.'

'Then what will Mercy do for sandwiches?' demanded Rose.

'She'll have to buy her bread until we get your oven installed in the new bakery.'

'What! Buy bread from the food hall! That rubbish? Are you mad?'

'It's only for a few days.'

'You told me that the new bakery won't be ready for weeks?'

This woman had wrangled with hardened truckers and suddenly Owen didn't feel six foot two any more. 'We've had to change our plans. The cave roof's got a fracture. Only the team stripping the place is allowed back down there.'

Rose threw up her hands. 'Why is this fracture so dangerous now?'

'Water from that flood caused movement in the ceiling. You wouldn't want Palace Parade down on top of you, now would you?'

'Dunno. Be a hell of a way to go.' Muttering to herself, Rose pottered off down the mill steps where she told Mo, her oldest son, to take a detour and find a decent baker.

That night the cave workshops were rapidly dismantled and their machines, tools, and materials crated and packed onto the barge. The lift to the storeroom was removed and the cladding in the shaft stripped off. The block taken out during its excavation was fitted into the head of the tunnel and large aggregate cemented into the space below it.

Early next morning a relay of trucks, vans, and lorries carried off everything that had been taken from the workshops to the new locations in Moltonford where it was either installed or stored in the properties Wentworth had bought up.

The river gate had its old fittings replaced, the landing bays were removed, the tunnel link to Bald Wendy filled in, and the gearing room floor made good. Any stock in the water mill was cleared out and alternative addresses sent for future deliveries.

By the end of the week no one but the odd cave shrimp would have known anyone had been there.

***

Unnerved by the consequences of the lie he had been caught up in, Preston managed to escape back home the next day. He preferred to have Lucy Tribble fluttering about him with cups of tea and Tiny sprawling across the bed than trying to cope with Ben's suspicions and Fran's bald demands for the truth. Grablatt may have been unable to make him talk, but his in-laws had a large family to practise emotional politics on. He wouldn't have stood a chance.

After a couple of days the jeweller was able to stand without visualising the monstrous shape of his attacker swooping down on him. Just in case Grablatt was waiting around the next corner to waylay him and finish the job, he always took Tiny with him.

When the aches and pains were reduced to dull, thudding reminders, he and Tiny surreptitiously slipped into the garden centre to see Ben's children's farm. He had given his dog a good meal first, as he had never been totally sure about the Alsatian's capacity for sheep worrying. Tinker left the animals alone because he was so well fed the only thing he could now catch was a well-aimed pork chop.

The Sunday morning was bright and too early for the aisles of spring bedding plants to be filled with customers. From the other side of the enclosure fence Tiny showed unsettling curiosity in the scampering rabbits, bleating goats and scratching chickens so, before it could cross his mind to get more closely acquainted, Preston took the Alsatian to a seat surrounded by a display of spring bulbs. He tied the dog's lead to the wrought iron leg of a bench outside the café, then called in for a coffee. There was no filter ready. As the jeweller's taste buds were still numb from the pounding his jaw had received, he brought back a cup of instant and sat beside Tiny who promptly slumped down on his feet.

The sun was warm. Preston sat basking for some time, watching the Sunday gardeners wander in to plan for the year ahead.

An elegant, middle-aged woman strolled over and seemed to take an interest in the spring bulbs. Although the sun was in his eyes, he could make out a trim figure in a blue suit of shot silk. Her hair, a natural silver ash, was immaculate and the sun's rays danced in her crystal drop earrings.

Preston felt uncomfortable, but Tiny's nose lifted enquiringly at the light perfume wafted towards them.

'Preston, don't you know me?'

Did Preston know her? The voice was terrifyingly familiar, although now it had a firm edge. There was no longer that acquiescence that used to permeate her unassuming manner.

The jeweller clutched Tiny's collar as though the dog could fend off the apparition. 'Deirdre!'

With the tunnel from Bald Wendy blocked and the entrance no longer opened by the electronic key, Toni Zelinski had some trouble freeing the old hinge and easing the gate wide enough to allow her inflatable through. The thoroughness of her work force could be frightening at times and she wondered whether she was still cut out to keep up with them. The civil engineer had the suspicion that she should really be wearing heels and behaving badly, like Priddy but, by the time she had put in enough practise to get that act together, she would be at least eighty.

As not even troglodyte bats needed to see what she was up to, Toni waited until the dinghy was well inside the tributary tunnel before switching on the prow lights. Grablatt's phantom might well have been infesting the place, yet there was more than one way to lay the ghost of a thug. It was a pity Preston Niblock could never know that the man would be unable to beat him up again.

Conrad Makepeace and Miss Priddle realised all too well that matters couldn't rest as they were. Somewhere, at some time, someone involved in the Bald Wendy conspiracy would have one jar too many and let the odd word slip. But what to do about it?

Toni Zelinski had the solution. Unfortunately she would have to keep it to herself. If Priddy knew that her friend was capable of behaving this badly, the accountant would feel her status as the region's most devastating female being threatened.

Toni had always been easy to work for and pleasant to know. However, a civil engineering contractor could not remain solvent on diplomatic turns of phrase and winning smiles alone. Those agents who had negotiated contracts with the builder soon found that out. Zelinski's had been brought to the verge of bankruptcy more than once by some corrupt speculator or other. Now, with the help of Preston Niblock, the business had recovered and she was damned if another Co-operative development was going to be ruined or burnt out again by Gideon Enterprizes.

Toni reached the main cave. She beached her dinghy and walked the underside length of Palace Parade, examining the roof with her flash torch. Eventually satisfied, she went back to collect her knapsack from the dinghy.

***

The next morning a stranger arrived in Moltonford. He was a short jolly man with the flu who asked in several pubs about the whereabouts of a certain councillor whose distant relative had left him a modest bequest. No one had seen Neville Grablatt and few missed him. Most proprietors thought he intimidated the regulars and took up too much space.

After searching Moltonford all day, the jolly little man went to the deserted Victoria Square where he sat in the chill evening air and pulled out his mobile phone.

'Boss, I reckon he's done a runner.'

'How could he know you were coming?' demanded Tucker, as though he hadn't already given the councillor enough warning of his intentions.

'Only confirms you were right. Want me to track him down?' asked the assassin.

'When was he last seen?'

'Several days ago. Apparently left his flat without bothering to cancel the papers. His wife hasn't seen him either, but then, she's not lived with him for over five years.'

Tucker sighed. 'Okay. With luck he might come back and try to blackmail Gideon, then we'll move in.'

***

'Will you come out of that bathroom, Preston! You have to face this sooner or later.'

The jeweller ignored Fran and continued to glare at the pale blue sea horses on the bath surround. At that moment he would have rather been swimming through some deep coral reef with them.

Fran went back into the lounge. 'I told you this would happen.' She slumped down on the sofa opposite her sister. 'Why couldn't you just let him carry on believing you were dead?'

Deirdre sighed - she had been doing a lot of that lately. 'It would have been so... dishonest.'

'You think that running off and letting everyone think you were dead was honest? To top it all, he'll now have to hand back all that insurance.'

'I know I shouldn't have done it. But Jenny was the same height and weight. When I collected Una's locket and left her upstairs with Frank sorting out old clothes, nothing could have

215

been further from my mind. Then I reached the other side of the park and saw the flames. I knew nobody could have survived that, and I was only two streets from the station.'

'Save it for Preston. You've told me about it enough times.'

Fran picked up a newspaper and irritably riffled through its pages. 'It wouldn't be so bad if you intended to return to the poor fellow.'

'But he doesn't need me. He never did. I'm surprised he hasn't found someone else by now?'

'Well, he's got Tiny and Lucy Tribble. Take it from me, that triangle is strictly platonic, just somewhat eccentric.'

Fran was annoyed because she could no longer browbeat her older sister. Something had happened to Deirdre, and it hadn't necessarily been bad. In fact, she was twice the person Fran could remember. Waiting until your mid fifties to find a life may have been leaving it a little late, but it had worked.

The women sat in awkward silence, listening to the distant chattering of plant buyers, children having pony rides, and a braying donkey. Then Jim's budgie started to chatter raucously at its mirror.

Fran glowered at it. 'That bloody bird has the knack of perking up when you don't want it to.'

'When do Jim and Josey come back?'

'Monday. After EuroDisney I doubt they'll be interested in the farm any more.'

Deirdre smiled. 'Of course they will.'

Tiny gave a warning whimper.

The sisters turned to see Preston standing in the doorway.

Deirdre started to rise. Fran pushed her back down and went to collect him. He refused to be collected and held onto the doorframe as though about to fall into an abyss.

Fran had to resort to reason. 'Don't stand there, Preston. It's not helping.'

Preston fixed his wife with an icy glare. 'So you're not staying? Thought you'd just drop in to let me know how well you're doing, did you? I should have known you were too wet to burn.'

'Preston!' snapped Fran.

He paid no attention. 'I could have made you anything from a Tiffany's catalogue - sprays of emeralds, starbursts of diamond, even a jade Donald Duck if that was all you wanted. But what do you do? Run off to earn a few pounds and wear plastic!'

Deirdre defensively touched her brooch. 'It's amber, Preston.'

'No it isn't! I can see from here! It's plastic!'

'You'll have a relapse,' warned Fran.

'Good! Then she can scrape up what's left of me and feed it to that bloody dog!'

Until then, Tiny had been sprawled out on the other side of the room. Hearing his second name, "that bloody dog!" he came over and nuzzled up to Deirdre. The Alsatian returned Preston's glare and growled.

'Bloody turncoat!' The effort with which he swore at Tiny made him clutch his fractured ribs.

Taking her life in her hands, Deirdre went to him. 'Preston, this isn't like you?'

The explosions going on inside his brain stopped him from answering.

Fran helped him to the sofa and took advantage of his momentary incapacity. 'Look Preston, Deirdre has done very well for herself since she left. She didn't even have a suitcase with her. Now she's in charge of a large hotel. You were the one who made out she was too dim to walk along the road without a compass. All she has done is prove you wrong.'

Having put so much effort into suppressing his guilt, Preston wasn't ready to take the blame just yet. 'She should have told me!'

Deirdre risked taking his hand. 'You never listened to anything I said, Preston. You could always persuade me to do what you wanted and make me feel awful if I disagreed.'

'You were happy enough, weren't you?'

'Well, yes, I suppose I was, but...'

'But what?'

'I don't know how to put this.'

Preston's expression was infused with a fierceness his wife had never seen before.

She paused.

'Well, what monstrous aspect of your husband's personality drove you to disappear like that!'

Deirdre gave him that melting look that could have dissolved away the resolve of a charging bull. 'Oh Preston - you were so boring.'

'Is he with you?'

Conrad Makepeace was pleasantly inebriated and hadn't a clue what was going on. 'Yes, and virtually incapable.'

'Good, don't let him out of your sight.'

'All right.' He returned the mobile phone to his pocket and ordered another short for Palace Parade's maintenance engineer. If anything went wrong in the mall tonight, it would have to wait until the morning.

***

Ron Acton now viewed all large supermarkets with the same suspicion. 'I still say that if a large store, however well known, is allowed into our new shopping centre they should sign a non-aggression pact.'

Sonia Cupit waved her order paper. 'But we'll need a well-known name like that to bring people up here. The only food shops will be Mrs Silvestri's delicatessen and Rose's bakery, and everyone has to have something with their bread. We need grocers to complete with the food hall in Palace Parade.'

'And what damage could it do us if we own the lease?' added Monty Golden. 'Sorry - Preston Niblock, who owns the lease.'

All eyes turned to the master jeweller sitting at the end of the head table. He was fighting dragons in another universe.

Toni Zelinski, who was chairing the meeting, stood up. 'Perhaps we should take a vote on it.' There were murmurs of approval. 'Motion; should Wentworth Developments allow a ten year lease to the aforementioned company?' The show of hands ratified the proposal. 'Motion carried.'

'Can we add a clause about them stocking our goods?' Mr Becker, being a publisher of specialist books, was on always on the look out for any opportunity.

'This is a food store, Mr Becker.'

'Some people who buy chips might be able to read.'

Lucy Tribble nervously raised her chubby hand. 'Perhaps we should stipulate that they carry Mr Becker's books if they intend to retail other publications?'

That motion was also carried. By the time clauses had been added to cover everyone else's goods, trading hours, licensing limitations and rules about feeding the pigeons, the meeting came to a close. The supermarket would have probably found it easier to establish a branch on the moon.

Before leaving, the gathering milled about, chatting over coffee and biscuits, except Preston Niblock who continued to sit, staring into infinity. Consistently under the impression that his main problem was dehydration, Lucy Tribble tried to interest the jeweller in a cup of tea. He remained somewhere in the reaches of outer space.

When it was ten o'clock, and parking meters were due to click over, the gathering started to wend its way into the darkness of the half paved plaza that now presented a splendid view of Palace Parade in all its monumental plate glass glory. Lit from below, the façade seemed to hang in the air by its upper storeys.

Suddenly the ground shook - San Andreas Fault fashion.

In the cave beneath the shopping centre, a fissure appeared in the length of its ceiling. Momentarily the crevice gaped for half-kilometre as though the limestone had been holding its breath for a hundred million years.

For a split second the stalactites and stalagmites valiantly took the weight of Palace Parade, then shattered like barley sugar. The two vast ceiling slabs that had fractured away from each other, and the cave collapsed. Fossils of beasts that had once ruled the world before falling into a bog were once again committed to water as the bedrock that had supported the centre of Moltonford rained into the River Nox.

Above, in the still night air, most of the Catalogue Co-operative stood watching. They heard faint snapping sounds, like thin ice breaking on a pavement.

The rest of the gathering in Mercy's function room rushed outside. Even Preston Niblock dropped back down to earth and followed the others. On the slopes of Moltonford, residents drew aside curtains to look down and see what was making the ground tremble.

The large plates of multi-strength glass below the hideous crown surmounting Palace Parade fractured and shattered in a volley of whip cracks. Shards rained into the air and embedded themselves in the forecourt and flowerbeds. Fortunately nobody had reason to be in the centre of town at that time of night. When Palace Parade closed there was nowhere else to go. All the shopping complex did was sparkle and give the surviving pigeons a place to roost. Not tonight. Acres of window continued to explode and several flocks took to the sky.

As the shopping centre's outside walls toppled inwards, away from their load-bearing columns, the beams of light illuminating Palace Parade became tangled. Inside, the shallow columns supporting the centre of the mall fell into the gap. With nothing to rest on, the raft foundations gave way and the middle of the mall floor cracked, unbalancing the large marble clock, which was sent rolling lopsidedly down after the central columns.

Inside the stores of Palace Parade the glass shelves of lead crystal ornaments and Royal Daulton at first vibrated, then tumbled, tinkling into each other. As the floor to ceiling cases were compressed, they shattered one by one, sequining the air with glittering shards. Frying pans, woks, and saucepans clattered from their hooks and rumbled across the heaving floors in an avalanche of aluminium. The floors tilted, double beds stood on end, and duvets, pillows, and sheets tumbled after them.

The escalators at first sagged, resembling limp bicycle chains. Then the loops of metal treads were pushed into the air to make bizarre Chinese lanterns, while the clear plastic lift walls folded up like enraged origami before fracturing. The decorative wrought iron supporting the elegant galleries snapped and they twisted like so many Tacoma Bridges.

In the food hall the odd tin toppled from its shelf and started to roll before whole stacks avalanched to their new centre of gravity somewhere on the other side of the security shutters. They were followed by jam and pickle jars, coffee, cheeses, frozen foods - many still in deep freezes - then the lighter merchandise; newspapers, toilet tissue, cornflakes, talcum powder, chased by milk, cream, fruit juices and cottage cheese from the rear of the store.

As the shopping mall continued to jack-knife down its centre, the symphony of breaking glass was accompanied by the tinkling of mosaic briquettes being spat from the falling galleries.

The stores' security shutters eventually gave way under the weight of goods and everything, from track suits to microwaves, spilt through the resulting gap, down into the inky waters of the River Nox.

Eventually the dislocated raft foundations fell away from the outer columns. The remaining walls of Palace Parade slid down into the vast cave below like two ocean liners being launched sideways into each other, leaving the half kilometre of pillars sunk deep in the bedrock isolated like the ribcage of some suddenly filleted monster.

The spotlights on the shopping mall's roof were last to tumble into the gaping ground. Not yet severed from their power source, shafts of light stabbed the water bubbling up through the rubble.

Having briefly surfaced as though merely inquisitive, the River Nox's tributary quickly found its way through the remains of Palace Parade to the other end of the exposed cave.

The shopping centre's maintenance engineer had staggered from the pub with only Conrad Makepeace's grip to keep him upright. He grimly watched the water swirling over the rubble that had briefly been Moltonford's heart.

'I told them to fix that cistern in the office loo.' Then he passed out.

On the other side of Moltonford, the silence that followed was broken by Lucy Tribble's squeal of delight. Suddenly the Catalogue Co-operative broke into applause. Tiny barked until Preston dragged him back home.

Next morning the jeweller stocked up with dog food, handed Lucy the keys to the shop and left to spend a fortnight at Deirdre's hotel where she had introduced a policy that anything left over from a banquet was given to the local down and outs.

THE END

www.ingramcontent.com/pod-product-compliance
Lightning Source LLC
Chambersburg PA
CBHW051052050726
47592CB00002B/498